CONTENTS

ALL MY TOMORROWS

ALL MY TOMORROWS

THREE HISTORICAL ROMANCE
NOVELLAS *of* EVERLASTING LOVE

Worth the Wait · KAREN WITEMEYER

An Awakened Heart · JODY HEDLUND

Toward the Sunrise · ELIZABETH CAMDEN

BETHANYHOUSE
a division of Baker Publishing Group
Minneapolis, Minnesota

Worth the Wait © 2017 by Karen Witemeyer
An Awakened Heart © 2017 by Jody Hedlund
Toward the Sunrise © 2015 by Dorothy Mays

Published by Bethany House Publishers
11400 Hampshire Avenue South
Bloomington, Minnesota 55438
www.bethanyhouse.com

Bethany House Publishers is a division of
Baker Publishing Group, Grand Rapids, Michigan

Printed in the United States of America

ISBN 978-0-7642-3101-8 (trade paper)
ISBN 978-0-7642-3174-2 (cloth)

Library of Congress Control Number: 2017938454

These are works of fiction. Names, characters, incidents, and dialogues are products of the author's imagination and are not to be construed as real. Any resemblance to actual events or persons, living or dead, is entirely coincidental.

Scripture quotations are from the King James Version of the Bible.

Scripture quotation on pages 101–102 is from the Holy Bible, New International Version®. NIV®. Copyright © 1973, 1978, 1984, 2011 by Biblica, Inc.™ Used by permission of Zondervan. All rights reserved worldwide. www.zondervan.com

Karen Witemeyer is represented by Books & Such Literary Agency.
Jody Hedlund is represented by Natasha Kern Literary Agency.

Cover design by Brand Navigation
Cover photography by Serg Zastavkin / Shutterstock

18 19 20 21 22 23 24   7 6 5 4 3 2 1

WORTH *the* WAIT

A
LADIES OF HARPER'S STATION
NOVELLA

KAREN
WITEMEYER

To all the ladies who helped me
brainstorm plot ideas for this story on
the Inspired by Life and Fiction blog.

Special thanks to Alexandra, Darcy,
Johnette, and Karen. Faithful, creative
readers are such a blessing!

Therefore if any man be in Christ, he is a new creature: old things are passed away; behold, all things are become new.

2 Corinthians 5:17

1

A re you sure it's safe?" Victoria Adams stared down at her exposed right leg as her friend Grace Mallory fit the Remington Model 95 over-under double-barreled derringer into the small holster affixed to her garter. "I'd hate to hit a rut in the road and shoot off my foot."

Grace peered up at her with a reassuring smile. "You could carry it in your handbag, if you prefer, but after all that trouble we had with Angus Johnson a few months back, I decided I'd rather have mine secured in a place more readily accessible."

Grace adjusted the stocking gun a final time, then reached for the bunched-up skirts Tori held against her thigh and arranged them smoothly over her handiwork, erasing all evidence that a weapon lurked beneath the layers of cotton and muslin. "A handbag can be out of reach in a critical moment or torn away from your grip before you can avail yourself of what's inside." Grace straightened to her full height, which put her light brown topknot below Tori's chin. "Better to have it close at hand at all times, and in a place no one knows about." She lifted her own skirts to reveal an identical pocket pistol strapped above her knee. "I've been carrying mine like this since July,

11

and I haven't shot my foot off yet." Grace's eyes sparkled with teasing humor, and Tori couldn't help but relax.

"You probably think I'm foolish, taking such precautions with a man who's been nothing but kind to all of us." Tori dropped her gaze as her insides clenched. She knew she was overreacting, but she just couldn't help herself. She hadn't been alone in a man's company for over five years—not since . . . No, she wouldn't think about it.

Tori fisted her hands at her sides, willing her mind to slam the door closed on those memories. The past would not control her. She had a future to create, a son who depended on her provision. The livelihoods of the women of Harper's Station depended on her ability to sell their goods.

Benjamin Porter was a good man. An honorable man. He'd been delivering goods to her store for over a year, since Emma Chandler first established the women's colony at Harper's Station. For months, Mr. Porter had been the only male allowed into their sanctuary, and never once had he betrayed that trust.

The freighter charged fair prices, and when her regular market in the neighboring town of Seymour dried up, he went the extra mile to find new places for her to sell the eggs, canned goods, and quilts the ladies of Harper's Station manufactured. And when Angus Johnson attacked their community, Mr. Porter stood beside them. Fought for them.

Warmth spread across Tori's face as she remembered the freighter standing guard day after day in front of her store. He hadn't been protecting the community at large. He'd been protecting *her*. He'd made no effort to hide his growing interest in her, and that, perhaps more than anything, was what had driven her to seek Grace's counsel regarding concealed weapons.

The gentle touch of Grace's hand upon Tori's arm cleared away the conflicting thoughts fogging Tori's brain. The young telegraph operator met her gaze with an intensity that spoke of secrets the normally shy woman took great pains to hide.

"Taking precautions is *never* foolish. Better to have a way to defend yourself and not need it than to need it and not have it."

The quiet statement rang with the truth of experience, making Tori question, not for the first time, what had led Grace Mallory to Harper's Station.

"You're right, of course." And she was. If Ben Porter remained a gentleman during today's excursion, there'd be no reason for anyone to know about the miniature gun hidden beneath her petticoats. She prayed that would be the case, that Mr. Porter's character proved to be as impeccable as it appeared and wasn't just a sham to convince her to drop her guard.

Surely no man would invest a year of his life charming a woman who'd made it clear on several occasions that she'd not welcome courtship of any kind. No dalliance was worth that kind of effort. *She* wasn't worth that kind of effort.

Forcing that pathetic, self-pitying thought back into the dark region of her heart where it belonged, Tori placed her hand atop Grace's, where it rested on her arm, and squeezed. "Thank you so much for sharing your expertise. I never would have found the courage to embark on this particular business venture without your help."

Grace's lips curved up at one corner. "Emma's always saying that we ladies can do anything we put our minds to, as long as we stick together. I guess after nine months of living here, I'm finally becoming a believer."

Tori smiled and allowed a soft chuckle to escape. "It's about time."

Grace joined in the laughter only to immediately attempt to stifle the sound when the curtain separating the back storage room from the area behind the general store's counter floated sideways.

"There you are!" Emma Chandler—Emma Shaw, now, since she and Malachi married two weeks ago—swept into the back room, her eyes alight with teasing. "I *told* Lewis you hadn't locked yourself in your room, but he didn't believe me. Begged me to fetch you before you changed your mind."

"That boy." Tori shook her head even as her heart warmed. Her son might be only four, but he knew his mama well. Too well sometimes. He picked up on her moods faster than a flapjack soaked up syrup. It was one of the reasons she tried so hard to keep her emotions under firm control. She wanted his childhood to be happy and free, not fraught with suspicion and mistrust inherited from his mother. "He's been talking about this trip nonstop since I agreed to it last week. You'd think we were embarking on an expedition to discover unknown lands instead of making rounds to drum up new customers. I couldn't back out now if I wanted to."

Emma came forward and clasped Tori's hand. "Do you want to back out?"

Tori kept her face serene as she shook her head. "Of course not. I made a promise, and I never go back on my word. You know that."

Of course Emma knew that. The two of them had been friends, confidants, and business associates for the past three years. Which was why Emma also knew how much Tori dreaded being alone in a man's company. Especially a large man. One built like the pair of giant Shires he had pulling his freight wagon. One who could overpower her with a flick of his wrist.

Tori's free hand fisted into the fabric of her skirt as her gaze sought out Grace and confirmation of the secret they shared. Grace dipped her chin in a nearly imperceptible nod.

Even large men weren't impervious to bullets.

Slowly forcing air back into her lungs, Tori relaxed her fingers and returned her attention to Emma, offering her a small smile of reassurance. "I won't say I'm comfortable with the whole idea, but it won't be the first time I've set my personal preferences aside in order to do what's best for the business."

Tori extracted her hand from Emma's and leaned over to collect the luncheon basket she'd prepared for the trip. "Mr. Porter's idea of delivering goods to area farm and ranch families has merit. If I can offer greater convenience at reasonable prices, customers who normally travel to Seymour or Wichita Falls to stock up on supplies might decide having a few staples delivered once a month at a slightly increased rate merits doing business with a woman. Especially if it means saving them the loss of a day's work."

Emma raised a brow. "Are you convincing me or yourself?"

Tori sighed inwardly. It really was dreadfully annoying having such a perceptive best friend. "Myself, I suppose." Her shoulders sagged a bit as she let a touch of her uncertainty creep into her posture. "I've been running logical arguments through my head all week. Increased business is not only good for me—it's good for the entire town. Nearly every lady in Harper's Station relies on my ability to sell the goods we produce. A larger market means larger profits for all of us."

"But not at the expense of your peace of mind." Emma reached out and took the picnic basket from Tori's hands, but it was her unconditional support that left Tori feeling unburdened. "If you want, I can ask Aunt Bertie to ride along with you. She'd be happy to act as chaperone. She could help mind Lewis while you and Mr. Porter broker your deals."

Tori shook her head. "No. This is something I need to do." Though she had to admit to being tempted by the offer. Alberta Chandler was a dear woman, always so kind and positive. She'd make the perfect buffer between her and the freighter. But this was a business trip, not a scenic excursion. She needed to treat it as such. "If I were a man, I'd be traveling alone. I'm a shopkeeper. A business owner. There is nothing improper about accepting Mr. Porter's escort, especially since he knows the route far better than I do and has already made contact with many of the families."

Tori reached an arm around Emma's shoulders and squeezed. "You're a good friend, Emma, but it's time. Time for me to venture outside the cocoon of this place and prove to myself that I'm strong enough to stand my ground in the real world."

Emma grinned a full-fledged, teeth-baring grin that glowed with all the inner radiance personified by the incredible woman who had given so many ladies power back over their own lives. Tori most of all.

"You're the strongest woman I've ever met, Victoria Adams." Emma leaned into the brief hug, then stepped back to face Tori straight on—her expression, her posture, everything about her oozing with confidence. "You're not just going to stand your ground, my friend. You're going to soar."

❖

Benjamin Porter did his best to hide his nerves by double- and triple-checking the security of the goods packed into the front of

15

his freight wagon. Assorted bolts of fabric, rolls of ribbon, scented soaps, creams, and a host of other female fripperies he couldn't begin to identify lay carefully stored in crates lined with cotton batting to keep them protected from the jostling that was bound to occur over the rutted roads that lay between Harper's Station and Wichita Falls.

It had to be one of the smallest loads he'd ever hauled, yet it was easily the most significant. His entire future rested on the outcome of this venture. Well, not his *entire* future, but certainly the most interesting parts. After months of patient hint-dropping and carrot-dangling, today was the day he would finally break through Tori's resolve and convince her to take their partnership from strictly business to something more. He'd been aching for that something more for over a year now, but every time he'd broached the subject, she'd made it clear she had no interest in pursuing a romantic relationship with any man.

He supposed he should take comfort in the fact that it wasn't *him* she objected to but his gender as a whole. It still didn't sit well, though. It wasn't fair of her to paint him with the same brush that she painted every other trouser-wearing yahoo who crossed her path. Especially the one who had put her off men in the first place.

Ben had no idea who the scoundrel was or what he had done, but he didn't doubt the man's existence. She'd never spoken of a husband, and always introduced herself as *Miss* Adams, not *Mrs.*, so he figured whoever had fathered Lewis had probably not seen fit to put a ring on her finger first.

And he'd remembered the terror in her eyes when they'd first met. He'd once worked with a horse that had that same look, who'd spooked every time he'd tried to get close. That gelding would kick and bite and run every chance it got. Turned out, its previous owner had taken pleasure in applying his spurs and whip. It took months to earn that roan's trust—months where he'd endured bites and kicks, months of letting the animal run away without forcing his coopera-tion—but in the end, the roan came around and became the best saddle horse Ben had ever owned.

Tori had suffered at a man's hands—of that Ben was certain. But now that she'd had months to get used him, to stop spooking every time he spoke to her or walked into her store, it was time she ceased viewing him through the lens of her past and saw him as his own man—strengths, flaws, and everything in between.

Well, maybe not the flaws. Not all of them anyway. He wanted to recommend himself to her as a potential husband, not scare her off for good.

"If you check those boxes one more time, I'm going to arrest you for disorderly conduct."

A strong hand gripped Ben's shoulder. He turned around and mockingly glared at Malachi Shaw, the newly minted town marshal.

"What do you mean *dis*orderly? These crates couldn't be more orderly." Ben crossed his arms over his chest, flexing his biceps for good measure.

Mal raised a single eyebrow, unimpressed with Ben's display. "It ain't the boxes that's disorderly. It's your conduct. But then, I guess that's to be expected. Waiting on a woman would send any man off his feed." The marshal cracked a grin, and the two friends slapped each other's backs in sympathetic bonding.

"So true." Ben stepped away from the wagon, relieved to have some other way to distract himself. He'd never admit it to Mal, but he was half afraid Tori would march outside and announce in that no-nonsense voice of hers that she'd changed her mind. Even after Lewis helped Ben load all the crates she'd packed up the night before, he had no guarantee that she'd actually go through with the trip.

"Mr. Ben! Mr. Ben!" Lewis sprinted toward the wagon, a pile of old quilts spilling from his arms. "Is my ma ready yet?" He nearly tripped over a quilt corner that dragged the ground right in front of him, but with the adroitness of a boy used to hopping stones in streams and balancing on store railings when his ma wasn't looking, he danced sideways, then slung his load upward in a sweeping arc to clear the path for his feet.

Ben snagged the blond-headed scamp around the waist and hoisted him in a sweeping arc of his own, off the ground and into the back of the wagon. "Not yet, but I imagine she'll be along soon. Why don't you arrange that bedding so you'll have a comfortable place to ride? I've got the boxes tied off, so you don't have to worry about them sliding around."

Lewis dropped the quilts in a heap right where he stood, then scrambled back over to the edge of the wagon and leaned far enough over the side to make Ben nervous about him toppling. Apparently the boy thought a lumpy mass of bedding would be sufficient for his needs. Ben doubted Tori would agree.

"Do a better job straightening those quilts, Lewis. If your ma sees that mess, she'll insist on straightening it herself, and then it'll take us even longer to get on the road."

"Aww, Mr. Ben . . ." the boy whined.

Ben gave him the eye. The one that made it clear he wouldn't be changing his mind. Lewis heaved a dramatic sigh, pushed away from the edge of the wagon, and set about creating a pallet. Not that Ben expected it to be much better than the current heap—a four-year-old could only manage so much neatness—but it kept the scamp occupied and taught a bit of responsibility.

"Don't just wad them up, now. Fold them like your ma would do."

Another sigh and a woeful glance over a shoulder. "Yes, sir."

Ben bit back a grin and returned his attention to the marshal. "Sending Lewis to fetch those quilts was brilliant. He was about to drive me crazy with his constant questioning about when we would leave."

Malachi's chest puffed out as he tilted back on his heels. "My Emma's a smart one. Always has been. She'll get your woman out of that store, too. Just watch."

An unwelcome heat crept up the back of Ben's neck. "She's not my woman. We're just business partners." Though he wished like anything that he had the right to change that claim.

"Uh-huh." Mal sounded less than convinced. "We'll see." He gave a little nod toward the store.

Ben followed his gaze, and his heart gave a familiar hiccup. Tori stood on the boardwalk outside the store, the autumn breeze catching a strand of her blond hair and blowing it across her face. She reached a hand up to capture it and fit it back into one of the hair pins holding the knot of hair at her nape. The straw bonnet she wore sat primly at the top of her head, the red ribbon around the middle the only adornment.

Tori wasn't one for drawing attention to herself. Dressed in a tan business suit with a white blouse buttoned to her chin, she was the very picture of unassuming. Or would be to anyone but him. She might try to downplay her feminine assets, but he'd been around her long enough to recognize the slender shapeliness of her figure and the beauty of her blue eyes and creamy complexion. And when she smiled? She became radiant. Not that he'd witnessed many of those rare events. She usually just curved her lips slightly to indicate pleasure or contentment. But every once in a while, especially if her son was involved, a genuine smile escaped all restraints and transformed her into a true beauty.

"I'm sorry for taking so long." Tori straightened her shoulders as if readying herself for battle, then traipsed down the steps to the street. "I had a few last-minute details to see to."

Ben hurried around the back of the wagon to meet her and had opened his mouth to offer assurances that the delay was no problem when Lewis popped his head up.

"About time! Sheesh, Ma. You took for-ev-er."

Ben cast a warning glance at the boy. "I'm sure whatever your ma was doing was important." He turned back to Tori and gave her his most charming grin. "She's worth waiting on."

Her lips tightened at that, but into a shape that looked more like disapproval than appreciation of a compliment. So much for his charm.

"Yes, well . . . I suggest we delay no longer." Tori lengthened her stride, giving him no chance to assist her into the wagon. She scrambled up the wheel spokes and onto the bench before he could even think about fitting his hands to her waist and hoisting her up.

Unfortunate, that.

Ben shrugged off his disappointment and moved forward to give his team a final check before climbing into the driver's seat. Emma handed a large basket up to Tori and wished her farewell while Grace Mallory waved from behind the store railing.

As he clucked to his Shires and set the wagon in motion, Ben grinned to himself. One of the best parts of this plan to call on area homesteaders was the sheer number of times they'd be required to enter and exit the wagon. Tori might have escaped him this time, but he'd have a couple dozen more chances to wrap his fingers around her slender waist. He could wait.

2

After forty-five minutes of maintaining ramrod straight posture and six inches of distance between herself and Mr. Porter, Tori's lower back throbbed. She couldn't keep this up for an entire day, not if she expected to have any energy available for winning new customers.

Pretending to smooth her skirt, she felt along the edge of her right thigh until her fingers encountered the small, hard lump above her knee. Reassuring herself of the derringer's presence, she allowed herself to relax, just a bit. Enough so she could sway with the natural movement of the wagon instead of forcing a rigidly proper posture. Because, really . . . what did being that stiff actually accomplish besides wearing her out and making her appear ridiculous? A lady might utilize such an unbending posture to communicate firm resolve and a standoffish manner when sitting in a parlor chair, but in a freight wagon such measures were far from practical. And she'd always prided herself on her practicality.

Tori chanced a glance out of the corner of her eye to the man at her side. His attention appeared riveted to the road in front of them. Good. He probably didn't even notice.

His head suddenly swiveled her way as if he sensed her gaze. He winked at her. Winked!

"I gotta say your stamina is impressive." His voice held a warm, teasing lilt. "I didn't think you'd make it past Mrs. Cooper's chicken farm with that iron-poker spine, and here you lasted three times as long."

Tori stiffened, then realized the irony of the action and settled for pursing her lips instead. "I'm sure I have no idea what you are talking about."

Mr. Porter chuckled. "And here I'd always thought you the honest type."

Tori couldn't decide whether she should be more upset over the fact that he'd called her out on her prim yet completely false denial, or the fact that he'd been aware of her to such a degree that he'd noticed the change in her posture the very moment she let herself relax. The latter was certainly more disturbing, especially because a tiny, foolish part of her couldn't help but be flattered by it.

"Look," he said. "If it makes you feel better, set that food basket on the bench between us." He nodded his chin toward the floorboard between their feet where the basket rested. "I don't want you to be so stiff and sore that you can't make it through the day. Hard to make a good impression if you're permanently bent at the waist with muscle spasms."

There he went being insightful again. And instead of trying to assure her with words that he was not a threat, he gave her a tangible way to feel safe. A barrier to replace the one she was forfeiting.

He understood her . . . on a frightfully deep level.

Tori's stomach clenched at the implication.

Then the fighter inside her, the one who had defied the odds by starting her business while raising a child on her own, roused. "I don't think that will be necessary. I'd hate for our lunch to topple and spill if we hit a deep rut in the road." And she'd hate even more for him to think her so emotionally fragile as to need a flimsy wicker box between them to feel secure. She wasn't fragile. She was cautious. There was a difference.

"Fine by me." He shrugged and turned his attention back to the road. "I think I see the turnoff for the first farm up on the right, anyhow. We'll be getting out in a few minutes."

Tori placed a hand against her middle in a vain effort to still the sudden bout of nerves dancing through her midsection. She twisted slightly and craned her neck to see into the wagon bed.

"We're nearly at the first house, Lewis. Remember what I told you. Don't interrupt the adults while we're talking, and stay where I can see you."

He aimed his popgun at a knothole in the side of the wagon, squinting one eye to sharpen his aim, and pulled the trigger. A tethered cork shot out and hit the knothole dead center. Lewis let out a small *whoop*, an ecstatic grin spreading.

"Did you see that one? I got it right in the middle!"

Tori smiled slightly even as she narrowed her eyes in motherly sternness. "Yes, I saw it. But what I need to know is if you heard what I said."

He tamed the grin into submission, yet his eyes continued dancing with little boy excitement. "Yes, ma'am." Lewis gave a vigorous nod that slammed his chin into his chest. "No talkin' to the grown-ups and no runnin' off."

"Very good. I expect you to be on your best behavior today."

"I know." Lewis smiled at her—that private, only for his mama smile that never failed to melt her heart—then turned back to his target practice.

Tori's heart swelled with love and pride. He really was a good boy. Bright. Obedient. A bit rambunctious at times, but never rebellious. Most shopkeepers wouldn't dream of taking such a young child with them on a business trip such as this, but Tori had no qualms. It had been just the two of them for so long, she would have been lost without him.

"I'll help you keep an eye on him." Mr. Porter's deep voice rumbled near her ear, bringing Tori's head back around. "So you can concentrate on selling our services without the added distraction."

Some ornery part of her wanted to turn down his offer, to argue that her son wasn't a distraction, and that she didn't need his help. But that bit of irrational feminism served no practical purpose. The truth was, having an extra pair of eyes keeping track of Lewis's whereabouts would be a blessing.

"Thank you." She dipped her head graciously to the man seated beside her, hoping he had no inkling of the thoughts that had just run through her head.

He nodded back without a word, but the suppressed laughter in his gaze hinted that he probably suspected her true feelings. Annoying man.

Mr. Porter turned his team of giant black draft horses down the rutted lane that led to a farmhouse nestled between a pair of large oaks. Sunlight winked off the window glass in a welcoming fashion, and Tori's pulse hummed a little faster. She sat straighter on the bench seat and raised a hand to check the simple chignon beneath her bonnet. She'd used a pile of hair pins to ensure it didn't move, but the wind always managed to tug a few wisps free.

"You look fine," Mr. Porter mumbled.

The gruff compliment would have lifted her spirits if the man's tone hadn't given her the impression he considered her efforts at tidiness frivolous. She stretched her chin forward and continued checking her appearance by running a hand along the ruffled collar of her shirtwaist, then down the center of the bodice to her skirt, brushing away any travel dust that might have accumulated. Though, thanks to the rains a couple days ago, the dust had been minimal so far.

"Might as well get used to the ritual," Tori announced in regal tones. "A businesswoman must always be cognizant of her appearance when dealing with customers. A tidy appearance gives the impression of capability and competence. Your muscles and height might be enough to recommend your abilities to tote and carry heavy crates and supplies, but for money to change hands, customers need to be assured that they are dealing with a professional."

Tori folded her hands in her lap, proud of her little speech until she realized she'd basically insulted her business partner, implying that all he was good for was hauling heavy objects, as if he were no better than the draft horses pulling their wagon. She knew for a fact the man had a keen mind. Why, this entire venture was his idea.

Her posture sagged a bit as she turned in the seat to face him. "I didn't mean that the way it sounded. I . . . "

He glanced her way, a cocky half grin making her belly tighten. "Like my muscles, do you?" He waggled his eyebrows. "Too bad we didn't bring along a few sacks of flour on this run. I can carry two at a time. 'Course, if someone loads me up, I can do twice that many. Two on each shoulder."

Good heavens! That was nearly four-hundred pounds. Not that she doubted his word. All one had to do was look at him. His coat barely contained the width of his . . .

He flexed just as her attention drifted to his biceps, stretching the already strained material even tighter around the impressive bulge of muscle. Tori jerked her gaze away, hating that he'd caught her looking. For pity's sake. She didn't even like big men. They were too powerful. Dangerous.

Yet Mr. Porter looked far from dangerous when he wiggled his eyebrows in that ridiculously overblown fashion and puffed up like a tom turkey showing off his feathers.

Well, this hen wasn't impressed with a bunch of fluff and gobble. That swirling in her belly was simply nerves about meeting her first potential customers of the day. Nothing more.

She wouldn't allow it to be anything more.

Tori cleared her throat. "I'm afraid the heaviest item you'll be required to lift today is a bolt or two of fabric. You'll probably waste away from lack of use."

He laughed. The deep, resonant sound poured through her like a long swallow of hot cocoa, rolling through all the cold places inside and warming them as it passed. Thankfully, she didn't have long to ponder the ramifications of her reaction, for the farmhouse door opened as the wagon rolled into the yard. A woman stepped out onto the porch, wiping flour-coated hands on a white apron tied about her waist. A little girl of about three years followed, her pudgy arm wrapped firmly around her mother's skirted leg.

"Can I help you?" The woman finished cleaning her hands and brought one to rest on her daughter's head.

Tori waved a greeting as Mr. Porter brought the team to a halt. The instant the brake was set, Tori stood and set about climbing down from the bench. Unfortunately, the freight wagon stood several feet taller than the wagons she was accustomed to, and since she had to exit backward, her right foot groped for a wheel spoke with no success.

Wonderful. Nothing like making a competent first impression. She adjusted her grip on the seat back and stretched her toe down a little farther, not liking the feeling of falling that assailed her when her shoe failed to connect to anything solid. Twisting her head sideways to better gauge her aim, she stretched a little farther.

Where was that confounded spoke?

Her palms began to perspire, and her grip grew slick. She slipped downward. A desperate prayer for help soared from her spirit at the same instant a pair of very large, very strong, very warm hands pressed into her waist.

He didn't say a word. No teasing comment whispered in her ear. No flirtation. Just a firm grasp and a smooth descent to the ground. The next instant he was gone, busying himself with the horses. A perfectly gentlemanly action that no one would think twice about. Except her.

She feared she'd be thinking more than twice about it over the course of the day. It had happened so fast and in such a matter-of-fact manner that she hadn't had time to be afraid of his intentions. In fact, with the graceful way he'd conveyed her to the ground after she'd started to flounder, his touch had actually made her feel . . . safe.

She couldn't remember the last time she'd felt safe when a man touched her.

But she didn't have time to ponder that small miracle at the moment. Not when her first customer and her daughter were making their way down the front steps.

Tori brushed a hand down the front of her bodice to still her jitters and stepped forward with a smile. "Good morning. I'm Victoria Adams. I own the general store in Harper's Station, just a few miles southwest of here. It's a pleasure to meet you." She extended her hand.

The farm woman hesitated a moment, then fit her palm briefly to Tori's. "Hazel McPhearson." She tilted her head toward the moppet at her side. "My daughter, Sarah."

Tori bent at the waist. "Delighted to meet you, Miss Sarah. My son, Lewis, is assisting Mr. Porter with the horses." She pointed in the direction of the menfolk a few feet away. Lewis grinned and waved with exuberance. "He's four, not much older than you, I would guess."

The girl craned her neck to better evaluate the strange boy who'd come for a visit, then looked back at Tori, her blue eyes wide. She released her mother's leg long enough to hold up three fingers.

"Ah." Tori clapped her hands on her knees. "Three years old. I thought so. Such a grown-up young lady." She glanced back at Mrs. McPhearson. "I brought some ribbon samples with me to give away to all the ladies I meet today. Would it be acceptable for me to give Sarah one? At no charge, of course."

Emma McPhearson eyed her suspiciously. "What do I have to do to earn it?"

Tori shook her head. "Absolutely nothing. Though, if you'd be willing to give me just a couple moments of your time, I would like to explain what brought me here today. If not, you can have the ribbon, and I'll be on my way."

She held her breath. It was a risk to give a customer the chance to send her away without listening to her sales pitch, yet Tori refused to bribe or manipulate another woman for her own financial gain. She knew all too well how few choices women had in this life. She'd not steal one more from Mrs. McPhearson.

The wagon creaked behind Tori. She glanced back to find Mr. Porter climbing into the back. As if completely unaware of Mrs. McPhearson's regard, he whistled softly as he went about uncovering the crate containing the fabric bolts, then proceeded to do the same for the toiletry items and seed packets.

Lewis came alongside the wagon and held up his hands. Mr. Porter gave him the wooden box Tori had packed her lengths of ribbon in. As if the two males had worked out this scheme ahead of time, Lewis accepted the box and traipsed over to Tori, wearing an expression that would make any businessman proud.

She accepted the box from her young assistant and opened the lid to show Mrs. McPhearson the rainbow of colors available.

The woman's hungry eyes said it all. She glanced down at her daughter's dark brown braids, then back to the box. "All right," she finally said. She turned to Sarah. "Just one, now. And be sure to thank the nice lady."

Tori held the box in front of the girl, whose gaze darted back and forth through the box as if unable to land on any one ribbon. She swallowed, then with a cautious flick of her eyes back toward her mother, reached her hand into the box and pulled out a bright pink ribbon. "Fank you," she murmured in a soft voice before darting back behind her mother's skirts.

Mrs. McPhearson collected the ribbon from her daughter and placed it in her pocket. "Why don't you show Lewis the puppies, Sarah? Let Mama talk to Mrs. Adams for a few minutes."

The girl dashed off toward the barn with only a small wave at Lewis as invitation. Lewis looked to Tori for permission. Unsure, she hesitated. She'd not be able to see him inside the barn.

Mr. Porter hopped over the tailgate, a pair of tin pails dangling from his right hand. "Would it be all right for me to fill these water buckets at your trough, ma'am? For the horses?"

Mrs. McPhearson nodded.

Porter bowed his head. "Thanks." He shot a meaningful glance at Tori.

The trough was right next to the barn. He'd be able to watch over Lewis.

Sarah stopped halfway to the barn when she realized no one was following her. "You comin'?" she shouted back to Lewis.

Tori gave him the nod he'd been waiting for. He grinned and sprinted after the girl. "You bet!"

Mr. Porter tipped his hat to both ladies, then followed the children.

That unexplainable safe feeling returned to Tori as she watched the freighter traipse after her son.

"So what brings you out here, Mrs. Adams?" Hazel McPhearson's voice brought Tori back to the matter at hand.

Tori ignored the twinge of shame that always jabbed when someone addressed her as *Mrs. Adams*. She insisted the ladies of Harper's Station address her as *Miss* since she'd never been married, but when trying to win over new customers, sometimes it was better just to let the misunderstanding slide.

"I'm expanding my business," she explained, allowing her enthusiasm to pour into her voice. "Thanks to a partnership with Mr. Porter's freighting company, I'm offering goods delivered directly to homes for those living between Harper's Station and Wichita Falls.

It would save you the time and hassle of having to make the long trip into town by bringing the store to you. We can provide ordinary staples or even the occasional extra item." She raised up on her tiptoes and reached over the side of the wagon to collect a bolt of green calico that seemed to have snagged the woman's attention.

"For a very small delivery fee, you can—"

"Put yer stuff away," a harsh voice growled behind her.

Tori spun around. A tall man marched straight for them, his face tight, his eyes belligerent. Her gut clenched. She dropped the cloth and backed up a step.

"We don't need any of yer fripperies." He stomped straight up to Tori, his arm raised.

Panic stole her breath. Her heart thumped painfully in her breast. Her mind flew to the pocket pistol holstered at her thigh. Should she?

3

On top of them now, the man brought his arm down.

Tori whimpered and threw herself to the side. As she staggered out of his reach, she grabbed the fabric of her skirt, determined to defend herself and Mrs. McPhearson from the brute who must be her husband.

Only the brute didn't notice her dodge. He didn't become enraged when his blow failed to meet her flesh. In fact, a grim look of satisfaction etched his features as his hand connected with . . . the calico?

As if the unassuming cloth were a plague ready to unleash against his farm, he shoved it back into its crate and lunged against the side of the tall freight wagon as he stretched out his powerful arm and grabbed hold of the lid. With a deep grunt, he snagged the cover and dragged it over the box, then stepped back and crossed his arms over his chest.

Tori released the skirt she'd raised to midcalf and fought for composure. He'd never intended to touch her. He'd been after the calico. Not her.

"Colin McPhearson! You've got no call to treat our guest with such rudeness." Hazel rammed her hands on her hips and glared at her husband, obviously not intimidated in the least by his rough manner. "And how dare you handle her goods without permission. Your hands are probably filthy."

Mr. McPhearson's face lost a shade of its belligerence as he shuffled back a step. "I ain't no crusty backwoodsman," he grumbled. "I washed at the pump."

Hazel huffed but ceased her tongue lashing. She turned to Tori and offered an apologetic smile. "My husband, Colin." Her eyes narrowed as she twisted to face her man again, apparently warning him to behave. "Colin . . . this is Mrs. Adams, a shopkeeper from Harper's Station."

"And I'm Benjamin Porter," a deep, wonderfully assertive voice said from behind Tori, "the freighter who transports Ms. Adams' merchandise."

Ben. Strength soaked into Tori like rainwater into a wilted flower, firming her resolve and shoring up her confidence. The height and size that once made her uneasy now acted as a balm to her brittle nerves. She hadn't seen him come around the back of the wagon. Her full attention had been fixed on Mr. McPhearson. But however he came to be standing behind her, she thanked God for providing an ally. Ben wouldn't let anything happen to her. She might not feel completely comfortable alone with him, but to face an outside threat? She'd choose no other.

Ben stretched out his hand toward the other man. McPhearson glanced at the offering, grunted, then reluctantly unfolded his arms and shook it.

"I don't mean to be inhospitable," McPhearson grumbled, "but ye got no business danglin' yer fripperies in front of me wife, temptin' her with things we can't be affording."

Hazel drew in an outraged breath. "Are you saying I'm too weak-willed to be trusted with financial decisions, Colin McPhearson? 'Cause if you are, I'll—"

"Calm yerself, woman." McPhearson held both hands up as if to placate his wife. "I ain't sayin' any such thing. Ye know I trust ye with our money. It's just . . ." He leaned closer to Hazel angling his face away from Tori and Ben, yet the air was so still, Tori could make out his words. "A man's got 'is pride, wife. Don't ye think I want to buy ye all them pretty baubles? I'd fill the house with 'em if I could."

Hazel visibly softened at his words. She moved closer and took his hand.

"In a few wee years, I'll 'ave this place turnin' a profit. Then we'll 'ave money fer more than the necessities."

Hazel peered up into her husband's face. "I love you, Colin McPhearson, and never once have I doubted your ability to provide for our family. But winter's coming, and both of little Sarah's dresses are inches too short and worn paper thin. New fabric *is* a necessity."

McPhearson blew out a breath and ran a hand over his face. He looked toward the barn, where Sarah and Lewis scampered about, each chasing a different puppy around the horse trough. Tori recognized the guilt lining the man's face as well as the frustration balling his hand into a fist.

She'd been there. More times than she cared to remember. Wanting desperately to give her child everything he could possibly need yet falling short time after time. For two years she'd scoured dirty laundry, the only job she could find that would allow her to keep her son with her. She'd slaved over boiling pots until her back ached, scrubbed on washboards until her hands grew raw and cracked, and pressed wrinkles until she perspired so much she forgot what it was like to feel clean. And all the while, her wages barely covered room and board.

Nevertheless she'd been determined to create a better life for her and her son, so she saved every penny she could spare, and a few she couldn't, praying she'd one day have enough to convince a bank to give her a loan so she could open her own store. Having grown up a shopkeeper's daughter, she knew the business inside and out, from creating displays to managing inventory, from keeping the accounts to brokering the best deals with suppliers. Yet bank after bank turned her down, labeling her a bad investment simply because she wore a skirt instead of trousers. If it hadn't been for Emma, she might still be sweating in a laundry somewhere, struggling to make enough to buy Lewis a new pair of shoes.

McPhearson was no different.

"I just finished putting in the winter wheat," the man murmured to his wife. "The account's been paid off and our credit extended with the store in Wichita Falls. We won't 'ave ready cash 'til June."

Tori's heart ached. She had to find a way to help them. Her attention darted to the children, laughing and carefree, unaware of the pressure weighing on their parents. She knew better than to offer charity. There was no faster way to insult a hardworking man or woman than to offer a handout. She should know. She'd been on the receiving end several times in those early years, and never once had it failed to raise her ire. If only she could work around . . . *That's it!*

"I'm willing to barter." Tori took a step away from Ben's solid presence, finding her footing and confidence once again. Negotiation. That's what the situation called for, and she could haggle with the best of them.

The McPhearsons turned their gazes toward her, Hazel's full of hope and expectancy, Colin's doubtful and suspicious.

"We don't 'ave nuthin' of value we're willing to trade." His words emerged in a gruff tone, as if they scratched his throat as he gave them voice.

Tori lifted her chin and stared him straight in the eyes. "It's been my experience, Mr. McPhearson, that one rarely sees value in the items constantly at hand. The everyday becomes mundane. But an outsider with a keen eye for what might be attractive to others sees things differently." She gave a little tug to her jacket hem to punctuate her words. "I know what my customers are looking for in Harper's Station, what I'd be able to sell at a profit. I daresay, if you give me a chance, I'm sure to find something we can agree upon as a fair trade for a few yards of calico."

Hazel released her husband's hand, slid her palm up past the crook in his arm, and tightened her hold to hug him into her side. "Please, Colin? It won't hurt anything to look. Surely we can find something suitable."

The man took one look at his wife's face and relented with a nod. "All right. But keep away from me tools. Those ain't up for discussion."

Ben hung back as Tori took charge and followed the McPhearson woman toward the house. The husband trudged along behind.

Halfway across the yard, McPhearson turned back and called to Ben. "Ye comin'?"

Ben shook his head. "Nope. I'm just the driver. Ms. Adams owns the shop. She makes all the buyin' decisions."

McPhearson nodded. "Seems my woman's determined to make a few buyin' decisions of her own." He shrugged. "I'll have to keep an eye on her. If Hazel has her way, she'll probably trade away me favorite chair. Finally got the thing fittin' me backside just the way I like it."

"Colin McPhearson," his wife scolded from the porch, where she and Tori had paused to eavesdrop on the men's conversation. "No one in their right mind would take that lumpy, broken-down thing. There's a better chance of me breaking that old chair up for kindling than there is of a sensible woman like Mrs. Adams taking it in trade."

"Don't be criticizing me chair, woman," McPhearson blustered, raising his voice but putting no real heat behind the words as he stomped the rest of the way across the yard.

Ben contemplated going after them to keep an eye on things—his heart had plunged into his gut when he'd spied the angry farmer barreling down on Tori a few moments ago—but McPhearson had proven to be more bark than bite, and Ben had promised to watch over Lewis.

Besides, Tori seemed to have things under control. Ben grinned. The woman was brilliant. Barter, indeed. He shook his head as he made his way along the side of the wagon up to the team. He had no doubt she'd find a way to make the trade. He'd seen her eyes go soft as she gazed at the little girl running around in her too-short dress. She'd hid her compassion well from the McPhearsons, the slight relaxation of the lines around her eyes practically imperceptible. They'd detect no pity from her, only a determined businesswoman keen on making a sale.

He saw more. Oh, it wasn't easy. Not with a woman who hid nearly every emotion she felt. The first few times he'd delivered supplies to her store, he thought her cold. Aloof. Until he'd noticed the way she interacted with her son. Her reserve didn't completely disappear even on those occasions, yet warmth and affection oozed through it, as if slipping through the cracks of a retaining wall.

That's when he'd recognized the truth. Victoria Adams was a warm, caring, beautiful woman hiding herself behind a shell of stoicism. Why, he didn't know. But ever since that day, he'd made it his aim to study her, to learn her tells as if she were a poker player sitting across from him in a high-stakes game. It had taken months of careful study, but he'd finally learned to decipher the small nuances of posture and expression that escaped her defenses.

"She's a tough one, Hermes," he murmured to his lead horse, a giant black Shire that stood over seventeen hands, "but I think she'll be worth the trouble." He patted the beast's neck, his gaze searching out Lewis to make sure the boy was keeping out of trouble. "Ma would like her, don't you think? Seeing as how they're cut from the same cloth. Smart, hardworking ladies, dedicated to their boys. Tori would fit right in at family dinners."

Helios, the second Shire of the team, raised his head and turned to look at his master as if asking to join the conversation. Ben obliged, stepping around to the front and petting the second animal's white blaze. The two horses were nearly identical, both in looks and temperament. Black coats, white blaze and socks, docile, strong, obedient. They were the best team he'd ever owned, and he babied them like they were his kids. The only difference between the two draft animals was the white belly on Hermes, and Helios's preference for carrots over apples.

He'd searched long and hard to find the perfect pair for his freighting business after scraping and saving for two years to accumulate the funds needed to purchase them. He knew what it was to work for something he wanted, something he valued. He'd expend no less effort to win Tori's trust and affection. And God willing, her hand in marriage. She was his matched pair. He felt it in his bones.

"Mr. Ben, Mr. Ben. Look!" Lewis ran up, a fluffy black-and-white pup cradled in his arms.

The pup barked at the horses and squirmed in the boy's arms as if to get free. Helios snorted and yanked his head up at the unexpected commotion. Ben grabbed hold of the Shire's cheek strap with a firm hand. It wouldn't do to have him upsetting Hermes as well.

"Easy, boy," Ben crooned as he patted Helios's neck. "There's nothing to worry about. It's just a pup." He turned back to Lewis. "Not too close to the horses, scamp."

Lewis backed up a step as he got the dog under control. Ben nodded his approval. Even reached out a hand to pat the cute little fluff ball on the head. Looked like an Australian shepherd. Good stock dogs.

"Sarah said I could name him." Lewis grinned, all trepidation vanishing as excitement took over. "He's the biggest pup of the litter, so I thought I'd call him Hercules. What do you think? Just like the strong man in the stories you tell me."

Satisfied that the horses were calm, Ben put a hand to Lewis's shoulder and steered him a couple paces away. He hunkered down and offered his fingers for the pup to smell, enduring the friendly licks and shameless begging for attention before giving in and ruffling the dog's ears.

When he and his brother had been kids, they'd run across a book on Greek mythology in their teacher's collection and had enjoyed the adventure stories so well, they'd started naming all their animals after the ancient characters. They still did as adults, though Bartholomew had more of an opportunity, running a livery in Seymour. Ben had saved the names he'd chosen until he'd found the draft horses that lived up to them. Hermes for the Greek god of trade and the guardian of travelers; and Helios for the Greek god of the sun who relied on mighty steeds to pull his golden chariot through the sky.

"Hercules is a big name for such a little pup." Ben raised a brow in feigned concern. "You sure he deserves such a tag?"

Lewis looked down at the fuzzy fur ball, scrunched his forehead in thought, then lifted his chin in the same stubborn way his ma did. "Well, even Hercules started as a baby." He lifted the puppy into Ben's face until they practically touched noses. "He'll grow, just like the other Hercules did. He'll get strong and brave and be the best dog ever!"

"I reckon you're right." Ben eased the pup away from his face and pushed to his feet, rubbing Lewis's hair as he stood. "It was Hercules's actions that made him a legend, not his name. A man should always remember that. It isn't his name or his clothes or how much money he has that matters. It's the way he conducts himself—with honor, kindness, and courage—that makes a lasting difference in the world."

"So you like the name?" The boy blinked up at him, giving Ben no idea if his attempt at conveying a life lesson had penetrated.

Oh, well. He winked at the boy. "I think it's an outstanding name." He tilted his head and scrutinized the pup a second time. "This one's definitely hero material. You picked well, Lewis."

The boy beamed and ran back to the little girl waiting for him by the trough. Ben's heart gave a tug as he watched the two put their heads together and giggle over the puppies' antics. Lewis had wormed his way into Ben's heart months ago. It hadn't taken long. The kid was so eager to please and so hungry for male attention, a rare commodity in a town full of womenfolk. Now Ben couldn't imagine his life without the little guy.

Although . . . a secret smile slid across Ben's face as he watched the two young'uns crawl around in the dirt like pups themselves . . . he *could* imagine giving Lewis a little brother or sister to play with. That would be a pleasure indeed.

4

Half a dress length of royal blue calico sprigged with yellow flowers and another of gray-and-pink-plaid wool remained behind at the McPhearson homestead when the wagon rolled out. Tori glanced over her shoulder to wave farewell to Hazel and Sarah, who watched their departure from the porch. Lewis called out his own good-bye, which was quickly seconded by a tiny yip as the boy snuggled his new puppy to his chest and raised one white paw in a doggy wave.

She must have temporarily lost her sanity. As if a four-year-old boy running through the shop wasn't bad enough, now she had a pup to watch out for. Tracking mud everywhere, getting into mischief, and—she took in the rapture on Lewis's face as he held the dog close to his heart and murmured little-boy secrets in its ear—and making her son happier than she'd ever seen him.

She turned back around in her seat, her own joy swelling inside. Sanity was overrated.

"Pleased with yourself, I see," Ben said as he guided the horses back onto the main road.

Ben? When had she started thinking of him as Ben? And how was it that the irritating man could read her every thought as if she were a plate-glass window without even a lace curtain to dim his view? It was unnerving.

"A dog is a good investment," she answered primly. "It will teach Lewis responsibility and provide him with a playmate when I'm busy in the store. Besides, Hazel knew I was being generous in offering the gray wool in exchange for the five pints of blackberry jam she brought up from the cellar. I could see it in her face. When we came out of the house and she saw Lewis with the puppy, I swore I could hear the calculations clicking through her head. She recognized she had a chance not only to balance the scales but to get the calico, as well."

Ben . . . *Mr. Porter* . . . grinned at her, a grin that implied he knew her answer only told half the story. He leaned close and spoke in a low voice that rumbled in her ear. "Mrs. McPhearson wasn't the *only* one to notice how taken Lewis was with that scrap of fur. Your heart was breaking right along with his when he set the pup aside and bravely ordered the tiny thing to stay when he thought it was time to go."

She wanted to deny it, but he was right. And since Mr. Porter had proven himself immune to her demurs anyway, there really was no point in trying to hide behind such a flimsy barrier of politeness. He'd just call her out on her truth-bending—like he had last time.

"You're right," she said, careful to keep her gaze directed on the road rather than on the man beside her. Openness was one thing, actual connection was far more dangerous. "When the poor little thing ran after him, yapping as if he were losing his best friend . . ." She shook her head and let her words trail off as her heart clenched in her chest at the memory. Thankfully, Hazel had chosen that moment to offer the animal in exchange for the second length of fabric, and Tori had been able to rein in her weakness and focus on business. "I'm glad it worked out."

"You might change your mind if Hercules decides to christen your crates."

Tori's gaze flew to the freighter. He nodded with a tip of his head and a quirk of his lips toward the wagon bed behind them.

Hercules staggered about on shaky legs sniffing suspiciously at the crate that held her scented soaps and bath salts. Was that back leg inching upward?

"Lewis!"

The boy jumped and spun around. "What?"

"Keep that animal away from my crates." Tori drew in a breath and deliberately calmed her voice. "Have him play on the other side of you, dear, where there's more open space for him to explore. And if you think he might need to . . . um . . . water the flowers, let me know at once and we'll—"

Masculine laughter cut off her words. "Water the flowers?" Ben tipped his head back and laughed all the harder. It didn't take more than a heartbeat for Lewis to join him.

"Your ma's sure got a way with words." The freighter wiped at his eyes, and for the first time Tori found herself envious. Envious of his unfettered emotion.

She used to laugh like that, so hard tears leaked from her eyes. She missed it. Missed the innocent girl who saw the world as full of possibilities instead of threats.

Lewis picked Hercules up and dutifully moved him to the other side of his sprawled legs to keep the pup away from the crates. "Aw, she just don't like talkin' about—"

"Lewis." Tori gave him a stern look, her warning tone eliciting a pair of irritating male grins.

"Womenfolk are like that," Ben said, turning back to face the road, but not before he winked conspiratorially at her son. "My ma used to say, 'answerin' the call of nature.' And she always blushed when she said it." He aimed a sideways glance at Tori, and her cheeks immediately heated. Traitorous things.

"Well, I don't think Hercules will need to *water the flowers* any time soon." Lewis snickered. "He watered the porch steps at Sarah's house before we left."

Tori bit back a groan. She better find a way to turn the discussion in a more appropriate direction. "I like the name you gave him," she said, pouncing on the first thought that came to mind. "Very classical."

Lewis scrunched up his nose. "What does *classical* mean? It sounds like school."

She'd been teaching him his letters in the evenings and called it their class time. He caught on very quickly for one so young, but he hated having to sit still at the table when there were forts to build and popguns to fire at invisible invaders.

"Anything related to Greek or Roman culture is considered classical," Tori explained. "Hercules was a hero from Roman mythology."

"Mr. Ben? I thought you said he was one of them Greeks, like your horses were named after."

Tori waited for Mr. Porter to contradict her. After all, men rarely admitted to being wrong, especially if they considered themselves an expert on the subject. She'd prove herself correct when they returned home. She knew exactly where the book was that had the Roman and Greek mythology chart inside. It would be a simple matter to—

"I think your ma's right." Ben's brows drew together as if he were truly pondering the question. No cockiness. No condescension. "The Greek and Romans stole stories from each other all the time," he said, "so the same heroes are in both, they just go by different names. The Greek names are usually more famous, but not always." He turned to Tori. "What was the Greek name for Hercules? I can't recall."

He was actually asking her for input. Openly admitting that she might know more than him about his own pet subject. And without a hint of shame. As if he fully accepted the fact that a woman's intellect could equal a man's. The novelty of the situation stunned her so completely it took a moment for her to remember the question he'd asked.

"Heracles," she blurted, thanking God for allowing her to retrieve the name before it flew from her brain with the rest of her thoughts.

Ben nodded. "That's right. Heracles."

"It's almost the same," Lewis said, "but I like Hercules better."

Tori stretched her arm along the bench to relieve the pinch in her back that ached from her facing backward and ordered herself to get a grip on her scattered wits. Hoping the man beside her couldn't see how much he'd rattled her, she asked, "How did you come to pick that name?" The pup really was a handsome little thing. Black fur on his back and face, accented with touches of brown around the edges.

White paws and belly. Big dark eyes that were impossible not to melt over when he tilted his head just so.

"Well . . ." Lewis scooped up the puppy when the little adventurer tried to crawl across his legs to get back to the crates. He plopped Hercules into his lap and stroked the animal's soft fur. "Since he looks so much like Hermes and Helios, I figured he needed a name to help him fit in with the family. Hercules starts with an H and matches the stories Mr. Ben tells, so it just seemed right."

Ben turned to look at her. She saw the motion out of the corner of her eye and felt his gaze upon her, but she didn't glance his way. She couldn't. Not when everything inside her had frozen at the words that slipped so casually from her son's mouth.

Family.

Oh, heavens. Did Lewis think of Ben Porter as family? As a father? Panic pounded through her breast, restricting her chest, closing her lungs. She'd told him over and over that the freighter was just a friend. Nothing more.

But what had Mr. Porter been saying? He'd made no secret that he wanted to court her. Had he been planting ideas in her son's head to use as weapons against her?

Ben felt Tori stiffen. He wasn't sure *how* he felt it since her body sat a good foot away and no part of her actually touched him, but he was aware of the change nonetheless. Then, out of the corner of his eye, he saw her fingers curl into a fist and crush the fabric of her skirt as she slowly turned to face forward. He adjusted his grip on the driving lines and tried to act as casual as possible, hoping by some miracle the storm brewing beside him would blow over. But he knew it was wishful thinking. Tori had to be truly furious to display her anger in so overt a fashion.

What had her so riled? Ben hadn't missed the kid's untimely wording—he'd secretly rejoiced over the fact that Lewis thought of him in family terms—but surely that little slip wasn't enough to get Tori this bent out of shape.

"How dare you use my son as a pawn," she ground out between clenched teeth, her voice low and shaking with rage.

Ben jerked around. "What are you talking about?" He matched her volume, not wanting Lewis to overhear whatever it was they were discussing.

Her eyes flashed blue fire as her delicate brows formed a tight vee of disapproval. "I've made it abundantly clear that I have no intention of ever marrying. You or any other man. Yet instead of accepting my word on the matter, you skulk around like an underhanded snake and use my son as a pawn in your stupid game. Do you think that if Lewis begs prettily enough that I'll bring you into my home like that pup of his? I'm not some weak-willed female ruled by her emotions. You've miscalculated if you think I'll be herded like a blind sheep into a pen of your making."

The words spilled out of her like a flash flood rushing through a dry creek bed, stirring up dirt and debris as it rushed heedlessly on. Stirring Ben's temper. He clamped his jaw closed and gripped the lines so tight Hermes missed a step. But the woman wasn't done.

"And what happens when I turn down your suit? After you build up ideas in my son's head of having a father, a family—you leave. What happens to Lewis then?"

Ben glared at her, a muscle ticking in his jaw. "I already care about that kid as much as if he *were* mine. I'd never hurt him. *Ever.*"

She opened her mouth to argue. He stopped her with a look.

"No, ma'am. You had your turn to spout unfounded accusations. You'll sit there and listen to my side without interruption."

She crossed her arms over her chest, but her mouth snapped closed. He'd count that a victory. She probably would have stomped away in a huff had they been back in Harper's Station. The woman had a talent for avoiding uncomfortable situations. But praise be, he had a captive audience this time, and by all that was holy, he was going to have his say.

"I've never said a word to him about the future. Never called him *son* even as a figure of speech. Never mentioned my feelings toward his ma in his hearing." Feelings that were rather heated at the moment but plenty strong.

Ben took a breath and forced a level of calm into his low-pitched words. "I know what it's like to grow up without a father, Tori. To envy other boys who had a pa to teach them how to fix a leaky roof or hunt pheasant for Christmas dinner. To feel a weight of responsibility press down on my shoulders that I was too young to understand. If it weren't for Marlow Hutchins, the old livery owner in Seymour, I doubt I would have made it to manhood."

Childhood memories swamped him.

"Ma had taken a job in the café after my pa died, cooking meals to all hours just to keep the mortgage paid and food in our bellies. Without her supervision, Bart and I ran wild. Skipped school, played pranks, caused all kind of havoc. Until old Marlow caught us shearing the mane off his best mare."

Ben chuckled. "He was livid. Demanded we work off our crime by shoveling manure for a month. Hounded us about goin' to school, too. Even went so far as to escort us there every day and check with the teacher every afternoon to make sure we did our lessons. If we didn't, he'd pile on extra chores and make us work past supper. We thought he was the devil incarnate.

"Then we reached the end of the month, and he paid us wages. Honest-to-goodness wages. The first we'd ever seen. I wanted to run to the general store and spend it on candy and a ten pin set. But Marlow told us to use the money to buy our ma something special. Said she deserved it for puttin' up with our shenanigans."

He slanted a look at Tori. "That one statement opened my eyes. I'd been so wrapped up in my own anger and loss, I hadn't noticed what my ma was going through. Not only had she lost the man she loved, but she'd been left to support two boys who couldn't see past the end of their noses. Yet she'd done what needed to be done without a word of complaint. And how had I thanked her? By adding to her burden.

"In that moment, I changed. I vowed to do whatever I could to lighten her load instead of adding to it. I begged Marlow for a permanent job, for me and my brother, promising I'd never pull a prank again. The old man agreed. He taught us everything we know about horses, freighting, and running a business. He helped us become men.

"That's what my friendship with Lewis is all about. Mentorship. Not manipulation."

Tori's posture relaxed slightly. Lines continued to mar her forehead, and her lips continued to press against each other in an angry line, but the vee of her brows eased and the fire in her gaze dimmed to mere coals.

"I admire you, Tori. I have for a long time. You're strong and beautiful and the best doggone businesswoman I've had the honor to meet. But you're not the reason I spend time with Lewis. He's worth my attention all on his own."

5

*ou're not the reason I spend time with Lewis. He's worth my
attention all on his own."*

Tori couldn't get the words out of her head. Or the earnestness
with which they'd been spoken. They haunted her the rest of the
morning as she and Ben stopped at house after house.

She dutifully went through the motions, smiling at the people she
met, conversing, selling. She collected orders for future supplies, sold
a few small items from her wagon stores, and in two cases, graciously
accepted the owners' wishes not to be visited in the future. She'd
known such requests would come. It would be unrealistic to expect
success at every stop. Still, she couldn't help feeling a small ding to
her pride each time her business was rejected.

The one request that truly got her dander up, though, came from
the rather odiferous bachelor farmer at their last stop. He'd been more
than willing to allow her to deliver goods to him if she left her boy at
home and drove the wagon herself. The leer accompanying his words
left no doubt as to what he intended to *buy*. She'd briefly fantasized
about shooting the lecher with her pocket pistol strictly on principle
but decided that having a mother in jail would not be good for Lewis.
So instead, she'd marched back to the wagon, ordered Lewis inside,
and waited for Mr. Porter to return to the wagon and whisk her away.

Ben had lingered behind, however, waiting until she and Lewis were out of earshot. Then he had a few choice words with the foul fellow. The freighter's back had been to the wagon, so she couldn't gauge his expression, but she could certainly gauge the effect his conversation had on the farmer. The man's expression transformed from one of bawdy amusement, to outrage, to blanching panic. He visibly flinched when Ben raised a hand to tip his hat, obviously expecting a much more violent intent from the motion.

Neither she nor Mr. Porter said a word about the incident as they made their way back to the road. Truth was, they hadn't spoken much at all since her earlier recriminations. Somehow that made his actions all the more heroic.

He'd defended her. Even after she'd lashed out at him, he still protected her. Whether it was because he cared for her personally or just for women in general she couldn't be sure, but either way, his actions spoke well of him—further proof that she'd been out of line with her accusations. She'd let her prejudice influence her judgment, allowing her distrust of men to overshadow the truth she'd gleaned with her own eyes over the last year. Ben Porter was a man of honor.

Dependable. Kind. Trustworthy. He'd done nothing to deserve her censure.

"I'm sorry." She blurted the apology as the wagon dipped into a rut. The jarring motion squeezed the end of the statement into a high-pitched squeak.

Ben glanced her way, his brows lifted. "What was that?"

"I'm sorry," she repeated, taking care to enunciate each word, wanting him to hear her sincerity. "For the things I said earlier."

He made no response, just kept looking at her with an unnerving level of intensity.

"I . . ." She swallowed hard then forced herself to form the words. "I've learned to be guarded around men, and sometimes that guardedness leads me to suspect dishonorable motives where there are none." She dropped her gaze to her lap, his attention too unnerving. "Over the past year, you've been nothing but kind to Lewis and to me. I had no reason to accuse you of deception and trickery."

He remained quiet for a long time. Even turned his attention back to the road. Tori bit her lip. Was he still so angry that he'd refuse to accept her apology? Or had her unthinking words injured him more than she'd thought possible? The man was so large, it was hard to imagine anything as puny as a few words inflicting damage. Yet she knew better than anyone how barbed comments could zing past one's defenses to slice into the tender places inside.

Contemplating whether or not she should try again to gain his forgiveness, she nearly missed the quiet offering that rumbled between them.

"Thanks for that. The words, I mean. I've . . . waited a long time." He glanced her way, and the raw emotion in his gaze obliterated her well-constructed shield as if it were no more substantial than papier-mâché.

He'd waited a long time for what? Not an apology, surely. She hadn't wronged him like that before. Recognition of his kindness, perhaps? She shifted uncomfortably on the bench. Had she really never expressed appreciation to him? Surely, she'd commended him on his timely deliveries or thanked him for his efforts in opening new markets for her goods at the very least. Hadn't she?

Good heavens. Shame lashed her. All this time, she'd been so set on protecting herself, she'd never once considered how prickly her armor made her. Politeness wasn't the same as kindness. Over this past year, Benjamin Porter had repeatedly bent over backward to help her—offering protection when their town had been threatened by outlaws, seeking new customers when her largest account refused to do business with her after Harper's Station agreed to take in Stanley Fischer's runaway mail-order bride. Time and again Ben Porter had gone the extra mile for her, and what had she offered in return? A smattering of porcupine quills in the face every time he came too close.

Why in the world did he wish to court her? He should brush her aside and find a woman who wasn't so emotionally barren.

An odd moisture gathered in the corner of her eyes. She almost didn't recognize it. She never cried. Ever. Tears were a weakness that failed to solve problems. But this wetness felt different. The tears blurring her vision hadn't emerged in response to something that had happened *to* her, as the pointless tears she'd wept in her youth had done. No, these had spawned from contrition, an altogether different source. And one that apparently had not been drained completely dry within her.

Tori blinked. Again. And again. Desperate to rid her eyes of the moisture that threatened to crest the spillway. Her heart thumped a wild staccato beat against her ribs.

Get yourself under control. You're out in the middle of nowhere. You can't afford to be this vulnerable.

Yet a secret longing deep inside urged her to set aside her rigid habits. To let her guard down just for a moment and remember what it was like to live without the constant weight of her self-imposed armor.

"I know you've been hurt in the past, Tori."

She closed her eyes against the compassion radiating from the man beside her, fumbling for the shield that used to fortify her so well. She couldn't relive the past now. Not when her emotions were closer to the surface than they'd been in years.

"I know you're afraid of being hurt in the future."

She could feel him looking at her. Feel his gaze like a caress against her sleeve. Her cheek. Her hair.

"I'll never ask you for details," he continued, and a tiny coil of tension unwound inside her. "Your secrets are yours to keep or to share as you will. But know that whether we remain simply business partners or someday move to a more personal relationship, I will *never* think less of you for what you've gone through. Whatever happened, you will always hold a place of highest esteem in my eyes."

The prickle along her arm dissipated, and she knew he'd looked away. She cracked her eyes open just enough to stare at her lap, the sensible taupe fabric of her skirt offering a much-needed anchor to the flamboyant thoughts and feelings splashing about in her mind.

Whatever happened? Ben might think he wouldn't think less of her, but if he knew the truth, he'd change his mind. How could he not? Her past was ugly. Slashed red with selfishness, disobedience, and willful stubbornness. Sprinkled with a healthy dose of youthful folly and naïveté. And over it all, smeared black with evil. With pain. With betrayal and abandonment.

The only purity that escaped the blackness of that time came from Lewis. She was sure she would have lost her faith entirely had God not seen fit to bless her with a child. Through Lewis, the Lord had proven he really could bring beauty from ashes.

As they drove on in silence, Tori prayed. Prayed that she not be so consumed with protecting herself that she failed to see the needs of others. Prayed that the man beside her would be showered with blessings in reward for his faithful kindness to her and her son. Prayed that somehow the pain that had kept her prisoner for so long would finally release its hold.

The wagon rocked, its rhythmic sway lulling Tori into a semi-doze. Her prayers gradually faded, her mind instead filling with the verses she'd memorized the day Lewis had been born.

"*. . . he hath sent me to bind up the brokenhearted, to proclaim liberty to the captives, and the opening of the prison to them that are bound . . . to comfort all that mourn . . . to give them beauty for ashes, the oil of joy for mourning, the garment of praise for the spirit of heaviness; that they might be called trees of righteousness, the planting of the Lord, that he might be glorified.*"

She believed with all her heart that God had sent Lewis to her for just those reasons—to bind her broken heart, to provide comfort, to turn her ashes into something beautiful that she could be proud of, to plant her firmly back in the Lord and allow her the chance to live righteously moving forward. And with God's help, her beautiful boy had done just that.

Or she thought he had.

So why did she still feel imprisoned?

Tori slanted a hidden glance at the man beside her. Could it be that God had sent her another messenger to finish the job? A rather handsome, overlarge freighter with kind eyes and a patient spirit?

A little shiver coursed through Tori's midsection. She named it dread, but that quiet voice deep inside whispered a different label— anticipation.

6

Ben did all he could to look nonchalant. Rested his forearms on his thighs as he drove. Kept his fingers loose and relaxed on the reins. Added just a touch of a smile to his mouth so his expression would give away none of his inner turmoil.

Had he said too much? Prodded old wounds when he would've been better leaving them alone? He didn't know. And the not knowing was driving him crazy. Tori hadn't said a word since he'd brought up her past. Not even an angry one. Nothing. It was unnerving.

'Course he hadn't said anything either.

He gave his head a nearly imperceptible shake. She'd finally admitted that he might actually have a few admirable qualities, despite his male status, and he'd gone and ruined the moment by reminding her of the reason she distrusted his kind in the first place.

Brilliant, Porter. Absolutely brilliant.

Yet he couldn't regret his words. She'd needed to hear them, whether she was ready to accept certain truths or not. He didn't judge her for having a son with no husband—however that occurrence came about. Heaven knew, he'd made enough mistakes in his own life to keep him from tossing stones.

He'd never thought it right for society to condemn a woman for bearing the consequences of a sin that obviously took two participants. To his way of thinking, any man who used a female in such a

51

way, then abandoned her deserved society's derision more than she did. And if the man had forced the issue against the lady's will . . . ? Ben clenched his jaw. He'd not throw stones. He'd throw boulders.

"Mr. Ben?"

Thankful for the distraction from his dark thoughts, Ben straightened his posture and leaned back against the seat to close the distance between him and Lewis. He raised his chin and twisted slightly. "What you need, scamp?"

"We gonna stop soon? Herc and I are gettin' hungry."

Ben glanced at the scenery around him, getting his bearings as he registered landmarks. "I think we can manage that. If I remember right, there's a real pretty spot by the Deer Spring turnoff. We should be there in about—"

Tori grabbed his arm. Her nails clawed at him with such force, they nearly cut through the sleeve of his shirt.

His gaze shot to her face. Her cheeks had drained of color. Her head slowly wagged from side to side, but her gaze seemed cloudy, unfocused.

"What is it, Tori?" Ben whispered not wanting to alarm Lewis.

Suddenly her gaze sharpened, pinning him to the seat. "We are *not* going to Deer Spring." Her voice shook, but her grip on his arm nearly cut off his circulation. "You said we'd be taking the route to Wichita Falls. Deer Spring lies too far east. We can't go there. There isn't time."

There wasn't time to go all the way to Wichita Falls, either, but somehow he didn't think that was the issue. Something about Deer Spring spooked her. She had the look of a mare ready to bolt, no matter how badly she might injure herself kicking free of the stall.

"We're not going to Deer Spring." Ben took one hand from the reins to cover hers where it clawed at his arm. He rubbed back and forth in a soothing motion, doing everything he could think of to calm her. "I promise. We don't even have to stop at the turnoff, if you don't want. We can drive straight past and find another place to have our lunch."

Lewis popped his head into the space between the two adults, oblivious to the underlying tension. "But, Mama, I'm hunnnngry. And I think Hercules needs to water the flowers." He snickered at his ma's prissy phrasing, but Tori barely blinked.

Ben clasped Tori's hand, peeling it away from his arm just enough to wrap his fingers fully around hers. He didn't care about the pain from her grip, or the marks her nails had surely left in his hide. All he cared about was communicating that he was by her side. He wouldn't leave. And he would guard her from whatever threat Deer Spring posed.

"You can wait a bit," Ben said, keeping his tone light. "Your mama wants to go a little farther before we stop. Maybe she can dig out a snack for you from that basket of hers." He turned his attention back to Tori, thankful to see a touch of color returning to her cheeks. He gave her hand a gentle squeeze. "What do you think, Tori? Can the boy have a bit of bread or something to tide him over?"

"A snack won't keep Hercules from peein'."

Ben shot Lewis a stern look.

"What?" The boy shrugged. "It's true."

"It might be, but we don't use words like that in front of ladies." What Ben really wanted to scold him for was pressing the issue of stopping when it caused Tori such distress, but he couldn't do that without causing the boy worry. Something Tori wouldn't want.

So, he opted for unilateral authority. "We'll stop in about thirty minutes, scamp. Sit down and try to keep Hercules away from your mama's boxes. We don't want him—"

"It's all right," Tori interrupted, her voice a little shaky, but her intent clear. "We can stop."

Ben peered at her. "Are you sure?"

She nodded. "Yes." She cleared her throat and tugged her hand free of his hold. Ben let her go, though he immediately grieved the loss of contact. "Let's stop at the turnoff," she said, her voice steadier now. "There's a stream there, if I remember correctly. It will be a good place for the horses." Her lips curved in a smile that was no doubt meant to reassure, but her eyes told the truth—she was still shaken. "We're all hungry. And heaven knows, I don't want Hercules watering the flowers before we stop."

Lewis giggled, and Tori's smile finally reached her eyes.

What had possessed her? Tori nibbled the edge of her bottom lip as she straightened the edges of the tablecloth she'd just spread over a grassy patch of ground near the stream. She'd known their journey today would take them in the direction of her old home. She'd made the trip to Wichita Falls before, for pity's sake. Yet when Ben mentioned the turnoff to Deer Spring, she'd panicked.

Tori frowned. She never panicked. Panic meant a lack of control, and she treasured control above all else. Yet she'd lost that control. For a few awful moments, the terror she'd fought so hard to abolish from her life sunk its poisonous fangs into her again. It must have been the timing. It was the only thing that made sense. That horrible man with his leering and suggestive proposition left her feeling soiled, the same way Paul had left her feeling after . . .

Don't think of it, Victoria.

She grabbed the mental door to slam it closed as she always did when memories tried to surface, but this time she couldn't quite shut it all the way. It was as if someone had stuck his foot into the door, and no matter how hard she slammed, the boot didn't budge.

Tori glanced over to the stream where Ben stood with his giant horses, patting their necks and talking to them as if they were people. Her heart softened a little. He really was a good man. A gentle man. That's why she couldn't close the door on her memories, not completely. Because Ben Porter had wormed his way into them.

Standing up for her against the lecherous farmer. Taking her side without question, even against Lewis. When thoughts of her past life in Deer Spring had pounced on her like a mountain lion on a jackrabbit, she'd reached for him. And he'd been there. Solid. Strong. Solicitous. He'd not pulled away from her touch, even though she knew she must have left marks with the force of her grip. Heat flared in her cheeks as she recalled how he'd had to peel her fingers away from his forearm in order to clasp her hand.

And, oh, how it had felt to have his large hand surrounding hers. Warm. Supportive. Wonderful. As if she had an ally. One who'd stand by her side no matter what came. She'd only ever felt that way with Emma and a handful of the ladies in Harper's Station. Never with a man.

"Keep an eye on your pup, Lewis." Ben's warning sharpened Tori's focus, bringing her out of her fuzzy reverie. "Helios spooks easier since that accident a few months back. Best to keep Hercules away."

She remembered that accident, precipitated by the same outlaws who had tried to drive the ladies out of Harper's Station. They'd destroyed Ben's freight wagon, nearly killing him in the process, and had sent his horses careening off into the countryside. The black-bellied one, Helios, had fallen and been pinned to the ground when Hermes, still connected via the harness, had fallen atop him. She didn't blame the animal for being a little skittish. Being pinned down by a hulking beast, unable to free yourself, was a horrifying experience. Tori rubbed her suddenly cool arms. One that left scars.

Thankfully, Lewis responded quickly to Ben's warning. He scooped up the puppy and moved a few yards upstream. Satisfied with her son's obedience, Tori turned her attention back to the picnic arrangement and lowered herself onto the spread cloth as she reached for the waiting basket. She unpacked the ham sandwiches she'd made that morning along with a covered dish of potato salad, a dozen molasses cookies, and two canning jars of what by now was sure to be tepid lemonade. Oh, well. At least it was wet and sweet.

"Lunch is ready," she called.

Ben was the first to turn. His grin set off an odd fluttering in her belly. He'd smiled at her before. Hundreds of times. So why did this one suddenly make her knees weak?

Because he's still got his foot stuck in your heart's door. Better dislodge him soon before he finds a way to sneak completely inside.

"Be right there." He touched the brim of his hat and dipped his chin. The gentlemanly show of respect only intensified the quivering in her midsection. Battling his gallantry was hard enough, she didn't need him to pour on the charm as well.

Tori dropped her gaze to the basket, determined to put the man back in his proper place—outside her heart. But as she collected the flatware and napkins, her head came back up, her eyes drawn against her will to the man who threatened to circumvent her defenses.

He led Hermes and Helios up the shallow embankment, their pace plodding and slow. The Shires remained in harness, but he'd unhitched them from the wagon to make it easier for them to graze and drink from the stream. They steadily drew nearer. Ben's gaze locked with hers. She tried to look away but couldn't. It was as if something inside her had remained connected to him after the episode in the wagon where she'd clasped his arm.

A yapping echoed in her ears. Loud and shrill, but she paid it no mind. Then out of nowhere, Hercules bounded across Ben's path. Lewis chased the pup, only inches behind.

"No, Herc!" the boy cried. "Stop!"

But it was too late. The pup rushed straight at Helios. The monster horse neighed in fright and reared back on his hind legs, his giant hooves flailing. Right above Lewis's head.

Tori screamed her son's name. She scrambled to her feet, desperate to get to him, stumbling over the food she'd so carefully arranged. But he was too far away.

The sharp, massive hooves descended. Lewis stood frozen beneath. Eyes wide, mouth agape.

"Noooo!" Her heart tore from her chest.

But in the same instant the hooves came down, a dark shadow engulfed her son, carrying him to the ground, and taking the blow upon itself.

Ben.

7

⬥————⬥————⬥

Instinct demanded she run straight at the horses, but Tori resisted the deadly urge and slowed her approach. If she spooked the team further . . .

Chancing a quick glance downward, she spotted Ben curled in a ball on the ground. Not moving. She swallowed the agony rising inside her. He would be all right. Lewis too. They had to be.

Helios shied sideways, his hooves banging against Ben's back and hip. The horse's nervous dancing set Hermes to snorting and pawing as well. Fearing one of the animals would rear again and inflict more damage, Tori held her hands up, palms out, and spoke as calmly as she could manage.

"Easy, now." She took a step forward. "Nothing's going to hurt you." Another step. "You're safe." One more.

The horses balked, tossing their heads and stamping their feet. Tori froze and silently begged the Lord to still the beasts like he had the waves of the biblical storm. Carefully, stealthily, she inched her way around Ben until she stood between him and the restless team. Leaning away from the horses' massive heads, which hovered so close to her own she could feel the warmth of their agitated breath, she slowly reached for the cheek straps on the bridles.

"That's right," she crooned. "Good boys."

She reached again. Her fingers closed around the harness, and she swore she heard angels singing. Probably just the rush of blood pounding in her ears as relief mixed with intimidation at being so close to such large creatures.

"Back," she urged as she straightened and applied light pressure to the bridle straps. Helios pawed the ground, nearly taking off her toes. Steeling herself, Tori inserted herself between the team and increased the pressure. "Back, boys." She leaned closer to the horse on her right. "Come on, Hermes. Take charge." She clicked her tongue. "Back."

Hermes took a step backward.

Thank you, Lord.

Helios followed, finally regaining his composure and obedient nature. She reversed their path a good ten feet before letting go of the bridle straps and easing away from them.

"Lewis?" she called softly, walking backward several steps before trusting the horses enough to turn and hurry to where she'd left Ben and her son. "Lewis? Are you all right?"

The puppy sat beside Ben, nosing at his midsection and whining. Tori pushed Hercules aside. "Ben? Can you hear me? I need to get Lewis."

No answer.

She reached into the crevice between Ben's arms and legs, where she spied the dark blue of her son's shirt. "Let go, Ben," she whispered, wincing as she jostled the brave man who had sacrificed himself to save her son. She didn't want to hurt him, but she needed to get to her son.

"Mama?" The tiny, muffled voice shot a healthy dose of joy through Tori. Joy and a desperate need to get him free. To hold him and assure herself that he was really all right.

"Yes, darling." She tugged on his arm, but the weight of Ben's torso held him captive. "It's safe now. The horses are settled." Tori tried to slip her own arm into the crevice to get a better grip on her child, but she couldn't find an opening. "Lewis? Help Mama get you out."

Little boy grunts echoed beneath her. "I'm stuck." As Lewis struggled, Ben's body shifted slightly but not enough to allow escape. "Mama, I can't move!" His fear spurred Tori to try a new tactic.

Bracing both hands on Ben's shoulder, Tori dug her toes into the ground for greater leverage and pushed with all her might.

Ben flopped onto his back. Tori's momentum sprawled her atop him, sandwiching Lewis in between. Ben groaned. Tori scrambled off as fast as she could, whispering apologies as she went. Lewis crawled away from his protector, too, and threw himself into his mother's eager arms.

Tori lifted him off the ground and hugged him tight. His legs clung to her waist, his arms strangled her neck, and his bony little chest pressed into hers. Nothing could have felt better. She held him close for a long moment, savoring the feel of her child alive and well.

But there was another who was not so well. One to whom she owed a debt she could never repay.

She kissed the top of Lewis's head, then loosened her grip and leaned back to see his face. The tears flowing down his cheeks sent a jolt of alarm through her. "Are you hurt?"

She immediately scanned him for injury, but he shook his head. "Mr. Ben s-saved me." He glanced behind him to the man still lying on the ground. "Is he . . . d-dead?"

"Oh, no, honey. No." Tori hugged Lewis once again, the guilt and anguish on his young face breaking her heart. "I heard him groan when he rolled over. He's just hurt. We need to help him."

"It's my f-fault." Lewis sniffed and his arms tightened around her neck. "I shoulda watched Hercules better."

"It was *not* your fault." Tori wasn't about to let him carry that burden. "It was an accident. That's all. You understand me?"

Lewis sniffed again, then nodded.

"Good." She juggled him a bit in order to reach into her skirt pocket and retrieve a handkerchief. After she wiped his tears away and helped him blow his nose, she stuck the soiled cotton back into her pocket and lowered Lewis to the ground. "Now. Let's see what we can do to help Mr. Porter."

Lewis hovered behind her, sniffing occasionally as she bent down to examine the freighter. She didn't see any blood or damage on his front side, but then, it had been his back that had taken the horse's blows.

"We need to roll him onto his side so I can see his head and back." She twisted to look at Lewis. "Think you're up to it?"

He glanced once at the horses, who grazed a few short feet away, his face filled with apprehension, but then he looked to his mentor and set his jaw. When his eyes met hers, they glowed with determination. He nodded.

"Good boy." Tori stood and walked around to the opposite side of Ben's fallen form then crouched down near his shoulders. "I need you to be here," she said pointing to a place on the front side near Ben's legs. Lewis hurried to take up the position. "When I say go, I want you to grab his denims at the top of his hip and pull him toward you as hard as you can. All right?"

Lewis squatted down and moved his hands into position.

Tori slid her palms beneath Ben's back and shoulders. She glanced across at her son. "Ready?"

He nodded.

"Go!"

Together they strained, pulling and pushing, until Ben's body finally started to roll. Tori wedged herself beneath him, not wanting to give up any ground they gained.

Why did he have to be such a large, solidly built man? If rolling him over was this hard, they'd never be able to get him into the wagon.

As the big man rolled slowly onto his side, Tori adjusted her hand position so she could gain greater leverage. Bent low, she pressed up into his back, pushing with her legs. Ben let out a groan. Something warm and wet oozed beneath her palms.

Blood.

Heaven help her. She was hurting him!

She wanted to let go immediately, but that would serve no good purpose. So she continued on, murmuring apologies he couldn't hear and promises he couldn't appreciate in his unconscious state. But his lack of awareness did nothing to dim her determination to keep her word. She would do everything in her power to see him restored to health. Whatever it took.

With one last push, they got him on his side. His head lay at a crooked, uncomfortable-looking angle, but it was the misshapen lump on the back of his skull that caused her the most concern. That and the bloody lines soaking through the back of his shirt.

Keeping an arm on his shoulder to ensure he didn't roll farther,

Tori met her son's gaze. "Go fetch the jars of water and the lunch napkins. Put them in the basket and bring them here."

Lewis shot to his feet and ran over to the picnic she'd laid out.

"Oh, and bring the tablecloth, too," she called as an afterthought. She could use it as a pillow of sorts to prop Ben's head up. The poor man deserved as much comfort as she could manufacture.

While Lewis collected the items she'd requested, Tori reached around to Ben's front and unbuttoned his shirt. She needed to see the wounds on his back.

Once the buttons were disengaged, she eased his left arm out of his sleeve. The task was much more difficult to perform with a heavily-muscled, grown man than a sleepy four-year old, but she managed. Slowly, she peeled the cotton away from his skin.

A deep angry groove in the shape of a horseshoe marred the space between his shoulder blades. There wasn't much blood, thank the Lord, just a few shallow places where the skin had broken. And since the blow had hit the high part of his back instead of the lower fleshy areas around the kidneys or liver, she had every hope that the internal damage had been minimal. It would cause him considerable pain and would no doubt turn half his back black-and-blue, but it shouldn't be a cause of major concern. Just to be sure, though, she ran her hands over the expanse of his back, feeling for any fractures that might exist in his shoulder blades, ribs, or spine. All while trying to ignore the impressive contours of muscle she traced. And the alarming amount of pleasure she derived from her exploration.

Thankfully, the clanking of canning jars and high-pitched puppy yaps announced Lewis's return.

"I got it," he huffed as dropped the basket to the ground beside Tori. He dragged half of the tablecloth behind him in the dirt, but she supposed Ben wouldn't mind a little dust. She'd just have to keep the worst of it away from his head wound.

"Good job, Lewis. Thank you." She took the tablecloth from him and eased it under Ben's head, taking care to fold the cleanest section on the outside where the freighter's head rested.

"His back is real scraped up, Mama." Lines of concern grooved Lewis's forehead.

All Tori could do was nod agreement. There were several smaller abrasions along the lower section of Ben's back, but the red marks were superficial and most were not even bleeding. It was the lump on his head that worried her.

After taking a couple minutes to clean the larger wound on his upper back, Tori shoved aside her dread and faced the challenge she'd been avoiding. His head.

She inhaled a deep breath and tried to recall everything Maybelle had done for him the last time he'd sustained a head injury—the day Angus Johnson had ambushed him and wrecked his wagon. Probe the wounded area for tenderness. Clean away the dirt and blood. Stitch up any gash that might exist.

Nibbling on her bottom lip, Tori gently tunneled her fingers into Ben's blackish brown hair at the back of his skull. As she neared the swollen area, wetness spread over her fingertips. A lot of wetness. She pulled her hand away. Red covered her hand.

"Mama?" Lewis's voice wobbled.

Tori immediately hid her hand in her skirt. "It's all right, honey. Miss Maybelle says that scalp wounds bleed a lot. It's nothing to fret about." Not that she was doing a good job of following that advice. Her pulse had ratcheted up when she'd seen all that blood on her hand. "Why don't you find Mr. Porter's hat and take it back to the wagon for him. Take the picnic food, too. You and Hercules can eat a couple of the sandwiches. I'll call you if I need more help."

"Okay." Lewis turned to his puppy. "Come on, Herc. Time to eat."

As soon as he left, Tori returned to her examination. A lump wider than the palm of her hand had swollen up at the back of Ben's head. A large, arc-shaped gash splayed open at the top of the area, deep enough she could see the white of his bone.

A gag rose in Tori's throat, but she fought it down. There was no time for squeamishness.

She poured a stream of water over the gash to wash away the blood and used a napkin to clean away the worst of the dirt. She wished now she'd never rolled him onto his back in order to free Lewis. What if the wound got infected because of her? She should have taken off her suit jacket and laid it beneath him. Protected him as he'd protected her son. But at the time, she'd been too desperate to free Lewis to think clearly.

She needed to get him to a house. Someplace where they would have spirits to clean the wound and salves to help it heal. She'd brought needles and thread in her sewing notions crate, but she dared not stitch his wound closed before it was adequately cleaned. Maybelle never stitched any wound without treating it with some kind of alcohol. She soaked the needle and thread in it, too, if Tori recalled correctly.

For now, she'd have to bandage it up as well as she could and figure out some way to get him into the wagon.

Lord, you're going to have to work that part out.

Dealing with the impossibility of getting Ben up into the wagon bed was beyond her capabilities. One worry at a time. His injury came first.

She folded the last clean napkin into a thick square and set it in the basket. As she did so, her hand knocked up against the knife she'd packed for cutting the sandwiches. Perfect. That would make tearing a strip from her petticoat much easier. She needed something to act as a bandage, a strip long enough to wrap around Ben's head. The napkins were too short and the tablecloth too dirty. She supposed she could use some of the calico she'd brought, but somehow she just couldn't imagine a pattern of tiny flowers wrapped around Benjamin Porter's head. The white cotton of her underskirt would be much more dignified.

Tori slowly got to her feet, lifted her skirt, and grabbed hold of her petticoat. Taking the knife, she cut a slit in the cotton directly below the seam that held the three-inch ruffle in place. Once she had a hole large enough to get her fingers inside, she fisted her hand around the fabric and pulled. The rending sound filled her with satisfaction as the ruffle pulled free. Using her knife again, she sliced vertically through the fabric at the bottom of the loop and created a long, wide strip of cotton ready to be made into a bandage. Holding it high to keep it from touching the dirt, she gathered it into a wad and folded it into her belly as she crouched back down. She returned the knife to the bottom of the basket and retrieved the dressing she'd made moments ago.

"Sorry, Ben," she murmured. "This is going to hurt." She pressed the dressing firmly against the gash and the swollen area beneath.

The big man moaned and mumbled something. She couldn't understand him, but the thought that he might have spoken, speared her with hope.

"Ben? Can you hear me?" *Please, God, let him wake up.*

Holding the dressing in place, Tori scooted around to the front of him to better see his face. His eyes were still closed, but he grimaced as she jostled his head. That had to mean he was semiconscious. Right?

"Ben. Please. Open your eyes." She stared at his lashes, willing them to lift. Maybe if she kept talking. . . . "You've been injured. Helios became frightened and reared. You took a blow to your head and another to your back. I've cleaned the wounds as best I can, but we need to get you somewhere where I can tend you properly." His eyelids twitched but didn't open.

She cradled his head while holding the dressing in one hand, then fed the end of the bandage into the fingers cupping his skull and started wrapping the fabric around his forehead, careful to steer clear of his eyes. Not knowing what else to do, she started chattering again, saying whatever popped into her mind.

"I need you to wake up, Ben. We have to get you into the wagon, but you're too heavy for me to lift." She reached the end of her bandage and tied it off. She should probably leave him laying there and see to hitching up the horses. It was a task she could actually manage, and one that would have to be done before they could seek help, but she couldn't bring herself to leave him. Not yet.

She leaned closer and gently took his face into her hands. His rugged, beautiful face. "Thank you," she said, her voice suddenly growing husky as moisture collected at the back of her throat. "Thank you for saving my son." She touched her lips to his bandage-covered forehead. "You're the best man I've ever known, Benjamin Porter. And I'm frightened by how much you are coming to mean to me."

"Don't be afraid, Tori." The low mumble of words brought her head up like a shot.

"Ben?"

His mouth quirked a half smile even as his eyes fluttered open. "I like hearing you say my name."

Never had she seen such beautiful gray eyes. "Do you remember what happened?"

He tried to nod, then winced and stilled. "Helios got spooked." Tension suddenly stiffened his muscles. His gaze zeroed in on hers. "Lewis?"

She smiled. "He's fine. Worried about you, though."

He sighed, and relaxed. His eyes slid closed, and Tori started to panic. He couldn't lose consciousness again—not before they got him in the wagon.

"Ben!" she ordered. "Open your eyes."

Praise the Lord, he complied.

"I need you to stand up. We've got to get you into the wagon."

His jaw clenched, and he rolled forward slightly, catching himself with one arm. Tori hurried to help. Moving as smoothly as she could to minimize the jarring to his head, she helped him into a sitting position. He glanced down at his naked chest.

"Where's my shirt?"

Cheeks heating, Tori reached behind him and snagged the dangling shirt sleeve and held it open for him to push his left arm through. When she finally found the wherewithal to look him in the face again, the teasing look in his pain-filled eyes nearly toppled her onto her backside.

"Knew you liked my muscles."

Of all the . . . Oh, who was she kidding? She *did* like his muscles. Though they both knew that had nothing to do with his shirt being undone.

"Modesty is obviously not one of your virtues." She'd tried to make the statement sound prim, but it filtered through her smile and came out sounding flirtatious instead. Her. Flirtatious. Good grief. Head injuries must be contagious.

Offering herself as a human crutch, Tori managed to get Ben on his feet, and together they hobbled to the wagon. Lewis arranged the pallet of quilts for Ben to lie on and kept Hercules contained while Tori fetched the team. It took longer than she would have liked to get the Shires hitched, but twenty minutes later, she was finally in the driver's seat reaching for the reins.

The only question was which way to go. She wanted to turn back the way they had come, start heading toward home to Maybelle's capable doctoring, but the last house they'd passed was thirty minutes away and belonged to that awful lecher who'd propositioned her. A shiver coursed through her. She couldn't go there. It wouldn't be safe. Nor clean. She pulled a face as she recalled the vile man's poor hygiene. Ben was more likely to catch an infection than prevent one if they stopped there.

The Deer Spring turnoff called to her. Four years ago, there'd been a house not far from this very junction. A well-kept clapboard home, picket fence, garden. She'd passed it as she left her home behind and dreamt of raising Lewis in a place just like it someday.

Her gut clenched as she contemplated turning the horses down that road. A road she swore to herself she'd never set foot upon again.

But Ben needed help. And that house, if still occupied, was the closest potential source of help.

Steeling her nerves, Tori made up her mind. She clicked to the horses, snapped the reins, and headed down the road to Deer Spring.

8

B en gritted his teeth as the wagon bumped down the road, determined to hold onto consciousness. His head felt like a smithy's anvil with the blacksmith pounding a sledge against the back of his skull over and over. Yet even through the haze of pain, he'd noticed which direction Tori had steered the team. Whatever had her spooked about this road, he didn't want her facing it alone. Even if the only attackers were memories from her past. He might not be able to fight off a flesh-and-blood enemy at the moment, but he could battle ghosts. And he aimed to do just that.

"I see the house up ahead, Ben." Tori twisted slightly to toss the words over her shoulder. "We'll have you there soon. I promise."

He grunted a bit in response. It was all he could manage with the majority of his energy being spent staving off the darkness that kept encroaching. Her continued use of his given name served as a pleasant distraction, though. Ben's mouth quirked up just a bit at the corners. The fact that she hadn't reinforced the formality between them now that the initial scare had passed gave him hope that one barrier might have finally come down.

The wagon dipped to the left as Tori turned off the main road. Ben couldn't see much beyond sky, but he could hear a dog bark and children's voices. He relaxed just a bit. Kids generally meant womenfolk and family. Less chance of Tori running into another unsavory character.

Hercules added his yips to the orchestration as Lewis shuffled across the wagon bed and lifted up on his knees to get a better view.

"What do you see, scamp?" Ben mumbled the words, but Lewis seemed to understand.

"A big white house, and a tree with a rope swing! And kids. A boy who looks a little older than me and a girl. She's short. And she's got a doll." He reported the last with such a tone of disgust, Ben would have chuckled if he wasn't sure the vibrations would set off a cataclysm in his head.

"Any grown-ups?"

Lewis made a show of looking right then left. "Nope. Wait. A lady just came out the front door."

He heard a woman's voice calling to her children. "Michael. Daphne. Come up to the house."

The team slowed, and Ben grabbed onto the side of the wagon. As soon as they stopped, he was going to drag himself to a seated position. He didn't want these folks to think him completely incapacitated.

"Please, I need help." Tori started her plea before the horses halted. "My . . . friend is hurt. He was kicked in the head by a horse while protecting my son. If you could spare some medical supplies, I can tend him out here. I just need some soap and hot water—spirits, if you have them—and, perhaps, some salve and clean bandages."

"There's too much dirt blowing around out here," the other woman said, her voice closer now that the wagon had stopped. "Let's get him in the house. Michael, go fetch your pa. He'll want to help."

She came up alongside the wagon, and Ben finally got a look at his hostess while he slowly edged upward. Marching down to the rear of the vehicle, all business, she reminded him a bit of Tori. Blond, on the tall side, blue eyes. Eyes that widened when they fastened on him. She pulled up short at the tailgate.

"He certainly is a *big* fellow, isn't he?"

Ben attempted a smile, but the scenery seemed intent on spinning and playing havoc with his stomach. The smile turned into a grimace as he concentrated on keeping the nausea at bay. "Benjamin Porter . . .

ma'am," he managed to force out as he gripped the wagon side and closed his eyes. If the world would just stop spinning. . . .

"Ben! You should have waited for me." The wagon wobbled a bit, no doubt from Tori climbing up into the bed. An instant later, her hand clasped his shoulder. "Here. Wrap your arm around me." She reached for the arm that didn't have a death grip on the wagon side and wrapped it around her neck.

He cracked his eyes open a smidge. "I'd never . . . turn that . . . request down."

Her cheeks turned a lovely shade of pink. Score one for him.

"Lean on me," she said, not letting his teasing interfere with her mission. "The wagon edge is not far."

All thought of further teasing left him as he clenched his jaw and focused on keeping his head as still as possible as he inched his way toward the tailgate. As soon as his legs dropped over the edge, a second set of shoulders pressed themselves beneath his other arm. Ben forced his fingers to release the wooden slats at his side and let some of his weight fall on the woman whose name he still didn't know. Not that it mattered. She was helping. Names could be exchanged later.

As the two women aided his pitiful progression up to the house, Tori admonished Lewis to stay on the porch and keep Hercules in line. The second woman gave similar instructions to her daughter, telling her to welcome their young visitor and perhaps introduce her doll to his puppy. Ben could imagine how well *that* suggestion would go over. He just hoped the doll didn't end up a doggie chew toy.

Ten minutes later, the women had him sitting in a chair at the kitchen table, his head unwrapped, a box of medical supplies open and ready. Tori insisted on cleaning the wound, her thoroughness rather painful to endure, but Ben managed to tough it out by gripping the seat edge and clamping his jaw shut to keep any unmanly moans from slipping out. When she reached for the whiskey, he knew he was in trouble, but he braced himself and only let out a small hiss when the liquid fire hit his scalp despite the fact that it felt like acid eating a hole through his skull.

"I'm sorry, Ben," Tori soothed, her hand cupping his shoulder as she blotted the excess wetness from his nape with a towel and waited for the liquor to evaporate. "I'm almost done."

Too bad. He was rather enjoying her fussing over him. Well, except for the excruciating pain. Tori had never voluntarily touched him. Soothed him. Murmured his name in the affectionate tone usually reserved solely for Lewis. Getting kicked in the head seemed to have advanced his wooing. He could live with temporary pain if it helped him claim a permanent hold on the woman he loved.

Yet when he watched her fish a threaded needle out of a shallow tray filled with whiskey, a few dozen second thoughts reared their heads. He wasn't a fan of needles. Jabbing and poking and dragging thread where it didn't belong. He'd suffered through it a few months ago after the outlaw attack, and he remembered the squeamish feeling all too well. A shiver coursed through him.

Be a man, Porter. Men don't flinch.

Making sure his feet were planted squarely on the floor, Ben sat up tall and nodded to Tori when she asked if he was ready. The jab of the needle wasn't so bad. It was the long tug of the thread that sent his stomach swirling. Praying that the Lord wouldn't allow him to disgrace himself by puking all over his hostess's kitchen floor, Ben closed his eyes and inhaled long and slow, doing all he could to keep his innards under control.

Jab. Pull. Jab. Pull.

Breathe, man. Think about something else. Anything else.

Jab. Pull.

Unfortunately, nothing else came to mind. He tried to think about Tori, about holding her in his arms while she smiled adoringly up at him, about lowering his lips to hers . . . but since she was the one instigating his torture, the pleasure he usually derived from that particular fantasy fell a bit short.

"Just two more should do it," Tori encouraged.

The sharp prick of needle entering flesh for a fifth time registered a second before the back door opened and a man stepped in, the boy Ben had noticed earlier at his side.

"Frannie?" The man's gaze immediately sought out his wife. "Are you all ri . . ." The words died, and his eyes widened, no longer fixed on his wife but on Ben. Slowly the man raised his hands and stepped protectively in front of his son.

What was the fellow doing? Ben was no threat. He was woozy and bleeding and had a hole in the back of his head, for pity's sake.

"Easy, lady," the man said. "Put the gun down. You don't want to hurt anyone."

Lady? Ben slowly turned his head, ignoring the pain radiating through his temples.

There stood Tori. Face ashen. Eyes panicked. Hands clutching . . . a pocket pistol? What was she doing with a gun? And why did she have it trained on a man they'd never even met?

"Don't touch me," she whispered, the words broken, angry, desperate. "Don't touch me."

Ben eyed the man, then cast a quick glance at the boy cowering behind his pa. A boy that bore a striking resemblance to the one playing outside with his new puppy. Suddenly Ben's head was the last thing he cared about. Using the table as support, he slowly pushed to his feet and balled his hands into fists.

It was only the wife's indrawn breath and the way her eyes filled with empathy as she gently approached Tori that made Ben pause.

"Heaven's above. You're from Deer Spring, aren't you." The quiet words were more statement than question as the woman, Frannie, gently touched Tori's shoulder.

Tori didn't seem to notice the contact. Every ounce of her attention remained focused on the man in front of her.

"He's not Paul," the woman said, her voice firm yet compassionate. "He's not the one who hurt you. Look closer. His eyes are a darker brown. His nose has a bump on the bridge. He has an old scar along his chin from when he fell out of a tree as a child. He's not Paul. This is Jed. Jed Crowley. My husband. He means you no harm. Please. Put down the gun."

9

He's not Paul. He's not Paul. Tori repeated the words over and over in her mind, wanting desperately to believe them. But the man looked just like her attacker—a face scalded into her memory. Except . . . His eyes *were* darker. Paul's had been the golden brown of fresh-baked biscuits not the darker shade of maple syrup. And the tiny red line running along this man's jaw didn't fit her recollections, either. Paul's features had been perfection. Not a flaw in sight. Hence why her friends had died of jealousy when the youngest Crowley son started hanging around the store to chat with her before closing time.

The youngest Crowley. There had been an older brother. Quieter. Kept to himself. Worked at the grist mill until he married and left town to start a farm. Jed. Jed with the darker eyes, the childhood scar, and the crooked nose.

The derringer wobbled in her hand. She blinked. Saw the rest of the room for the first time since the man had entered.

Dear Lord! Is that Lewis? She dropped her gun arm immediately, even as her addled brain recognized that the boy was taller, his face slightly rounder, his wide eyes hazel instead of blue.

"Forgive me," she whispered, guilt stabbing her breast. Heaven above. She'd drawn her gun with a child in the line of fire! "I . . ." She had to leave. Had to . . .

"Tori?" Ben's voice. Calm. Strong. Supportive.

But she couldn't look at him. What must he think of her? A deranged lunatic waving weapons at innocents. Or worse . . .

She closed her eyes and groaned, the sound echoing in the still room like a wounded animal.

He would know. He would fit all the pieces together and *know*.

Ducking her head, she dropped the derringer on the table and ran. Straight out the door. She didn't stop when Ben called after her. Not when Lewis jumped to his feet, questions etched on his face. Not even when she reached the wagon. She ran all the way to the end of the drive, not stopping until she reached the road. The road that led to Deer Spring. She turned her back firmly against the town that had turned its back on her, crossed her arms over her middle and stared in the direction of home. Harper's Station. People who cared. Who needed her. Who saw her as a person of worth. Of value.

Gradually her breathing eased and the silence soaked into her soul. She stood there for several minutes, letting the warm southern breeze brush back her hair and calm her spirit.

"He hurt me, too."

Tori turned at the low, feminine voice. Frannie stood behind her, her gaze stretching up to the sky.

"Paul," she clarified, finally bringing her eyes down to meet Tori's. "He attacked me, too. A couple years before you, I would guess, judging by the age of your boy."

All Tori could do was stare at the woman, so shocked was she by what she was hearing. Why would this complete stranger tell her such a horrible, intimate secret?

Yet when she looked into Frannie's face, she didn't see anger or bitterness or the brokenness Tori so often felt deep inside whenever the memories of that day worked themselves out of the prison where she tried to confine them. No. What she saw in the woman's face was peace and compassion and astounding courage.

"Jed and I met at a church revival meeting up near Wichita Falls. I fell hard for him. So quiet and serious." The smile that bloomed on her face radiated adoration. "We started courtin' soon after. Jed would stop by the farm whenever he was out making deliveries for the mill. I would look for excuses to ride into Deer Spring." Her eyes sharpened. "Until I met his brother."

Tori finally found her voice. "What happened?"

Frannie lifted her gaze back to the sky, a shadow dimming her smile. "He was a cocky kid. Competitive, too. Sure any girl would prefer him to his brother and determined to prove it. He tried to woo me away from Jed with charm and wild promises. The attention was flattering, but Jed held my heart, so I turned Paul down. Gently at first, then more adamantly when he refused to accept my decision.

"Then one day when I rode into town to meet Jed at the mill, Paul intercepted me on the road. He told me Jed had been hurt while chopping wood out behind their house that morning and was in bad shape. I spurred my horse and raced to the Crowley house as fast as I could go. Only no one was at home. Mr. Crowley was at the bank, as usual. Mrs. Crowley was out making her social rounds. And Jed, not hurt in the least, was at the mill. Waiting for me. Only I never kept our appointment.

"Paul trapped me in the house and forced his attentions. When he finished, he left me lying on the parlor floor. Shattered. Numb. Destroyed.

"Jed tried to see me for weeks after that, but I told my mother to turn him away. I couldn't tell him what happened. He'd never believe his charismatic brother capable of such a terrible deed. And even if he did, it would destroy the love that had started to grow between us. I was damaged. Soiled goods. No decent man would ever want me. And I wasn't sure I wanted one to. The idea of being intimate with a man, even a kind, loving man like Jed, filled me with terror."

Tori drank in every word, the tale resonating deep within her. The fear, the self-loathing, the shame this brave woman voiced—Tori had felt it all. She still did on occasion.

"How . . ." A tightness in Tori's throat cut off the question she longed to have answered, the one she sensed could help her find true peace. She inhaled and steadied herself, then tried again. "How did you get past it?"

For the woman must have. Somehow. She was married to the brother of her attacker, a man who bore a horribly strong resemblance to the barbarian who'd hurt her. Yet not only was she married, she'd had children—at least one, if not both, by her husband.

Frannie smiled. "A lot of prayer, and one very patient man." She strolled a couple strides past Tori, then turned back, a look of regret darkening her eyes. "I never told my parents." She shook her head. "Foolish, I know. But I was so afraid that it would change the way they looked at me. That my shame would touch them. Defile them. So I kept the secret buried inside. And when my woman's time came, I thanked God, sure that I would never have to tell anyone. That somehow, I could piece my life back together and pretend that awful day had never happened.

"But secrets fester, and buried pain poisons the soul. Looking back, I'm sure my parents knew something was wrong, yet I think they were afraid of causing me more pain, so when I continued deflecting their questions, they eventually stopped pressing me for answers. But Jed . . ." A look of pure love flashed across Frannie's face as her lashes blinked back the moisture gathering in her eyes. "Jed never gave up on me."

Tori's heart beat a little faster, pumped a little harder. How many times had she thought the same thing about Ben? Wondered at his persistence. His patience.

"About a month after I told him I didn't want to see him anymore, Jed stormed my house. His face was battered, his knuckles bleeding, his shirt torn. I was so worried that he'd been seriously hurt, I forgot to keep my guard up. I let him in the back door and started fussing over his wounds. But he grabbed my hands the instant I moved within reach and refused to let me go.

"Earlier that afternoon he'd overheard Paul bragging to one of his cronies about how girls preferred him over his brother. I was proof. Paul claimed that, once he had shown me what being with a real man was like, I turned my back on Jed the same day."

Frannie bit her lip as if trying to keep her smile contained. "Now, my Jed is a peaceable man, as even tempered as they come. But when he heard Paul's boast, the truth of what had happened to me must have clicked into place. He suddenly understood that his little brother had forced himself on me, and that was why I'd turned away. Enraged, he lit into Paul like a man possessed. Later I heard that it had taken three men to pull him off.

"Jed's mama was so incensed over his violent treatment of and foul accusations about her youngest son, she took Paul and boarded a train the next day for an extended visit to her parents' home in Navarro County. She vowed not to set foot in Deer Spring until Jed was gone."

Frannie glanced off into the distance, back toward the town her husband had left in order to be with her. "I never knew whether his father believed in Paul's guilt," Frannie said, "or if he just wanted his wife back, but he helped Jed buy this piece of land and frame the house.

"In the meantime, Jed courted me. He told me he loved me—that nothing could ever change his feelings, that he wanted me for his wife. Even when I told him that I didn't think I could ever give myself to him the way a wife should give herself to her husband, he insisted that he wanted me anyway. That he would wait as long as it took."

Frannie turned her gaze back to Tori and sighed. "Deep inside, I still loved him. Still wanted to be his wife. And most of all, I didn't want Paul to win, to steal happiness from both Jed and me. So I took a chance and married him. We didn't consummate the union until our first anniversary. It took me that long to banish Paul's ghost. Those differences I pointed out to you when you thought Jed was Paul?"

Tori nodded.

"I made a list. A long list of every physical difference I could find. And over time, I trained myself to see the differences instead of the similarities. And I prayed. Every night I prayed."

Frannie inhaled a deep breath, and the last of the shadows melted away from her gaze. "Did you know that when God cursed Eve after her disobedience in the garden, he hid a blessing in between the pain of childbirth and her subjection to her husband's rule? He told her ' . . . thy desire shall be to thy husband.' I took that promise to heart and prayed for it every day, prayed that God would give me a desire for my husband. That he would heal the hurt inside of me and free me to love Jed with the physical closeness he deserved. It took months, but little by little my fear receded and my desire grew."

Frannie reached out and touched Tori's arm. "Unlock the secrets.

Release the shame. The fear. Only truth can fully set you free. And if you have a man who is patient and kind, he'll listen and understand."

"Ben." His name fell from Tori's lips so easily. She pictured his face. His kind eyes. His protective nature. His . . . *wounded head*. "Oh, my stars! I left him half-stitched with a needle stuck in the back of his scalp." Tori whirled around and lunged back toward the house.

Frannie's laughter echoed behind her. "Don't worry. Jed will have finished the job for you. I'm sure your man's all patched up by now."

Patched up and waiting by the end of the wagon. Tori stumbled to a halt when the large figure straightened and took a single step in her direction.

They both stood there, fifteen yards apart, eyes for no one but each other.

Could she do it? Tori fisted her hands in the fabric of her skirt. Could she tell him her secret? Her stomach knotted as old fear warred with new hope. He'd probably guessed most of it by now anyway, but he didn't know the worst part. That what had happened was her fault.

10

Ben's gaze never wavered from Tori as she slowly closed the distance between them. He wanted to reach for her. To hold her. Comfort her. Erase whatever ugliness that wastrel *Paul* had inflicted. But he kept his arms at his sides, not wanting to do anything to cause her further distress. He'd let her dictate what happened next.

She halted a few steps away, her attention flitting to the new bandage wrapped around his brow.

"How's your head?" she finally asked.

He couldn't care less about his blasted head. "Fine." He took a step toward her, his hand outstretched, not to touch her—just to swallow the remaining distance between them. "Tori, I . . ."

She jerked away from him, then caught herself and forced a false smile to her lips. "There's a . . . a log over there beyond the barn." She pointed to a spot behind him. "Will you . . . sit with me there?"

Her eyes pleaded, the blue depths a little timid, perhaps even fearful, yet there was a familiar spark of determination there as well. And something else. Something resembling a tender shoot of trust. His heart ricocheted in his chest. He could build on trust. Nurture it, feed it, help it grow into something sturdy, strong, and indestructible.

Suddenly eager for a chat, he nodded and gestured for her to lead the way, not even wincing when the motion set his head to throbbing again. Neither said a word as they strolled across the yard, past the barn entrance, and around to the side where the log lay in the dirt against the barn wall, obviously set there to serve as a bench of sorts.

Tori seated herself in a slight hollow positioned just left of center. Ben eased himself down beside her, leaving enough space so as not to crowd her, but sitting close enough that when he angled toward her, his knees nearly brushed hers.

She folded her hands in her lap then slowly, courageously, brought her gaze up to meet his. "I have a secret, Ben. I'm sure you've gathered some of the more pertinent details already, but there are other pieces that I've kept buried. Things I've told no one. Not even Emma."

Her focus dropped back down to her lap, and her hands fidgeted with the edge of her jacket. "I thought I could bury them deeply enough that they couldn't harm me," she said, her voice small. "But I was wrong. I've recently come to understand that secrets are like lies. They take a toll on their keeper. They erode one's soul until nothing is left but a brittle shell."

She raised her head, and her blue eyes pierced him with a craving so stark, he felt it in his gut. "I don't want to be a shell anymore, Ben. I want to be set free. And the only way I can do that is to voice the truth. Will . . . will you listen?"

Emotion swelled so high inside him, it nearly closed off his throat. She trusted him—trusted him enough to open the most hidden places of her heart to his view. It was a gift so rare and beautiful, he could scarcely fathom it.

Unable to keep still a moment longer, he reached out and gathered her folded hands into his own. He kept his touch featherlight, as if he were holding an injured bird. He didn't want her to feel trapped, but neither did he want her to feel alone. "You can tell me anything, Tori. I will hold your confidence sacred, and I will listen without judgment. You have my word."

She nodded then turned to stare at some invisible point in the distance. "I was sixteen when I met Paul Crowley. He was newly returned to town after being gone more than a year. There was talk about something scandalous in his past, but no one spoke of details. To be honest, the hint of danger surrounding him only made him more attractive to the girls in town, me included. He was rich, handsome, and he had this way of talking that made you feel as if you were the only person he saw."

Ben hated him already. Slippery flimflam artist. He knew the type. All shine, no substance. Just the kind of fella to turn a girl's head if she were too young or inexperienced to see through his charade.

"One day he came into the store, running an errand for his mother. It was late afternoon, so I was working the counter alone while my mother prepared dinner and my father started the nightly inventory tallies. I helped him select a spool of black thread and a packet of sewing needles, the type I knew Mrs. Crowley preferred. He was witty, charming, and so effusively appreciative of my assistance that I was instantly smitten. When I handed him his parcels, he took my hand along with them and brushed a kiss against my knuckles. My foolish heart fluttered like some kind of imbecilic dragonfly, too stupid to recognize his insincerity."

She spoke of her younger self with such scorn. Ben wanted to jump in and offer excuses on her behalf, remind her she'd been young and innocent of the manipulations of dishonorable men. However, he sensed she'd not welcome the interruption, so he held his tongue and gently rubbed his thumb along the edge of her hand instead.

"He made a point to stop by the store nearly every evening after that," she continued, her brow furrowed as if she were scowling at the memories. "He seemed to know when I would be alone in the store. He must have watched and waited for my father to go into the back room before coming through the front. I thought the stolen moments romantic. The more clandestine the better.

"After a fortnight of such visits, he invited me to go driving with him after church on Sunday. I begged my father to let me go, but he refused. He said he didn't approve of me spending time with Paul. That he didn't trust the man. I was sure my father was just being narrow-minded and overprotective. He didn't know Paul the way I did. Didn't understand our connection.

"So when Paul asked me to sneak out the next night and meet him down by the old pond, I did just that. I willfully disobeyed my parents and ignored every twinge of my conscience that tried to warn me of danger. I thought we'd walk together in the moonlight. Perhaps Paul would even steal a kiss. By the time I realized he had much more than kissing in mind, it was too late. I screamed and fought him as hard as I could, but he was too big. Too strong. And we were so isolated, no one heard my cries."

Helpless fury stormed through Ben. How he wished he'd been there to hear. To rush to her rescue, to spare her all that pain. But he hadn't been there. No one had been there.

With Herculean effort, Ben managed to keep his hold on Tori gentle instead of clenching his hands into fists as instinct demanded. Heaven knew he wanted to pound something. Preferably Paul Crowley. Tori didn't need his anger, though. She needed his understanding. So instead of balling his hands into fists, he merely clenched his jaw and continued stroking the backs of her fingers.

"My parents were awake and waiting for me when I came home," Tori continued. "Mama took one look at me and broke into tears. Daddy just looked disappointed, which made my shame all the greater. He turned his back and left the room without a word. Mama held me, cried with me, then helped me bathe. After she tucked me into bed, I heard her arguing with my father, demanding that he bring charges against Paul for what he'd done. But Daddy refused. He wanted to flay Paul's hide for what he'd done to his little girl, of course, but they couldn't risk crossing the Crowleys. They owned the bank that held the mortgage to the store. If he brought charges against Paul, the bank would call in the loan and send them into foreclosure. They'd lose everything. Better to pretend like nothing had happened."

Now Ben wanted to pound on Tori's father. Protecting one's livelihood was all well and good, but not at the expense of one's daughter. Family came first. Always.

"Daddy didn't let me work the counter any more after that. I stayed in the back room inventorying supplies and bringing the ledgers up to date. I didn't mind the ostracism. I wanted to hide. From everyone. But after a couple months, I realized that I'd not be able to hide my shame for much longer. I was carrying a babe."

Ben squeezed her hands lightly. "Lewis."

Tori nodded. "Yes. Another catastrophe for the store. An un-married girl in the family way would bring shame upon the Adams name and hurt business. So Daddy sent me away before my secret could be revealed. I moved in with his sister in Whitesboro. She took me in and treated me like a servant even though I knew my father was sending her money for my upkeep. She ordered me to keep my distance from my younger cousins, afraid they'd be tainted by my immoral influence. She insisted I call her Mrs. Stanbridge, too. Never Aunt Wilma. No one was to know we were actually related. She was simply a godly woman offering shelter to an indigent girl out of Christian charity.

"I put up with her self-righteous hypocrisy as long as I could, believing I had nowhere else to go. But when Lewis was born every-thing changed."

For the first time since this awful tale began, a smile touched Tori's face. She met Ben's gaze fully, pride and love radiating from her in waves. "Holding my son in my arms, I knew I would give my life to keep him safe. So when Aunt Wilma called him the devil's spawn and informed me that a man from the foundling home over in Denison would be by to collect him as soon as a wet nurse could be found, I knew I had to leave. I sold the brooch my mother had given me for my sixteenth birthday and left within the week.

"I made it as far as Gainesville and took refuge in the church there. The preacher and his wife found me a position working for one of the widows of their congregation, doing her laundry along with cooking and tending house. The same work I'd been doing for my aunt, only now I earned a wage. After the first year, Mrs. Barry allowed me to take in extra laundry to increase my earnings. I worked sunup to sundown and saved every penny I could spare.

"After two years, I'd put enough by to make a down payment on a small shop I'd had my eye on. Only, no banker in town would loan me the money I needed to stock it. Until I found Emma and heard of her dream of a women's colony."

"And ended up in Harper's Station," Ben said, "running a thriving business and proving all those fools wrong who doubted your ability to succeed." He expected her to smile, for her eyes to flash in triumph, but she slowly shook her head and tugged her hand free from his hold.

"That wasn't the point of the story, Ben," she murmured.

He disagreed. That was exactly the point. She'd overcome tremendous adversity to achieve success in a world where her youth, feminine gender, and motherhood would have handicapped others. She was the most amazing woman he'd ever met. But she was pulling away from him again, physically creating distance by separating herself from his touch.

"The point," she said as she folded her arms around her middle, "is that I brought all that trouble upon myself. I was a rebellious, disobedient girl. If I had just listened to my father—"

"Stop right there." Ben snapped, surprising both of them with the sharpness of his tone. Her eyes flew wide as her face jerked upward. "You made one mistake, Tori. One bad decision. But that does *not* make you responsible for what happened. The minute you said no, all the blame shifted to the snake who lured you away from the safety of your home. *All* the blame. He is the criminal, not you. He is the one who deserves to feel shame. Not you."

Ben captured her hands and gently unfolded her arms from around her waist. He clasped her fingers and brought both hands up to his mouth. He pressed his lips to the back of one and then the other. Her breath caught, but she didn't pull away.

She'd opened the inner recesses of her heart to him. He supposed it was only fair that he do the same for her.

"I love you, Victoria Adams. I have for a long time. And what you've told me today only makes me love you more. I admire your courage, your fighting spirit and inner strength. I hate the path that carried you to Harper's Station, but I thank God every day that he brought you to a place where we could meet."

He pulled her hands to his chest and placed them palm down against the thudding of his heart. "As steadfast as your love is for Lewis, that's how strong my love is for you. It's not going to go away. Ever. Someday, I'll convince you to become my wife, Tori. To let me be a father to your son. But today, all I ask is that you believe me when I say I love you."

"You . . . you love me?" Her voice trembled and her bright blue eyes swam with wonder.

Ben smiled and nodded. "With all my heart."

"Even after all I've told you?" She looked so bewildered, he worried she'd convince herself to push his words aside.

Ben flattened her hands more tightly against his chest, wanting her to feel his intensity, his desire to never let her go. "*Especially* after all you've told me."

She peered up at him, apparently at a loss for words. But words had their limits. Perhaps another communication style would prove more convincing.

Slowly, gently, Ben ran his hands up Tori's arms to her elbows. With a small tug, he brought her body closer to his, her face closer to his.

"I love you, Tori," he whispered an instant before he touched his lips to hers.

He felt her suck in a breath, but she didn't pull away. Didn't slap his cheek or shove against his chest even though her hands were already in position. So he did it again, brushed his lips over hers in a kiss so feathery it could have been the stroke of a butterfly's wing.

"I love you," he repeated, reaching a hand up to caress her cheek, to cup her jaw, and tilt her mouth more fully up to his. He felt a tremble course through her and thought to release his hold until her neck stretched, bringing her lips even closer.

Ben nearly wept at the invitation he'd waited so long to receive. Bringing his other hand up, he cupped both sides of her face and melded his lips with hers. His pulse thrummed in his veins as desire swept over him, but he kept the kiss soft. This was about giving, not taking. Someday there would be more between them, a completeness of trust that would offer greater freedom. But for now, he'd settle for tender and sweet.

When Tori finally pulled back, Ben lifted his mouth from hers yet didn't let her go. He rested his forehead against hers and whispered the words one more time.

"I love you."

She said nothing, but he hadn't expected her to. All he could hope for was that she would let the truth of his vow drift past her barriers to settle in a secure chamber of her heart where it could take up permanent residence.

He could wait to hear the words. After all, he'd waited over a year to come this far, and the outcome had been far sweeter than he'd ever imagined. He could be patient a while longer. A life with Tori and Lewis was worth the wait.

11

He loved her. Benjamin Porter—handsome, kind, godly, and infinitely patient Benjamin Porter loved *her*. It took the entire ride back to Harper's Station for Tori to accept that such a miracle might have actually occurred. She probably wouldn't have believed it at all if she hadn't met Frannie Crowley and seen with her own eyes the amazing goodness God had wrought from a situation instigated by evil. If the Lord could create a loving marriage for Jed and Frannie, maybe . . . just maybe . . . he could do the same for her—if she opened her heart enough to allow him the opportunity.

Tori glanced over at the man by her side, the one who'd stubbornly insisted he was strong enough to drive despite the knock he took to his head. She had to admit the man had admirable stamina. They'd been traveling for three hours, and except for a little pallor in his skin, he looked as fit and strong as ever. Which was very fit. With all those lovely muscles that, yes, she enjoyed looking at. His strong jaw. His warm, gray eyes. A little sigh eased through her parted lips. The way those eyes heated even further right before he had kissed her.

A shiver danced over her skin as she recalled the tender way his mouth had covered hers. The touch had been so different from Paul's forceful, selfish groping. She'd felt nothing but pleasure at Ben's kiss. No fear. No resurgence of harsh memories. Only a feeling of being utterly cherished. A feeling she could grow quite greedy for, if she weren't careful. But who wanted to be careful? Not her. Not anymore.

Feeling daring, Tori snuck another peek at Ben, her gaze zeroing in on the lips that had brought her such pleasure. Lips that were curving up at the corners.

She jerked her attention away from his mouth, embarrassed to have been caught staring, but before she could turn her head, his warm, teasing gaze captured hers.

"I haven't thought of much else, either," he said in a voice low enough not to wake Lewis, who dozed in the wagon bed.

Tori's cheeks heated. How did the man always know what she was thinking? If they were to marry, she'd have to find a way to even the playing field. Perhaps study him so closely that she could read his thoughts as well.

She turned back and stared at him until he squirmed, inwardly delighting at his growing discomfort. It was about time she got the upper hand.

"Tori? Everything all right?"

A true smile blossomed across her face, one that grew so wide it stretched her out-of-practice cheeks almost to the point of pain.

Ben blinked at her as if momentarily blinded.

"Everything's perfect," she proclaimed. And she meant it.

Frannie had been right. The truth *had* set her free. It had taken Tori several hours to recognize the change, but it was there. Inside. A lightness of spirit—one that felt foreign but, oh, so wonderful. And not just because a man she admired told her he loved her, though that was a miracle she'd be savoring for years.

There was more to it, a freedom that resonated in the very core of her soul. Her guilt and secrets had chained her in a dungeon of her own making. A dungeon she'd wrongly believed would keep her safe, when in actuality it held her prisoner.

But no more. She was out in the sunshine now, and she'd not go back. Freedom meant risking pain and disappointment and confrontations with evil, but it also enabled joy and a richness of life that superseded the mere existence she'd subjected herself to for the last several years. And perhaps, if God were very generous, it might even bring—she laid a hand on Ben's arm—love.

"Tori?" Ben's brows rose, disappearing behind the bandage he wore.

She tightened her hold and stared intently into his eyes. "We'll have some details to work out with the logistics of courting in a women's colony, but if your patience can hold out a little longer, and if you're still interested . . ." Her lashes dropped. She couldn't actually say the words. It would be far too forward. Wouldn't it?

Thank heavens she was sitting beside a man who had a tendency to ride to her rescue. She only waited a heartbeat before he cleared his throat and twisted to face her, leaving the horses to make their own way.

"Miss Adams?" He straightened his spine, and addressed her with such a formal tone she felt the need to bite back her smile and heed him with solemnity. Not that it worked. Her grin kept breaking free, even when she used her teeth to hold onto her bottom lip.

Ben had much more self-control. His face remained inscrutable. Well, except for the delight dancing in his gray eyes. A delight that made her heart race and her stomach flutter.

"Miss Adams." He repeated. "Are you giving me permission to call on you?"

Tori did her best to play along. She gave a prim nod. "I am, sir. As long as your intentions are honorable."

Ben dropped the façade, reached between them, and stroked the edge of her cheek with the back of his fingers. "Tori, I plan to honor you all the days of my life."

He leaned close and touched his lips to her forehead. A tremor coursed down her neck and over her spine.

"For better or for worse."

He kissed her temple, the tender caress stealing Tori's breath.

"For richer, for poorer."

He kissed the line of her jaw.

"In sickness and in health."

His lips hovered a bare hairsbreadth away from hers.

Please, she silently begged. *Please.*

He crooked a finger and placed it beneath her chin, then slowly tilted her face to meet his at the right angle.

"Until death do us part."

Finally his mouth met hers, and Tori caught her second glimpse of heaven that day. Warm, tender, and so full of love, her heart throbbed in response.

Somewhere along the edges of her awareness, she felt the wagon slow to a halt and silently rejoiced. If the horses didn't need their driver, she could keep his attention a little longer. And, oh, how she enjoyed his attention.

Tori wrapped her arms around Ben's neck and lifted herself closer to him, exulting at the feel of his arm circling her waist and his hand flattening against her back. This was where she belonged. In the arms of this man.

"Mama? Are we home?"

The sleepy voice jolted Tori. She jerked away from Ben, her cheeks warming even as her determination sparked. Instead of glancing into the wagon bed to address her son, she kept her gaze focused on the man beside her as she gave her answer.

"Yes, Lewis," she said, having no idea how far away they were from Harper's Station and not caring in the slightest. "We're home."

An
AWAKENED HEART

HEART

◆———————◆

AN
ORPHAN TRAIN
NOVELLA

JODY
HEDLUND

1

---•——————•——————•---

top prostituting yourselves and run to the loving Father who will embrace you with forgiveness." Reverend Bedell's voice rose above the sniffles and muffled weeping of the women crowded on trestle benches of Centre Street Chapel.

In the front row, Christine Pendleton clasped her hands together in her lap and inwardly wept at the depravity the women faced night after night. Even though she'd been volunteering at the chapel every Sunday for the past month, her heart hadn't stopped aching every time she came and witnessed the number of immigrant women who'd fallen into immorality.

At a tug on the folds of her black flounced skirt, she glanced down to find the grubby fingers of the toddler who'd been playing on the floor behind her, clasping the silky layers. His hands were not only filthy, but slimy.

"Don't touch the fine lady." The harsh whisper behind Christine was followed by a slap on the child's hand.

The toddler whimpered and jerked away from Christine's skirt.

"It's all right." Christine smiled at the young mother, who was holding a newborn babe in her bony arms. The woman didn't smile back but instead stared at Christine with eyes that seemed to have been drained of all emotion. She gave the baby in her arms a small bounce, though the infant, wrapped in an unraveling shawl, hadn't cried a peep the entire service. While Christine wasn't accustomed to children of any size or shape, she supposed a little squalling and squirming was preferable to lethargy.

The toddler on the floor peered up at her with glassy eyes. A goopy discharge from his nose curled over his top lip and had crusted on his cheeks. Christine tried not to think about the fact that the slime was now on her skirt.

"Here." She released her tight grip on her handkerchief only to find that the delicate linen was horribly wrinkled from the pressure and dampness of her hold. She shook the square, but the wrinkles remained. She held it out to the little boy anyway.

His slickened fingers touched the lacy edge hesitantly.

"You may have it," Christine whispered.

The toddler pinched the handkerchief between his thumb and forefinger. The unspoiled white contrasted with the boy's shirt, which had probably once been white but was now the gray of dirty dishwater. His trousers were cinched at the waist with a piece of twine and rolled up at the legs, clearly intended for a much larger child. In the wide material, his feet stuck out like twigs, the soles as black as coal.

"You can find happiness again," the reverend was saying. "There is hope. There is a better life available."

The boy laid the handkerchief across his lap and then began to trace the scallop pattern around the rim. Christine waited for the mother to pick up the linen and wipe the boy's nose for him, since apparently he had no inclination to do so for himself. But the young woman didn't bother to look at her child, almost as if she'd forgotten he was there.

What if neither of them had ever seen a handkerchief before?

At the startling thought, Christine shifted so that she was facing forward and attempted to focus on Reverend Bedell standing behind a simple pulpit. The poverty and misery of this place overwhelmed her again as it had since the day she'd heard the reverend speak at the Ladies Home Missionary Society meeting.

He'd spoken so passionately about the needs of the immigrants in lower Manhattan. He described situations he'd encountered, the drunkenness, theft, and degradation that existed in what he called the "infernal pit." Although he'd come to give his annual report, he ended his speech with an invitation to join in his evangelistic efforts by becoming "visitors" among the poor.

After hearing the reverend, Christine had been unable to think of anything else until she finally had her coachman drive her to Centre Street Chapel. Of course, her visit had nothing to do with Reverend Bedell himself. Even if the other ladies had gossiped about how fine-looking the widowed pastor was, Christine didn't pay attention to that sort of drivel anymore. At thirty, she'd long past resigned herself to spinsterhood. She'd buried her hopes and dreams of having a husband and children, and there was no sense in reviving them only to face disappointment.

Besides, she'd had the consuming work of taking care of Mother for so many years that she hadn't had time for anything else. Now that Mother was gone, she wanted to focus on helping these poor unfortunate souls and not get sidetracked with thoughts of handsome bachelors.

"I plead with you to abandon your sins." The reverend's face was taut with earnestness, and his brows furrowed above warm, compassionate eyes. He was a large man with the build of a giant—stocky shoulders, thick arms, and a wide but solid torso. While his muscular appearance was intimidating, there was a boyishness about his tousled blond hair and expression that softened his hard edges.

The weeping in the chapel was growing louder. Even though he was kind and tender in the way he spoke, his plain and powerful messages moved the women to tears every week. If only his messages would move them to make changes in their lifestyles . . .

Reverend Bedell paused and bowed his head. His large hands gripped the pulpit. The intensity emanating from his frame proclaimed his deep longing for God to move in the women too.

The narrow room was unlit except for the light that managed to dispense through the grimy front windows. The walls had been whitewashed, the wooden floor cleaned. Still, the room was dark, and the sickly sweet scent of liquor lingered, diminished only by the sour body odor of so many unwashed women in close confines.

"Reverend" came a voice near the back.

The women never spoke during the service, at least they hadn't since Christine had started attending the chapel services. So she swiveled along with everyone else to see who had dared to be so bold.

Near the back, a tall woman was standing. Her navy skirt was tattered, her ruffled bodice stained. The stitching and cut of the cloth told Christine the garments had once been of good quality, a testament to just how far the woman had fallen. Her hair was brushed into a sloppy knot, and her face was ashen and gaunt like the others.

"I beg your pardon, Reverend," the woman said with a slight English accent, "but every week you preach to us about the need to change our ways. And every week I sit here and pray I could change my ways—" Her voice cracked, and she swiped dirt-crusted fingers at a new trail of tears that rolled down her cheeks. "Please don't tell us anymore how happy we once were, or how wretched we are now, or how miserable we must be eternally. We know all that too well. But give us the means of earning an honest living, and we will abandon this life. It's intolerable for us to stay in it, if we could avoid starvation in any other way."

The other women began to nod and murmur their agreement. Some sat up straighter. Others called out "aye." Their sudden energy was unexpected, and it stirred something in Christine, the same something that Reverend Bedell's impassioned speech had awakened in her that day at the Society meeting.

These women wanted help. Desperately. But they were trapped like moths in a lantern globe. No matter how frantically they beat their wings, they had no place to fly.

Just before the service, Christine had heard the women whispering of two sisters who had lost their jobs and could find no other. Rather than resort to whoring to save themselves from starvation and homelessness, they'd bathed and put on their best clothing. Then after consuming a lethal drink, they'd lain down on their bed, held hands, and went to sleep. Forever.

All through the sermon Christine couldn't get the image of the two sisters out of her mind. And now her heart cried out that these immigrant women should have more choices than prostitution or death. Surely the reverend would have a solution to their dilemma.

Reverend Bedell released his tight grip on the pulpit and finally addressed the woman who'd had the courage to speak up. "Mrs. Watson, sometimes throwing off our old ways requires great sacrifice. Let us pray and ask God to give all of you the strength to do so."

The anticipation deflated from Christine's chest. As he started to pray, she bowed her head and closed her eyes but was too disappointed by his answer to hear anything else. When the prayer ended and the women rose to leave, they were somber. Gone was their brief burst of energy and life. Instead they shuffled out as though leaving a funeral rather than a worship service.

Christine helped straighten the benches and watched Reverend Bedell at the door say good-bye to the last woman and her child. He squatted, his hulky frame dwarfing a girl sucking her thumb. The reverend spoke gently and pressed a hand on the girl's crown, blessing her before rising and offering the mother one last smile.

The mother only nodded before ushering her child away. As the reverend watched the pitiful family leave, his smile faded and was replaced with the same sadness Christine had noticed before.

She knew she shouldn't stare. She ought to ready herself to depart like the other volunteers. Yet that something inside her chest seemed to burn hotter. As the reverend trudged back to the pulpit, she started toward him, then stopped and twisted her beaded reticule.

Who was she to approach the pastor? She was a diminutive woman of little consequence. She wasn't outspoken but instead labored quietly. With her rather plain features, petite frame, and unassuming dark hair, she never stood out in a crowd, and she was perfectly content with that.

Today, however, she felt different as she pushed herself forward again toward the reverend. She didn't stop until she stood in front of the pulpit, where he was tucking several sheets of paper into his Bible with an absent-minded frown.

She waited for him to acknowledge her as he gathered his notes, shut his Bible, and started to turn without seeing her. Part of her wanted to scuttle away like a mouse back to its hole. But she willed herself to be brave. "Reverend Bedell?" she said.

He halted and glanced at her.

She expected irritation or at least weariness to cross his features and was completely unprepared for his warm smile and the genuine kindness in his eyes. "Yes? Mrs. . . . ? Forgive me. I seem to have forgotten your name."

"Please don't concern yourself. You have so many names to remember."

His eyes had pleasant crinkles at the corners, belying his age in a way the rest of his appearance didn't. She'd overheard the other ladies at the Society meeting whispering that he had a grown son who was in seminary and studying to be a pastor. Yet he certainly didn't look old enough for that to be true. "I always try to learn the names of volunteers. It just takes me time, Mrs. . . ."

"Miss Pendleton," she supplied, shifting uncomfortably as he perused her black dress with its sloping shoulders, wide pagoda sleeves, and full skirt. Mother had passed away in March, and she hadn't yet finished the six months of mourning that was socially expected at the loss of a parent.

"Mrs. Pendleton," he replied. "I'm sorry for your loss. Your husband?"

"Oh, no. I'm not married. It's *Miss* Pendleton." She enunciated her title more clearly and loudly, but then realized she'd just announced her spinsterhood for all the world to hear and flushed at the mistake.

"I beg your pardon," the reverend said.

"My mother recently passed," she added and hurried to cover her embarrassment. "She was ill for many years and was finally released from her burdens."

"Again, I'm sorry for your loss."

From the compassion that filled his eyes, she had the distinct impression he was being sincere and not merely placating her. "Thank you." If only she needed the compassion. She dropped her eyes so he wouldn't view her guilt. The truth was she hadn't experienced any sorrow at Mother's death and still felt none.

"Time will ease the pain," he said, apparently mistaking her bowed head for grief. "Take it from someone who knows."

She didn't dare look at him. He'd surely think her calloused for her lack of true mourning. And he'd also see that she'd listened to the gossip about him and knew he was a widower. The ladies had mentioned that Reverend Bedell's wife had died at least ten years ago, but that he'd never had an inclination to get remarried. Of course, they'd declared what a shame that was.

He was silent a moment as though sympathizing with her. Then he surprised her by squeezing her upper arm. The contact was brief but warm. "Doing the work of the Lord helps ease the pain. Seeing the suffering of others has a way of taking the focus off our own circumstances, doesn't it?"

She nodded and finally lifted her eyes. "That's what I wanted to speak to you about, Reverend." This time when she looked into his empathetic eyes, she noticed the color was an interesting blue-green, the shade of eucalyptus. Even though the pulpit was between them, she was also aware of the breadth of his torso and the way his suit coat stretched at the seams of his thick arms.

She clutched her reticule, snapping it open and closed and then open and closed again, wishing he was much older, wizened, and prune-faced. As it was she was suddenly all too conscious of the fact that he was an entirely appealing man, and she was entirely socially inept at interacting with the opposite sex.

He tucked his Bible under his arm and waited.

"Yes," she said hurriedly. "I'd like to figure out a way to help the women."

"You're off to a very good start by giving of your time to minister to them during the chapel service."

"But there has to be something more I can do."

The reverend glanced at her small beaded purse, and then his eyebrows rose, revealing a light in his eyes that she prayed wasn't humor. "Miss . . . ?"

"Pendleton," she replied, not caring he'd forgotten her name already.

"Miss Pendleton, would you like to join us in passing out tracts next Saturday? Several other volunteers and myself walk the nearby streets, pass out tracts, and invite people to attend the service."

Pass out tracts? She refrained from looking at the pamphlets stacked in a box near the door. She'd been responsible for giving them to the women last week as they'd exited after the service. Most had declined. And the few who had taken the sheets had pocketed them without a glance.

"I shall consider it."

"Good. Then I'll expect you next Saturday at eleven o'clock in the morning." He started to turn away again.

"You'll beg my pardon for asking if perhaps we ought to consider other methods of helping them besides tracts and sermons?" The words spilled out before she could stop them. "The women and children look hungry. Many have no shoes. Their clothes are in tatters. And they need gainful employment."

When the reverend looked at her this time, he seemed to be taking her in, as if seeing her for the first time.

She squirmed, even though she admonished herself not to. She looked around the room and realized she was the only volunteer left. Her coachman stood in the doorway, apparently having grown worried when she'd neglected to exit with the others. Ridley had insisted on waiting for her each week, though she'd assured him she would be fine. He'd only shaken his head and told her he wouldn't leave her in the Sixth District alone, even if she fired him for it.

"You're correct, Miss Pendleton," Reverend Bedell finally said. "There are many needs. So many, in fact, that it would take the restructuring and overhauling of lower Manhattan itself to make a small dent in the suffering and poverty that exists here."

She'd had to drive through the squalor to reach the Centre Street Chapel. She'd seen the overflowing tenements, the drunks and beggars on the streets, the refuse that filled the gutters. The sheer mass of people who lived in the area was overwhelming. With hordes of immigrants arriving every day into New York Harbor, the city was crowded beyond capacity.

"You sound as though there is no hope for their suffering," she said.

"Oh no," he replied. "There is most definitely hope. The true hope found in Christ."

"I certainly don't mean to diminish their spiritual needs, but it appears we may be feeding their souls while allowing their bodies to languish." She cringed as she waited for the reverend to chastise her for being so outspoken. She was surprised when instead he returned to the pulpit, set down his Bible, and nodded solemnly.

"I understand what you are saying, Miss Pendleton. We may clothe and feed them, but without true repentance and a transformation of the heart, they will only return to their immoral ways."

She stood silently and pondered his words. She saw the reasoning in them. However . . . "Why can we not meet their spiritual and physical needs at the same time? Why must it be all one or the other?"

"The Spirit brings life and power to accomplish the other. Once people are truly set free from their sins, they will have the motivation and desire to seek a better life apart from sin."

"In light of your logic, then during Jesus's ministry on earth, He would have *only* preached. But did He not heal the sick and feed the five thousand? Doesn't that indicate His compassion moved Him to meet more than spiritual needs?"

Reverend Bedell rested his elbows on the pulpit and leaned down into them, which lowered him to her level. His eyes were wide and had turned a shade lighter, more blue than green now, as though sunshine had chased away any shadows.

She fiddled with her reticule, but then clasped it behind her back to keep herself from opening and closing it again.

"Miss Pendleton," the reverend said with a slow smile. She almost thought she caught a glint of admiration in his expression. "You're astute, and I appreciate your reasoning. But we cannot forget that Jesus was able to meet physical needs and change hearts simultaneously in a way we aren't capable of doing."

"But He clearly believed that meeting the physical needs of the lost was important." She reached for his Bible on the pulpit. "May I?"

"Of course." He handed it to her.

She flipped open the well-worn pages, noticing the frequent underlining of text and notes in the margins. She found her way to the twenty-fifth chapter of Matthew, cleared her throat, and began to read. "'Depart from me, you who are cursed into the eternal fire prepared for the devil and his angels. For I was hungry and you gave me nothing to eat. I was thirsty and you gave me nothing to drink.

I was a stranger and you did not invite me in. I needed clothes and you did not clothe me. I was sick and in prison and you did not look after me . . . I tell you the truth, whatever you did not do for one of the least of these, you did not do for me.'"

She closed the Bible and returned it to the pulpit.

Ridley was still waiting in the doorway. Etiquette demanded that she go. To stay and deliberate further would be unladylike.

And yet, even as she took a slight step back, the reverend said, "To be honest, every time I visit among them, I come back desolate, wishing and praying I could do more. There have even been times I've wondered what I'm doing here. I never see a difference. If I leave to minister somewhere else, perhaps a better man could come here and accomplish what I cannot." Once the words were out, he rubbed his hand across his mouth as if he wished he could take them back. "I'm sorry, Miss Pendleton."

"I can only imagine how discouraging this work is day after day." She was grateful for his honesty and felt the need to reassure him. "I'm sure at times I would want to give up too."

The muscles in his jaw flexed, and he nodded in response.

"But there are few others like you, Reverend Bedell, who are willing to minister here among the immigrants. Therefore, I doubt God will easily release you from this task."

His eyes locked with hers. The window of his soul was open, allowing her to see deep into his insecurities and fears.

"Perhaps rather than thinking God wants you to put your efforts into a new congregation," she continued hesitantly, "what if He's simply asking you to consider making some changes right where you are?"

His expression told her he was seriously weighing her words. "Just this week I prayed about whether to turn in my resignation. And I do believe God is giving me His answer through you, Miss Pendleton."

A small measure of satisfaction settled in her chest, and she couldn't keep from smiling.

His eyes lit and he smiled in return, a happiness radiating from him that hadn't been there previously. She was struck again as she had been earlier by what a fine-looking man he was, especially with the errant tousle of hair that had slipped down his forehead.

When he combed it back, she turned, embarrassed at having been caught studying him. "I should be on my way, Reverend. I've already taken up more of your time than I'd intended." She started down the center aisle between the benches toward Ridley.

For a moment the reverend didn't say anything, but she could feel him watching her with each step she took. Although she tried to act calm, her stomach began to flutter under his scrutiny. She'd almost reached the door when his voice broke the silence. "Wait."

She spun much too quickly.

He'd rounded the pulpit, looking as if he had every intention of chasing after her.

As she waited for him to speak, her breath hitched, although she wasn't sure why. And she wasn't sure why her skin felt overheated.

"Do you have any ideas for what I—what we—could do differently here?" he asked.

The satisfaction she'd experienced before came rolling back. Reverend Bedell was a good and humble man to request her advice when she'd already imposed. "I'm afraid I've already spoken too much today as it is."

"Not at all. If God brought you here as an answer to my prayer, then I have a feeling He has much more for you to say."

Reverend Bedell was giving her more credit than she deserved. She wanted to tell him she wasn't anyone special. But his expectant eyes stopped her from disappointing him. "Perhaps you should continue to pray. If God has answered your prayers once, I'm sure He'll do so again."

"I'll do that," he said.

She nodded and turned to leave again.

"I'll see you on Saturday then for the visiting?" The hope in his voice stopped her.

"Will you be ready for more bossing around by then?"

He chuckled. "Absolutely."

"Then I'll be here." Once more she became conscious of her bold interactions with this man and strode forward, anxious now to leave.

Her coachman opened the door for her. As she passed by, she tried not to notice that Ridley's eyebrows were arched high above his questioning gaze.

In light of her behavior with the reverend, her dear faithful friend probably suspected she was addled in the brain. She feared he was right.

2

The stench of death choked Elise Neumann. In the windowless bedroom of the tenement, the air was already dank and humid. The odor of vomit and the rottenness of the chamber pot filled every breath.

Elise clasped the frail hand in hers, not surprised that her mother's skin was cold in spite of the May heat.

"You won't die, Mutti." Marianne's strangled voice was muffled against their mother's chest. Marianne had thrown her arms across Mutti, but the dying woman didn't have the strength to return the embrace.

"I will go soon, Liebchen," Mutti whispered. "And I will be glad to see your *Vater* again."

"No!" Marianne cried. "You can't leave us."

Elise's eyes burned, yet she refused to cry. She hadn't shed a tear when their father had died two years ago. And she wouldn't weep now either. As the oldest of her sisters, she had to be strong. The others relied upon her steadfastness and her practical nature. If she allowed herself to fall apart, they would all be lost.

In the corner came Sophie's persistent sniffling. Even though Sophie was younger than Marianne, she hadn't resorted to the same weeping and theatrics. Elise suspected Sophie wanted to remain strong for her own charges, the two toddlers who clung to her as though she were their mother.

"Elise," Mutti said weakly.

"I'm here." Elise squeezed her mother's hand.

"Get my box, *bitte*."

Elise rose from the floor next to the only bed in the apartment. She supposed she ought to be grateful to Uncle Hermann for allowing Mutti the use of the bed during her dying moments. Normally, Mutti slept with them in the other room, which sufficed as a kitchen and parlor during the day and a bedroom at night.

The apartment wasn't big enough for Uncle's family. And it certainly wasn't large enough for their family in addition to the two children left by the last boarder.

Elise stepped out of the closet-like room that served as the bedroom. Her aunt sat at the table next to the coal-burning stove. Two of her daughters were mending with her, the garments having been patched until the original linen hardly remained.

The three glanced up as Elise sidled past them.

"She will not last long now," Aunt Gertie said in German without pausing her stitching.

I had no idea. Thank you for letting me know, Elise was tempted to retort. Instead she nodded and crept through the maze of furniture and belongings to the sagging sofa that was no longer green, if it had ever been. Like everything else, it wore a permanent layer of black soot. Without a vent, the smoke from the stove had nowhere to escape except into the apartment, which was already difficult to keep clean without running water. The only source of water for the entire tenement building was a faucet at the bottom of the stairwell that all the families here shared.

Elise knelt next to the sofa and reached for the box stowed underneath. She slid the container out amidst the clutter of blankets, shoes, and clothes that were also stored there. With trembling fingers she dusted the lid. The flat box held all her family's possessions—the remnants of a past life that had somehow slipped away no matter how hard Elise had tried to grasp it. They'd had to sell everything of value one item at a time, until now all that remained could fit into a single box.

With the container in hand, she retraced her steps to the bedroom, back to Marianne's weeping and Sophie's sniffles. The light coming in through the open doorway from the kitchen was scant, and the shadows of the room were deep.

As she knelt again next to Mutti's still body, Elise couldn't detect a trace of life, not even the gentle rise and fall of her mother's chest. Marianne was kissing Mutti's palm, tears coursing her cheeks, and sobs shaking her shoulders.

"Is she—?" Elise couldn't make herself say the word.

"I am still here, Liebchen." Mutti opened her eyes and somehow managed to lift her free hand toward Elise.

Elise grasped Mutti's fingers and pressed a kiss into her hand the same way that Marianne was doing.

"Would you take off my wedding band?" Mutti asked.

Elise started to shake her head.

"Bitte, Elise." The plea was soft but threaded with desperation.

Elise quickly did the dirty deed. The ring slid off too easily, even with the bit of scrap material wound around the back of the band to keep it in place. Elise silently berated herself, as she had a thousand times over the past week when Mutti hadn't been able to rise. She should have noticed Mutti becoming weaker and thinner. Of course, they'd all grown too slim since Vater had died. Even with Mutti, Marianne, and herself working twelve-hour days and boarding with Uncle, they still never had enough to completely fill their bellies.

Once Mutti became ill, her appetite had diminished, until all that remained was a skeleton of the vibrant woman she'd once been. Once upon a time. When they'd lived in Hamburg, when Vater had still operated his bakery, in the days before Count Eberhardt had destroyed Vater's business with one spiteful and false rumor.

Without customers, Vater had been left with little choice. He could watch his family starve to death, or he could sell his failing business and use the capital to sail to America and attempt to start over in the "land of opportunity."

Bitterness burned within Elise every time she thought about Count Eberhardt, with his protruding belly girded in place by a wide belt with a gold buckle, his fat fingers decorated with equally fat rings, and his fleshy jowls that were creased with a permanent frown. Like so many aristocrats he'd abused his power and wealth without a care for how he'd ruined others' lives. Even now he was probably feasting at his lavish estate manor on fresh apple strudel and hot cherry tarts while Mutti lay on a stinking, soiled mattress unable to keep down even the tepid water they'd spooned into her mouth around the clock.

"Elise," Mutti whispered, "I want you to have my ring."

Elise closed her fingers tightly around the band. The sharp edges of the cross bit into her hand.

"I want you to keep it as a reminder of the fullness of life found only in God, of the richness of forgiveness, and of the freedom that comes from surrender."

Elise knew what Mutti was asking her to do. Forgive Count Eberhardt for the pain he'd caused their family. But Elise also knew that she never could, especially now that she was losing Mutti. Mutti was too young, too beautiful, and too sweet to die. It was all the count's fault. Everything that had happened to them was the count's fault. And she'd never be able to forgive him for what he'd done. No matter how much her mother pleaded with her. However, she wouldn't say that to Mutti. She didn't want to disappoint her mother during her final moments on earth.

"Thank you, Mutti," she said before bending and placing a kiss on her mother's gaunt cheek.

Mutti closed her eyes. Even in the darkness of the room, Elise could see the haunted shadows of pain cross her mother's once-elegant features. Her brown hair that had been lustrous and full and wavy was now thin and greasy and gnarled with gray. Her skin that had been silky and soft and smelling like lavender was cracked and ashen.

At eighteen, Marianne was a reflection of what their mother had once looked like while she at nineteen and Sophie at fifteen had both inherited their father's fairness, with his hair the shade of buttercream, and eyes like ripened blueberries. Sophie could have been Elise's twin, except her younger sister had endearing dimples in her cheeks when she smiled, which unfortunately wasn't often enough in recent years.

"Now I need the music box," Mutti said.

Elise opened the container of their possessions and lifted out a pale oak pedestal with the wooden figurine of a young girl tending her four geese. The little carvings were hand-painted with detailed design work in bright green, red, and white.

"Turn it on," Mutti said weakly.

Elise rotated the wooden hand crank, and the geese and a tiny tree began to turn to the German folk song "Alle Meine Entchen," which translated to "All My Ducklings."

"Marianne . . ." Mutti fumbled for the young woman.

With swollen eyes and red splotchy cheeks, Marianne lifted herself from Mutti.

"The music box is for you," Mutti said. "I want you to keep it as a reminder to always sing and never lose sight of the music and joy that is found in living, no matter how difficult or hard your situation."

"Oh, Mutti!" Marianne burst into fresh sobs. "It's yours from Vater. I won't take away something so precious."

Elise set the box next to Marianne knowing full well that Marianne wouldn't accept either the gift or Mutti's death until after the dear woman was buried.

Mutti pressed her lips together, holding in a moan of pain. Mutti hadn't allowed Elise to send for the physician earlier in the week when she'd taken to bed. At first Elise had assumed that Mutti was in denial of her sickness. But as the week had progressed, Elise realized the opposite was true. Mutti knew how ill she was, likely had known for some time. And because of that, she hadn't wanted to waste their pitifully inadequate earnings on a doctor's visit that would be for naught.

Mutti's face contorted into tight lines. Her chest ceased rising and falling.

Elise held her breath and frantically tried to form a prayer. *Not yet, God. Please. Not yet.*

Mutti opened her eyes, and for just an instant Elise glimpsed the acute agony her mother was suffering. "Now. For Sophie."

At her name, the young girl in the corner swiped at her cheeks and crawled forward until she was kneeling next to Marianne. Without Sophie, Olivia and Nicholas huddled together. At two and a half, Olivia was already mothering her baby brother, who was hardly more than a year old. They hadn't fussed when their own mother had forsaken them weeks ago, if they'd even noticed.

Elise was proud of Sophie for pouring out her love and attention upon the two orphans, much the same way Mutti had always showered her daughters with her affection, smiles, and wisdom. When Olivia and Nicholas had first arrived with their mother and father to board in Uncle's apartment, the two children rarely spoke or smiled. They'd been scared and bruised. It hadn't taken long to see why. Mr. Olson, their father, beat them every time they so much as whimpered. He did the same to his wife.

In the already crowded apartment, the conditions had become unbearable. When Mutti had asked her brother to do something about Mr. Olson's abuse toward his family, Uncle Hermann had only brushed off her concerns. Not only was Mr. Olson one of Uncle's drinking partners, but having the extra income from the new boarders allowed Uncle to spend more at the beer halls along the Bowery every evening.

Since Sophie had already been appointed to watch the youngest children and babies during the day while everyone else worked, she'd readily gathered Olivia and Nicholas to her small flock of charges. When Mr. Olson had been found dead in an alley only two weeks after their arrival, no one had shed a tear. Without her husband's income, Mrs. Olson hadn't been able to afford the rent. At mother's pleading, Uncle had agreed to allow Mrs. Olson a week to find other arrangements. Apparently she had, except that she'd neglected to take her two children with her. And after four months she hadn't come back for them.

Mutti had attempted to locate the young mother. But finding one person among the thousands of poor immigrants crammed into lower Manhattan was like locating a grain of yeast already pounded into rising bread dough. Impossible. Useless. Futile.

Uncle had insisted that Mutti take the Olson children to the Orphan Asylum on Cumberland Street. But Mutti had assured Uncle that they wouldn't be a burden to him, that she'd provide for all the children's needs.

Elise didn't want to think about how she would take care of everyone after Mutti was gone. With just her and Marianne's income, they would be hard-pressed to pay Uncle's rent, much less buy food.

Sophie leaned down and kissed Mutti's cheek. Before she could pull back, a large tear dripped off her chin onto Mutti.

"Oh, *mein Engel*." Mutti always called Sophie her angel. "You are such a good, sweet child. I will rest easier if I know you will be a brave girl. Tell me you'll be brave."

"I will, Mutti."

Mutti lifted a hand and brushed one of Sophie's fine strands of hair away from her face. "I will miss seeing you grow up."

Sophie choked back a sob. "I will miss you too, Mutti."

Mutti's hand fell to the bed as though she'd used up the last of her strength to touch Sophie. "Elise, hand me the candleholder."

Elise hurried to retrieve the brass item from the box. She opened her mother's hand and laid it there gently.

"This candleholder is for you, Sophie." Mutti's voice was strained, as though every word cost her an enormous effort. "I want you to remember not to lose your way in the darkness. No matter how lost you might feel at times, always keep His light burning inside you."

Sophie clutched the heavy angel, which was kneeling and holding up a lampstand. The empty basin was polished and shiny compared to the angel that had become tarnished over time from disuse.

"All three of you," Mutti whispered. "Let me look at you one last time." Mutti's lips were cracked and dry. Elise reached for the tin pot and dipper, ladled out a small amount of water, and tipped it against Mutti's mouth.

"*Nein*, Elise. No more. I'm done."

"Please. One little sip."

Mutti shook her head. "I have no need for it. My only need now is to memorize each of your beautiful faces." Her hungry eyes took in Sophie's face first, then moved to Marianne's. And finally when Mutti devoured hers, Elise had to blink rapidly to capture tears that wanted to escape.

"I know you will find a way to take care of everyone," Mutti whispered through a tremulous smile.

Elise nodded. "Of course I will. I promise." She didn't know how she'd keep her promise to Mutti. And she certainly wouldn't admit that she was terrified that she'd fail. For now, the most important thing was making Mutti as comfortable and happy as possible.

She wasn't sure if Mutti believed her, because she closed her eyes and her face took on the serene expression that it always had whenever she prayed, an expression that announced Mutti's peace and pleasure in prayer.

Elise had never understood how her mother could remain so full of joy and peace in spite of all the difficult circumstances Count Eberhardt had set into motion for their family. She didn't understand why Mutti wasn't angry. Surely they had every right to be upset at the count. Surely there was nothing wrong with being incensed at the rich in this new country, who lived in opulence while she and her sisters slaved long hours day after day simply to survive.

Kein Konig da. No king there. That was what so many of her fellow countrymen said about America, this place of freedom and opportunity. But even if there wasn't a king here in America, there were those who lived like kings, those who took advantage of the masses of poor immigrants in order to line their own pockets.

Mutti's eyes opened, and this time they were hazy, as if she were already halfway to heaven and looking back down on them through the clouds. "I'm so proud of each of you."

A deep sob broke from Marianne, which echoed the cry of Elise's heart.

"God will take care of you." Mutti's lashes dropped. "Good-bye, my sweet girls. I love you."

"I love you too." Elise grabbed Mutti's hand, as if by doing so she could keep her from leaving them. But this time Mutti's eyes refused to open, and her chest refused to rise again. She was gone.

3

Guy Bedell opened the front door of the tenement and held it wide. The towering five-story brick structure was identical to all the other buildings crammed together on Avenue A. They were packed so tightly that sunbeams could hardly break through to bathe the narrow street in much-needed light. Instead the crowded buildings trapped the stench and shadows, which helped to spawn the filth, wretchedness, and mischief plaguing the avenue. He'd also heard that the tenements were so poorly built they couldn't stand alone and therefore, like drunken men, needed the support of each other to keep from toppling over.

He waved Miss Pendleton ahead of him. "Are you certain you want to do this?"

"I'm not certain at all, Reverend," she responded in that no-nonsense way she had. Like last week, she was wearing all black. And like last week, he couldn't keep from noticing the way the dark color highlighted her pale skin and grayish-blue eyes. She was petite and put together in every detail from her severe coif to her immaculate garments. Though she wasn't remarkable in her appearance, there was something in her delicate porcelain face that he liked. Perhaps her determination? Or compassion? Or honesty?

Truthfully, he hadn't noticed her at all before last Sunday, but now he was chagrined to admit he'd thought about her all week. He'd told himself that his thoughts had only to do with the way God had spoken through her to answer his prayer. He'd been battling such doubts recently regarding his ministry among the immigrants, and when she'd spoken to him after the service, it was almost as if she'd been delivering a message directly from God. He loved when God worked that way.

Regardless, his mind had wandered too many times from the answered prayer to the bearer of the answer. He hadn't met a woman in years who had arrested him quite the way Miss Pendleton had. And he was quite taken aback by his strange reaction. After Bettina had passed away ten years ago, he'd had little desire to think about courting other women. At first he'd been too filled with grief and had focused all his energy on raising Thomas. When Thomas had left home to pursue his studies at Union Theological Seminary, Guy had taken the challenge given by the New York Methodist Episcopal Conference. He'd accepted their position as an itinerant pastor to start a mission and chapel among the lions' den.

He'd left his comfortable pastoral position and embraced God's calling to raise the outcast and homeless, to be among those who had no friend or helper, and do something for them of what Christ had done for him. He'd focused all his time and attention on reaching the lost. Nothing and no one had shaken that attention.

Until last week.

Miss Pendleton passed ahead of him into the entryway, and he pulled the door shut behind them. She stopped abruptly and pressed a lacy handkerchief to her mouth and nose. In the tight quarters he almost bumped into her. His six-foot-three frame formed a solid wall that could easily surround and protect her.

He wasn't worried about anyone attempting to harm them in Kleindeutschland, Little Germany. Usually his sheer size kept any pickpockets or drunken brawlers away. But he wasn't afraid to pull out his knife or revolver when he had to on occasion.

Miss Pendleton heaved, and the distinct sound of gagging came from behind her handkerchief.

"Miss Pendleton, are you ill?" Perhaps he shouldn't have invited a woman of her frail sensibilities to visit after all. Most of the others who came with him, like the team visiting the building across the street, were comprised of middling class parishioners. Those with wealth were usually content to do their part by giving donations, not their time.

"I'll be fine in a moment," she said in a muffled voice that was followed by more gagging. "Perhaps you have advice on how to adjust to the foul odor?"

"Foul odor?" He breathed in a deep whiff and noticed the scent of cooked cabbage.

"Very foul." Her eyes were focused on the unlit stairwell ahead.

He examined the steps. The corners were crowded with refuse and stained with urine. He supposed he'd grown immune to the sights and stench over the years. "I'm sorry, Miss Pendleton." He touched her elbow to usher her back out. "I should have warned you." He hastily prodded the door open, but she shook her head.

"I don't wish to leave, Reverend." She squared off with the stairwell and lifted her shoulders as though preparing to enter battle. "If these people must live in this squalor day after day, then surely I can withstand it for a few hours." She removed the lacy square from her nose and crumpled it in her gloved hand.

Guy wanted to smile at her pluck. But at the gravity of her expression, he held his emotion in check. It wasn't that he was amused at her. Not really. He couldn't describe how he felt, except that he appreciated her attitude.

He nodded toward the second door on the right. "One of the tenants has a sweatshop in there."

"Sweatshop?" Her dark eyebrows shot up.

"It's a garment workshop for ready-made clothing."

"Here?" She stared at the closed door.

All traces of his mirth fled at the thought of the numerous sweatshops that existed all throughout the tenements of the Lower East Side. "A sweater, or contractor, picks up precut, unsown garments from clothing manufacturers. Then he supervises the sewing of the garments in his apartment. He hires basters, pressers, finishers, and buttonhole makers."

"They work in their homes and not with the manufacturer?"

"That's right. The manufacturer only hires more specialized tailors, who have skills at cutting the garments. I've heard that Brooks Brothers has less than one hundred 'insiders' who do the cutting and trimming of the material, but that there are thousands of 'outsiders' who do all the sewing."

"I had no idea such a system existed."

Guy couldn't fault her for her ignorance. As a member of the Ladies Home Missionary Society, she came from a wealthy and prominent New York family. Almost all the ladies shared a similar background. Such women wouldn't even consider buying ready-made clothing. They had tailors who came directly to their homes. He'd heard that some of the more fashionable ladies employed French seamstresses to handcraft the latest European styles.

"Most sweaters allow me to come in and visit for a few minutes with the workers," he said, "so long as they don't slacken in their sewing. I've found it's actually the perfect time to talk with them. I have a captive audience, so to speak."

She glanced at the door, and hesitation flitted across her features. "And what should I do, Reverend? What should I say?"

"Give them a tract and tell them the Good News of the gospel."

"I'd much prefer to give them a loaf of bread." On the walk over from the chapel, she'd asked him if he'd ever considered providing food to the people when they came for services. He'd explained his philosophy that he didn't want to grant people handouts. He believed giving them something for nothing lowered their dignity and fostered dependency.

While Miss Pendleton had listened to his principles, she'd also offered him well-thought-out objections, just as she had last week— objections that had left him strangely moved.

"Follow my lead, Miss Pendleton," he said, fighting back the uncomfortable nudge inside that had been growing until at times it felt more like a violent shove. "We shall deliver homilies about the evils of alcohol and the blessing of God's love, and the need to preserve young girls from experiences that might inflame their young passions." He started down the dark hallway toward the first sweatshop. "And we will pray that God, in His time and in His providence, will water and nourish all the seeds we plant."

116

By the time Christine had reached the third floor of the tenement building, her middle churned with nausea. She was no longer merely gagging from the overwhelming stench. No, she was sick to her stomach at all she'd witnessed. The conditions of the building and the apartments were beyond deplorable.

The two sweatshops they'd visited had each been so crowded that she and the reverend had hardly been able to maneuver through the people and stacks of cloth waiting to be sewn, along with the finished garments that were ready to be returned to the manufacturer.

In one of the shops she'd counted at least eight men and women working in what appeared to be the apartment's main room. She guessed the living quarters to be no more than ten-by-ten feet. Her dressing room was bigger than their living space, not to mention that her boudoir and bedroom were each twice the size.

Each apartment was identical with the parlor facing the street and a windowless interior room the size of one of her smallest utility closets. Not only were the apartments tiny and crowded, but they were coated with dust, loose threads, and dye from the cloth.

Reverend Bedell paused. "Are you sure you'd like to visit one more? We can leave now."

She brushed her hand over her skirt. The motion was useless to divest the skirt of the dirt it was accumulating. Every stitch would be embedded with the foulness of the place. But every chamber in her heart was also embedded with an acute ache for the people who must live this way.

As much as she wanted to run away and bury her face in her hands and cry, instead she straightened her shoulders. "I think we have time to visit one more, don't you agree?"

What else did she have to do? Especially now that she no longer had Mother to take care of. Although the physicians had never been able to properly diagnose what was wrong, Mother had taken to her bed not long after Christine's coming out at eighteen. And Mother had spent the next twelve years incapacitated, in her bed, never once leaving her chambers.

Mother's confinement had been a prison sentence for Christine, although at first she hadn't realized it. In the beginning, she'd wanted to do her duty as an only child to her widowed mother. But as time went on, she felt more and more isolated and cut off from the world. Whenever she made mention of visiting friends, going to the opera, or even attending a ladies' group meeting, Mother would have a setback.

Christine had tried to be sensitive to her mother's pain and illness. And she'd wanted to follow the Beatitude that said, "It is more blessed to give than to receive." But there had been times when she grew resentful of the constant demands that were made without a single ounce of kindness or gratitude.

Now all her childhood friends were strangers, long since married with families of their own. She was the odd one wherever she went, the socially inept spinster. She was woefully out of touch with fashion and the unspoken rules of New York City's elite society of which she'd never been very good at. Many of the ladies shunned her anyway as a result of her father's ruthless business practices in his last years of life.

Mother had slowly wasted away, her muscles atrophying and her bones growing brittle from so little movement. Her bedsores had festered until the pain and the ugliness of them had seeped into her soul.

"Miss Pendleton, you've already braved more than most women of your status would." Reverend Bedell paused before a door. In the dark hallway he knew just where to go. And he could obviously sense her discomfort. Or perhaps he'd noticed her nervous habit of fiddling with things. How could he miss the fact that her fingers kept returning to the cameo pinned to her high collar?

She quickly clasped her hands together in front of her to keep herself from fidgeting. "I'm ready, Reverend."

He smiled then, and it seemed to bring a glow to the hallway. "I admire your courage."

She wasn't sure if it was his smile or his kind words that infused her, but whatever it was warmed her heart.

The reverend had been a gentleman the entire time they'd been together. He'd seemed genuinely concerned about her well-being for which she was grateful. She rebuked herself not to read more into his kindness than he intended. He was simply treating her the same way he would any lady from the Society.

Even so, she found herself liking him much more than she ought.

His knock was answered by a diminutive man whom the reverend addressed as Mr. Hermann Jung. The man had a large nose that reminded her of a bulb onion. The tiny red veins crisscrossing it were the sign of too much imbibing, as was the nervous twitch in his eyes, the indication of a thundering headache that wouldn't leave him in peace until he imbibed again. She was well-accustomed to the signs, the sourness of his breath, the jaundice of his skin, the sharpness of his voice. She'd seen all that and more in her father before he'd drunk himself to death.

The sweatshop was nearly identical to the other two they'd already visited. Even though the window stood open, the room was stale, without a hint of a breeze. She didn't know how the women could hold the needles without them slipping from their fingers, which were surely slick from perspiration.

But as it was, each head was bent over what appeared to be dark vests. Two were sewing buttons up the front, another finishing the buttonholes, and still more were adding meticulously neat finishing stitches to the edges. Their fingers were blue from the dye but moved in and out of the material rapidly.

The women cast glances in her direction, clearly curious, but none made an effort to speak to her. Christine hadn't expected them to. From her month of volunteering at the chapel, she'd learned if anyone would do the reaching out, it must be her.

She spoke a few words to the closest woman, who only smiled and nodded, a sign the woman didn't speak English well enough to converse. Christine's education had begun in the first sweatshop after she'd spent five minutes in a one-sided conversation, only to have the woman finally reply but in German.

Christine stepped over outstretched legs and stacks of precut cloth and made her way toward one of the younger women. She'd also learned that most of the women under twenty spoke English fairly well. The assimilation into the new land with a new language and customs was apparently easier for them.

A woman with a coiled blond braid glanced up at her from her hard-backed chair near the window. Christine was immediately impressed by the beautiful face with fresh, natural features, as if the young woman belonged among the meadows and valleys of the Alps rather than sitting in a dimly lit room, slaving over garments for twelve hours a day, six days a week. Her eyes were a pretty shade of blue that hinted at violet.

Within them, Christine caught a glimpse of vulnerability and heartbreaking sadness. It was only then that she noticed the young woman was wearing all black. Mourning clothes. The plainer brown-haired girl sitting next to her was also donned in black. Something in the similar willowy build of their frames and the same elegant shape of their noses told Christine they were sisters. And she surmised that they'd recently lost someone they loved.

While Christine couldn't relate to their sadness, she could relate to their loss. With determination she directed her steps toward them. As she stopped next to them, both girls focused on the vests in their laps. Each of their stitches was even and perfect.

"I'm sorry for your loss," Christine said gently.

The younger of the two sisters looked up again, this time with glassy tear-filled eyes. Her bottom lip wobbled, but she pressed her lips together without saying anything. The older girl continued to work as though Christine hadn't spoken.

"As you can see, I lost someone recently too." Christine laid a gloved hand on her skirt to indicate that she was wearing mourning clothes.

Again the younger girl looked up, her brown eyes such puddles of sorrow that Christine wanted to bend down and draw her into an embrace. "Who did you lose?" the girl asked.

"My mother."

"We did too. She died just last week."

Christine crouched before the girls, glad that she hadn't worn her cumbersome hoops. Even though her position was entirely unladylike, she felt as though she must lower herself to their level to be able to genuinely offer the comfort that it was clear they needed.

"I can see you miss her terribly."

The girl nodded, and a tear slipped out and dropped onto the vest in her lap, forming a dark spot in the material.

"Marianne," chastised the older girl. "Keep working before Uncle sees you."

Christine glanced at the bulbous-nosed man who'd answered the door and was now talking with Reverend Bedell. The reverend was in the middle of one of his mini-sermons on the evils of alcohol, likely having caught the whiff of beer on the man's breath.

"Is your uncle the supervisor?"

"Not usually," the older girl responded curtly. "Only when Mr. Schmidt has gone to return a load of vests and pick up more work."

"So this isn't your home?"

"No, we board across the hall with Uncle."

"And your father, what does he do for a living? Does he work here too?"

Another tear dripped from Marianne's chin. "No, Vater died several years ago. And Mutti had no choice but to move in with Uncle."

"And now she's gone too." Christine understood then the depth of their grief. They'd lost both of their parents. At least they had each other. Christine had no one, no siblings, and certainly no relatives who cared about her except what they might gain from the wealth she'd inherited. "Then we are alike in more than one way, because I too have lost both my father and mother."

"Elise," Mr. Jung said sharply with a strong German accent, "I'll hold you responsible if your sister's work is sloppy."

The older girl nodded at her uncle and then slid Christine a look that told her to move on before she became the cause of more trouble.

Christine straightened and took a step back. Somehow the conversation felt unfinished, but she didn't know if she should venture to speak again since the older girl—Elise—had dismissed her. Christine's fingers fluttered to her throat, to the cameo pin. She grazed the outline of a woman's face framed by a finely detailed gold-filigree frame.

"If you ever find yourself in need of a friend," Christine said before moving on, "please come see me at the Centre Street Chapel." She didn't know what she'd be able to do to help them. She hadn't been able to help any of the other women who'd attended the services. Even so, she wouldn't retract her offer.

"Thank you," Marianne said, her hand growing idle, her needle only half through the seam.

"Ask for Miss Pendleton."

Marianne nodded, but then was elbowed by Elise, who grumbled something in German under her breath.

"Actually, I would love to see you any time," Christine offered. "Whether you need a friend or not, don't hesitate to visit me there at the chapel."

Long after she'd left Kleindeutschland, and long after she said good-bye to the reverend, Christine's thoughts kept returning to the two beautiful girls in mourning. As her brougham rolled to a stop along West Twenty-eighth Street, she peered out the window at her four-story home of red brick and white limestone trim, with its elaborate towers, spires, and mansard roofs. The dwelling had at least thirty rooms, not including the kitchen, larder, and other utility rooms in the basement.

How could she ever again enter this mansion and live alone in its many spacious, well-furnished rooms when a tenement building was smaller but housed dozens of families and their boarders amidst unsanitary conditions, which magnified the dangers of fire and disease?

The carriage door swung open, and Ridley's distinguished face appeared. "Shall I have one of the servants draw up water for a bath?"

She didn't budge from the plush velvet cushion. "Ridley, I'm completely at a loss for what to do for those people."

Ridley doffed his tall black coachman's hat, revealing a head of white hair that matched his shaggy eyebrows. He flattened the waves with his palm and regarded her with the seriousness she'd always appreciated about him.

"I need to do something more than offer those poor people platitudes. What good are kind words when they're sweltering under hardship and oppression?"

"I take it then that Reverend Bedell couldn't be persuaded to consider any type of charity at the chapel?" She'd discussed her frustrations with Ridley last week. She was grateful he never failed to stop what he was doing to give her his undivided attention.

"The reverend is of the mind that simply handing out charity to people will do more harm than good." Weary, she leaned her head back and closed her eyes, wishing she could as easily close her mind's eye to the horrible sights she'd witnessed during the visiting. "I understand his position. Really I do. But surely there must be something we can accomplish besides handing out tracts and then waiting for a miracle."

"Maybe instead of waiting for the miracle, you need to be the miracle." Ridley's confidence and faith in her was unswerving.

"Be a miracle?"

"Sometimes God calls us to wait for Him to act. And then other times He calls *us* to act."

"But that's the problem. I don't know what to do."

"You have a fortune, Christine." Ridley was not only her coachman and friend, but he'd also been her father's financial advisor for many years. After Ridley had retired from the bank, he asked Mother to hire him to help in any role she needed. Since he had no family of his own, he'd wanted to stay busy. In hindsight, Christine realized now he'd taken a job as their hired help so that he could remain close to her. Although he never said it, Christine knew he loved her like a daughter. He was more of a father to her than her own had ever been.

"Your father had many stipulations on the trust," he continued. "But I think I can find a way to pull some of it out for you to use."

"Then you think I should give the poor my money?"

"Not directly. I agree with Guy Bedell on that. They don't need a handout. They need good, honest work with fair wages and decent working conditions."

"Fair wages. Decent working conditions." Ridley's words rolled around her mind like carriage wheels bumping over cobblestone. She'd been grasping for a solution that jostled out of reach.

"Your father was an investor in D. and J. Devlin," Ridley said. "In fact, he was a personal friend to Mr. Devlin and loaned him money when his business nearly went bankrupt in '49. Now Devlin has one of the biggest businesses in the Second Ward."

D. and J. Devlin was a clothing manufacturer similar to Brooks Brothers. But what did that have to do with her?

Ridley's eyes sparked with a keenness that showed his mind was still as sharp now as it had been in the days when he was a sought-after investor. "I'm sure Mr. Devlin would have a very hard time saying no to Ambrose Pendleton's daughter."

Her thoughts bumped irregularly for another moment. Then the clattering ceased. She stared at Ridley and smiled. "I think I'm finally catching on."

Ridley returned the smile, his clean-shaven face still suave and sophisticated, the same as when he'd been a younger man. "You're a strong and intelligent woman, Christine. Much more than you allow."

She reached for his hand, and he clasped hers in return. "Thank you for always believing in me."

"I could do nothing less." He squeezed her fingers, and from the sorrow that flashed in his eyes, she knew he was remembering the harsh words her father had spoken to her over the years. His words had been a bludgeon, berating her for being a daughter instead of the son he'd coveted. Her father hadn't hidden his disappointment from anyone. In fact, quite the opposite. He'd been openly disdainful, making it clear to everyone that he wished Christine had never been born.

She could only thank God that He'd been gracious enough to bring Ridley into her life. The dear man had somehow looked past her stiff and severe façade into her aching little heart to see how rejected and unloved she truly was. He'd whispered words of encouragement that had brought healing to her soul. And he'd never stopped. Even now, though he surely had his own small fortune, he continued to wait on her every need.

"I'll outline the plan," she said. "And then shall we discuss it more at dinner?"

"It would be my pleasure." He helped her from the carriage and accompanied her up the brick walkway to the portico. "Just promise me you won't neglect Reverend Bedell in your plans."

"I don't think this venture will be to his liking." Even if the reverend had been kind to her again today, their philosophies about how to spend their time and resources clearly diverged.

The May sunshine lent Ridley's black hat a glossiness and warmed it enough to bring out a mustiness of the beaver pelt of which it was made. He opened the ornately carved mahogany door and held it wide, revealing the front hallway with its enormous chandelier glistening with dangling crystal jewels. It hung from the high ceiling above a wide, spiraling marble staircase.

"Besides," Christine said, pausing in the doorway, "if you help me, I won't have to worry about the reverend's assistance."

"I'll help you in any way I can. You know that."

She nodded.

"But," Ridley added, "we don't have the connections among the immigrants and the years of experience that Reverend Bedell has."

Everywhere they'd gone today, people had received the reverend with open arms. He clearly had developed trust within the immigrant community. "You're right, Ridley. I'll have to figure out a way to gain his cooperation."

"From what I could see, he already wants to cooperate with you."

Her ready response stalled. She wasn't sure if she'd heard Ridley correctly, but at the ensuing sparkle in his eyes, she shook her head and stepped inside hoping her friend couldn't see the flush that was surely creeping into her cheeks.

"He's a widower and completely devoted to his work. That's all." She tugged at the fingertips of her gloves.

"I suppose that's why he decided to have you accompany him rather than assigning you to another group?"

She slipped off the glove heedless of the fact that two fingers were rolled in. She dropped it onto the silver tray that graced the pedestal table, then began to pluck at the other glove. "I'm sure he meant nothing by his actions."

Ridley was silent as she finished divesting her fingers of the tight leather and carefully began to remove her hatpins and drop them in the silver tray with a clink. She could feel him watching her, waiting. Finally, after she had her hat off and couldn't avoid him any longer, she turned and met his gaze.

"You are not giving yourself enough credit," he said gently. "You're a delightful young woman."

"I'm old and unappealing."

"Thirty isn't old. And you're very pretty."

"Of course you would say so."

"I may be ancient and slightly biased," Ridley said with a return smile, "but my eyesight is still quite proficient. And I had no trouble seeing that Reverend Bedell had a hard time keeping his attention off of you."

Christine shook her head in disbelief. "Thank you for attempting to cheer me with your nonsense. But I've had many years to resign myself to my singleness and have no interest in entertaining thoughts of heartache." As she crossed to the spiraling staircase, her footsteps clopped with finality against the polished white tile. She might need Reverend Bedell to carry out her plans, yet she didn't need him beyond that. Most certainly not.

4

---•——————•---

Elise stroked Sophie's long hair, letting her fingers linger in the strands that were finer than freshly ground flour.

"And so when the orphans bit into the warm, chewy buns, they were surprised to find gold coins inside," Marianne whispered from the other side of Sophie.

In the dark, Sophie snuggled against Elise. It didn't matter that the night air was heavy and sticky with moisture. Elise relished her sister's slight frame against her.

They'd spread a blanket on the parlor floor for their bed near the sofa, as they usually did. But they didn't need a covering, not like in the bitter cold winter when their threadbare blankets did little to keep them warm from the drafts that whistled through the cracks around the window frames.

On the sofa, the soft even breathing of Olivia and Nicholas told Elise the two infants had already been lulled to sleep by Marianne's story.

"And then the children returned to the baker and his wife?" Sophie asked, even though she'd heard Marianne's story a dozen times and already knew the answer.

"Yes, the children went back to thank the baker," Marianne said. "And they told him they couldn't take his gold coins unless he allowed them to work for him."

For just a brief moment, Elise could picture the three of them back in Hamburg in the big feather bed they'd shared in their dormer room, cuddled together under a thick down blanket with the scents of sourdough and pumpernickel wafting up through the floorboards to permeate even the uppermost level. She could imagine the security of knowing Vater was awake in the bake shop below, tending his loaves throughout the night so that they would be fresh and hot in the morning.

"So he gave them a room above the bakery?" Sophie whispered.

Marianne's fingers joined Elise's in combing Sophie's hair. When they'd left the Fatherland, Sophie had been such a little girl. Now after living in New York these past seven years, she had learned English so completely that she no longer had even a trace of a German accent. Unlike Elise who hadn't been ready to let go of their old life.

Father had insisted that all his daughters attend the public school. Sophie and Marianne had benefitted the most. All Elise had been able to think about when she was sitting on the hard bench in the stuffy classroom full of immigrant children was how she missed working alongside Vater. She wanted nothing more than to bury her fingers in thick, sticky dough, kneading and twisting and shaping it into rolls, horns, and pretzels.

"The baker and his kind wife made a room for the children, who never went hungry again and who lived happily ever after." Marianne's story tapered to an almost inaudible whisper.

Elise could feel Sophie's body beginning to relax, her chest rising and falling in a peaceful rhythm.

Outside their tenement in the hallway and stairwell came shouts, mostly in Plattdeutsch. The footfalls and banging of doors and arguing hardly ever stopped, except perhaps in the early morning for an hour or two. The noise, the odors, the lack of privacy, the shortage of fresh air—sometimes it was too much to bear. The chaos only added to the bitter acid already eating at Elise's insides. This wasn't the kind of life they were supposed to have.

Someday, somehow, she'd find a way to make things better for all of them. She vowed it.

At the rattle of the doorknob, Elise stiffened. A muffled curse was followed by bumping and thudding. The hour was too early for Uncle.

He usually stayed at the beer halls until dawn. Then he came home and slept for most of the day, only joining them in the shop when Mr. Schmidt called for him.

Elise silenced her breathing and noticed that Marianne had done the same. Thankfully, Sophie was already asleep. And thankfully Uncle's sons weren't there for him to fight with anymore.

Uncle's two boys, Alexander and Erick, had run away from home several months ago. The warmer temperatures of spring had lured them to the streets, away from their father who demanded their labor in the garment shop but took every penny they earned. Once Erick had decided to hold back some of the pay for his own use, and Uncle had beaten the boy until he wasn't able to stand.

After Erick's wounds healed, he'd left and never returned. Elise didn't expect to see the boys ever again. At twelve and fourteen, they were old enough to survive on the streets. There were plenty of other runaway and orphan children who lived on the streets year-round and managed to eke out a living.

The door finally opened, and Uncle stumbled inside. Elise didn't move and neither did Marianne. They'd learned it was better to pretend they were asleep. When Uncle was in one of his drunken states, there was no telling what he might do.

He slammed the door closed behind him and careened forward. In the darkness of the room, lit only by the moonlight streaming through the open window, he always bumped into furniture. Usually his curses would foul the air, until he made his way to the bedroom where he passed out on the bed.

Elise often held her breath till he'd completed his course through the parlor. But tonight, he veered toward the sofa and their makeshift bed. His heavy boot connected with her spine. Though pain shot through her, she refused to cry out.

"I know you're awake, Elise," he slurred in German.

She extricated herself from Sophie and sat up. "Ja," she said.

"Do you know why I'm home already?"

It wasn't so much a question as an accusation. But Elise knew he'd expect an answer anyway. Although she didn't want to respond, she wanted his boot in her spine again even less. "Nein."

"I'm home because I'm out of money." Uncle wasn't a large or strong man, but somehow his drink gave him superhuman strength. With him towering above her, she must play this game or suffer the consequences.

"So you cannot buy any more beer?"

"I always knew you were a smart girl." He started to chuckle but ended up coughing. When he finally caught his breath, his boot connected with her again, this time her thigh. She considered standing up and moving out of his reach, but to do so would expose Marianne and Sophie, and she'd never do that. In fact, to get to them he'd have to kill her first.

"Since you're so smart," he continued, "then you'll tell me how we're going to come up with more money."

She'd already pondered that question numerous times since Mutti had died. None of the options had been viable. The only one that might work was to have Sophie join them in the sewing. But then who would watch the children? While Elise had considered the possibility of taking Olivia and Nicholas to the Orphan Asylum, she wasn't willing to break Sophie's heart to do so. She tried to tell herself that the two infants weren't a burden, that they didn't require much extra food or expense. But the truth was she couldn't take care of them indefinitely, not like this.

"I can't afford to provide charity to you and your sisters any longer," Uncle said. "And without your mother's income, that's what I'm doing."

"I'll have Sophie join us." Her throat closed around the words. But she knew no other way. "She can take Mutti's place."

"She won't be able to earn what your mother could."

Uncle was right. As women they already made less than the men. She and Marianne each made only $1.60 a week compared to the $3.50 the men earned. It didn't matter that they were swifter and more skilled than most of the men in the building. Sophie, as an inexperienced child, would make even less.

"It will increase our income until Alexander and Erick return for the winter," she said.

Uncle cursed his sons' worthlessness. "Maybe you can get another job."

130

Again, she'd already considered the option. But what else could she do?

Uncle spoke as if he'd heard her thoughts. "You can go sell yourself like all the other girls do at the beer halls."

Marianne gasped and gripped Elise's nightdress. Elise reached behind her and clasped Marianne's trembling fingers. She squeezed them, reassuring her sister as much as herself even as her stomach churned at the thought. Then she stood to her feet, fighting her revulsion and anger. "What would my mother, your sister, say if she heard you suggest something like that?"

The words seemed to sober Uncle, and he didn't speak for a moment. "I'm too nice," he finally said with a sigh. "That's my problem. Taking in all my family. Now look where it's gotten me."

"We have no money because of your drinking—"

The back of Uncle's hand caught her in the mouth, causing her lip to split against her teeth. Pain flooded her senses as blood gushed down her chin. Before she could duck, Uncle's hand connected with her cheek in a slap that knocked her head to the side. "Don't you ever talk to me that way again, young lady!"

She wanted to shout at him that if he stopped squandering their money and worked hard alongside them, perhaps they could begin to save for a better life. But she lifted her chin even as the blood dribbled off. It would do no good to say any more. If Uncle wouldn't listen to Mutti's pleas, he certainly wouldn't listen to hers.

Behind her, Nicholas began to whimper, but someone quickly silenced the infant. Elise had no doubt everyone was awake now.

"After all I've done for you," Uncle shouted. "After giving you shelter, food, and a job, how dare you repay me with belligerence? I ought to throw you out tonight. Then maybe you won't be so quick to disrespect me."

And what about disrespecting me? she almost asked. But she would have no place to go and no one to turn to if Uncle carried through on his threat. She was stuck here. With him. In the pit of hell.

Uncle began to berate her again, but then doubled over with a fit of coughing. With an exasperated wave at her, he stumbled toward the kitchen table. He steadied himself on the back of a chair before staggering into the bedroom. The thud of his body against the mattress was followed by silence.

Only then did Elise allow herself to collapse to the floor. Marianne launched herself against Elise with silent sobs, and Sophie, who was holding both Nicholas and Olivia, sidled against her. Elise drew them all into her arms, muffling their sniffles and crying against her chest.

She kissed the tops of their heads and thanked God they were all still safe and together. But for how long? She squeezed them tight. How long could she keep them safe here at Uncle's? And how would she protect them if they left?

She swallowed the lump that stuck in her throat. She had to find a way to provide a better life for them. But what could she, a single immigrant woman of nineteen years of age do? How could she provide a better life if both her parents had already failed to do so?

Despair threatened to bring tears, but she forced them back. She wouldn't cry. She wouldn't wallow in self-pity. And she certainly wouldn't give up.

5

---•—•—•---

"You've brought what?" Guy Bedell stared down at the delicate face of Christine Pendleton.

"A piano," she repeated even as she motioned at her coachman, who stood in the doorway. The white-haired man nodded and disappeared outside.

The Sunday service didn't start for another hour, and normally he used the time beforehand to pray and review his sermon notes in the relative quiet of the chapel. He certainly hadn't expected to see Miss Pendleton quite this early. Rather than feeling irritated at the interruption to his normal routine, he found his pulse thrumming faster at the sight of her.

After spending last Saturday with her and watching her interact with the immigrants, his admiration had risen to a new level. This week, like the previous, his thoughts kept straying to her. He'd tried to mentally categorize her with the rest of the volunteers, to view her platonically. He thought he'd succeeded, until now, when his body had betrayed him with the quickening.

Her lovely gray-blue eyes peered at him with the same determination and intensity he'd come to expect. "The piano was just sitting in a closet at church. It hasn't been used in years. So I asked the rector to donate it to the chapel, and he and the deacons readily agreed."

"That was very kind of them."

"I thought a piano would allow us to sing during the service."

"Yes, of course." Although he'd asked for a piano when he first opened the chapel, he gave up the pursuit mainly because, even if he'd received the donation, he didn't know anyone who could play it. "There's just one problem, Miss Pendleton."

"There's no problem. I've arranged for it to be delivered and tuned within the hour."

"That's all very gracious of you, but we don't have anyone here who can play the piano."

"Yes, we do." Her pretty mouth curled into the beginning of a smile. He'd learned that she doled out smiles sparingly, and so he gave himself permission to study her face, her dainty chin and nose and the slenderness of her lips. If he were to kiss her, he would have to do so tenderly, otherwise he might crush her.

Her smile faded. "Reverend?" Miss Pendleton's voice wavered with uncertainty. When he finally turned his attention and thoughts away from her mouth, he realized he'd made a complete fool of himself by staring at her like a schoolboy daydreaming about his first kiss. From the way she was twisting at her reticule, and the slight pink in her cheeks, he could see that he'd embarrassed her. He prayed she hadn't been able to read his thoughts.

Why in all that was righteous had he been thinking about kissing her anyway? What had overcome him?

He cleared his throat. "I'm sorry, Miss Pendleton. What were you saying?"

"I was going to tell you that we do have someone who can play the piano."

"And who is that?"

"Me."

Before he could respond, her coachman reappeared with four burly men, who were carrying the piano. They grunted and heaved and sweated as they deposited the heavy item near the pulpit. Soon afterward an older man with a long gray beard appeared. Dressed in a well-worn and ill-fitting suit, he sat down on the piano bench and began to tune the instrument.

"Miss Pendleton," Guy said, running a hand over the glossy light oak of the piano's frame, "I don't know how to thank you."

"I do." She glanced at her coachman. The man didn't have the build or face of one accustomed to manual labor, but instead had the suaveness and bearing of a gentleman. He gave Miss Pendleton a nod of encouragement. "If you'd like to thank me," she continued, "you could agree to help me in a new venture I've set into motion."

"And what new venture is that?" Guy appreciated her fine mind, her inquisitiveness, and even the way she challenged his own beliefs.

"You asked if I had any ideas for ways to make a difference here at the chapel."

"Yes, I did."

"I didn't have any ideas until I returned home last week." She plucked at the edge of her widemouthed sleeve. "I believe God has given me the answer that we've been seeking for how we can be of more help to the immigrant women."

"And the piano is a wonderful idea—"

"I'd like to open a garment shop on the second floor above the chapel."

His words stalled as his thoughts came to an abrupt halt. A garment shop, as in a sweatshop like the ones they'd visited last weekend together?

From the look of expectancy in her wide eyes and the way she peered up at him with such hope, he knew that was exactly what she had in mind. He forced himself to stifle the immediate rebuttal and swell of disappointment. "Miss Pendleton, I don't know what to say," he started with a shaky laugh.

His doubts and hesitancy must have been loud in that nervous chuckle, for her hopeful expression immediately deflated. "Do go on," he said hurriedly as he silently berated himself for hurting her feelings. "Tell me your thoughts."

She took a deep breath as though to fortify herself. "The women who come to our chapel have begged us to find them decent employment so they can leave their lives of sin without putting their children at risk of starvation. I believe we can provide them with employment. Here. We can be the contractors, the sweaters who get the precut garments from the manufacturers while they do the sewing."

The words came out like a well-rehearsed persuasive speech. The only trouble was, no matter how convincing she might be, such a prospect was out of the question. "Most manufacturers already have enough contractors. And even if we could find one who was willing to consider using us, the company wouldn't want these women working for them. Most have no training or experience."

He expected her lips to thin with displeasure at his news, but she pressed forward almost as if she'd anticipated his objections. "I've already located a manufacturer willing to provide me with the already-cut material for shirts. In fact, this week I spoke with the president of the company and have made him aware of the lack of training of the women. But he's assured me he'll provide a seamstress in the beginning who can train the women."

At her words, his face must have registered his astonishment, because Miss Pendleton continued on eagerly, her eyes lighting to a hazy summer blue with her obvious pleasure. "I've agreed to act as the supervisor during the workweek and will make deliveries to and from D. and J. Devlin."

"What about the deposit?"

"I will make it."

"Of course." She could likely do so without any hardship.

"The only drawback is that Mr. Devlin won't pay commensurate for the garments until he sees their quality equals that of more skilled seamstresses."

"So that means we won't be able to pay the women very well?"

"I calculated it and figured out that we can still pay them close to what other seamstresses make."

"And how is that?"

"As the supervisor, I won't require a percentage of the profits."

He stared at her then, not caring that his mouth was hanging open.

"What do you think, Reverend?"

While her plan seemed to grow more possible with every passing second, his initial doubts still swirled like a dust cloud that she couldn't sweep away. "I like your venture," he said slowly, "but I'm still not sure that I'm convinced."

"What are your hesitations?" She stepped closer in her eagerness.

But her nearness only caused his thoughts to scatter. What *were* his objections?

"Well, for one," he said, fumbling over his words, "I don't think it's feasible for you to be the supervisor. That means you'd have to work long hours every day."

"Only at the beginning," she countered. "Once our shop is running smoothly and bringing in a steady profit, I'll appoint one of the women to be supervisor in my place."

"It would take up so much of your day. It wouldn't leave time or energy for you to do anything else—to shop, go to parties, attend charity gatherings, visit with friends or entertain callers." Did she have callers? Certainly a woman as pretty as she had men vying for her attention.

"This is what I want to do with my time."

"But for how long? What happens when you tire of this project and decide to move on to something else?"

"If this is what God would have me do right now, then I'll see it to completion until He releases me for other work."

"You're amazing."

He didn't realize he'd spoken the words aloud and that he was staring at her again, until she averted her eyes, looking down at the floor while clicking her reticule open and shut several times. He was tempted to beat his forehead with his palm for speaking so forthrightly, yet her small smile and the flush in her cheeks stopped him.

She *was* amazing. He didn't know of any other woman who would consider sacrificing so much of her time and energy to do this. Certainly none of the other ladies of the Ladies Home Missionary Society would consider such a thing.

The Society . . . His pulse began to race.

She peeked up at him through her long lashes. "Does that mean you're in agreement?"

Oh, how he wanted to be in agreement. But his heart felt suddenly heavy, as though a chain had been locked around it. "I can see that you've thought through all of the details."

Her expression was steady and unruffled. "But . . . ?"

"But there is one thing you haven't taken into account, which is perhaps the obstacle that may be insurmountable."

"'If God is for us, who can be against us?'"

"The Ladies Home Missionary Society."

"And why would they oppose this ministry since it won't require any effort or contributions on their part?"

"Every time I've made minor suggestions for changes, they've repeatedly informed me they want the chapel to be a religious association and not a charitable one. They would entirely oppose your venture."

She shrugged. "Why should it matter what they think?"

"Because they are my patrons and I need their support."

For the first time since they began the conversation, her countenance sobered and she didn't have a ready answer. The only sound in the chapel was the repetitive plunking of the piano keys as the tuner worked.

There had been many occasions Guy chafed under the leadership of the Society. But overall, his philosophy had lined up with theirs. He'd viewed his mission as more spiritual than physical. However, after seeing the tenements and the poor immigrants through Miss Pendleton's fresh eyes, he had to admit his stance was beginning to shift.

"I have evaluated how I might carry forth my plans without your aid, Reverend." Miss Pendleton's tone was gentle but determined. "But I've come to the conclusion that God has brought us together for this purpose. I can provide the capital, and you can provide the connections with the people. They already love and trust you in a way I could not gain so readily."

Was this the plan God had for them? He'd been praying, as Miss Pendleton had suggested, that God would give them direction. Was this the answer?

Miss Pendleton nodded as though reading the question in his eyes. "I cannot ask you to endanger your relationship with the Society. Still, I ask you to consider that if I'm willing to step out in faith, that maybe it's time for you to take the next step as well."

Her rebuke went straight to his heart. And again, as he had the first time she'd approached him, he felt as if God were using this woman to communicate with him, to convict him of his complacency, and to challenge him to do more.

"You really are amazing," he said again, not caring that his voice was low and perhaps a little too intimate.

At his words, she sucked in a sharp breath that made her chest rise. She mumbled an excuse about needing to discuss something with the piano tuner. Guy stood unmoving at the pulpit and watched her walk gracefully away and speak kindly to the tuner still at the piano. Guy couldn't stop himself from staring, even though he was flustered at the thought that he was acting like an untried youth rather than the experienced once-married man he was.

"God help me," he whispered, finally tearing his attention away from Miss Pendleton to focus once more on his sermon notes. He liked her. Much more than he should.

6

Christine tied back the curtain. The freshly washed glass allowed sunlight to cascade into the room. She fluffed the cheerful yellow calico and then stood back and surveyed her hard work. She smiled with pleasure at the transformation that had taken place on the second floor of the Centre Street Chapel.

She'd hired construction workers to knock down as many interior walls as possible to enlarge the work space. They'd applied a fresh coat of white paint to the remaining walls. She'd arranged for several of her servants to help her scrub floors, windows, and every filthy inch of the second floor. They'd swept away debris, cobwebs, mouse droppings, dead cockroaches, and only the Lord knew what else.

Now after nearly two weeks of preparation, the work space was almost ready. Just that morning she'd had tables and chairs delivered and set up in tidy rows close to the windows to allow the women as much light and air as could be gained. She'd had lanterns strategically placed above each of the tables for dark, rainy days. And she still planned to have at least two stoves installed before winter arrived.

At firm footsteps on the stairway, her middle fluttered like the lacy curtains blowing in the breeze. After working at the chapel from dawn until dusk every day, she easily recognized the reverend's footsteps now. And she couldn't stop herself from anticipating seeing him.

She tried to rationalize that she was only eager to be with him to discuss their plans. But when he reached the top of the steps and offered her one of his easy, carefree grins, her heart skipped like a little girl jumping rope. She couldn't deny she looked forward to these moments every day when he came up to check on her progress and to report on his.

Returning his smile felt easy and natural now.

"I think we're all set," he said, removing his hat and combing his fingers through the messy waves of blond hair.

"Will the women show up?" she asked.

"Most of them will. I've told them the doors open at seven o'clock." He walked further into the room and around the tables and chairs. She was glad to see his large frame could maneuver in the new space without any trouble, which hopefully meant the women would have plenty of room to stretch out while they worked.

She ran her fingers over the smooth tabletop. "Even if we only have a few at first, word will spread. Don't you think?"

He seemed to be silently counting the chairs. "We'll have more than a few."

"Are you sure?"

"I'm positive." His blue-green eyes were warm and full of confidence.

"Do they seem excited?"

With a growing smile he rounded the table toward her. "You're nervous."

"Maybe a little."

He stopped in front of her and surprised her when he reached for her hands. His large fingers enclosed hers and he squeezed them gently. "We've done all we can, and now we must pray for God to bless our efforts."

He'd never held her hands before. In fact, they'd rarely been alone over the past couple of weeks since numerous workers had always been present. Or Ridley. Dear, faithful Ridley. She didn't know what she would have done without his advice and insights. Even now he would be soon arriving to take her to Devlin's to pick up the first order of precut shirts the women would begin sewing tomorrow.

"Why don't we pray right now?" Reverend Bedell suggested without releasing her hands.

How could she say no to such a request? Even though they were alone and holding hands, they were only praying. Surely there wasn't anything improper about that.

He bowed his head and closed his eyes. She did likewise. However, as he began his prayer, she couldn't think about anything but the warm pressure of his hands against hers. His fingers were strong but also contained a tenderness she'd grown to appreciate about him. In fact, there were many things she'd learned about him that she liked. He was humble, open to her ideas, and yet he wasn't a pushover. He always had insightful suggestions and advice to add to her plans.

He was also diligent and hardworking. He arrived at the chapel before her every day and left later. He was kind and merciful to all those he came into contact with, yet he hadn't hesitated to confront a couple of drunken men who'd disrupted the worship service. He was tough and intimidating when he needed to be.

She peeked up at him, taking a few seconds to study his features as he prayed. She liked the square solidness of his chin, the smile lines next to his eyes, and the peaceful look on his face. She found herself captivated by his mouth and the purposefulness of each word he spoke.

Suddenly his lips stopped moving, and she saw that he had one eye half open and was peeking back at her.

"I'm sorry," she said. "I was just . . . just . . ."

"You were just praying with your eyes open?"

"Yes, exactly."

"And reading my lips at the same time?" Mirth lightened his eyes.

"Of course. What else would I be doing?"

"Thinking about kissing me?" There was something in his tone that bordered on hopeful.

She gasped and tried to dislodge her hands from his.

Instead of releasing her, he chuckled and wrapped his fingers tighter. "I'm sorry. I shouldn't have assumed you were having the same thoughts as me."

She ceased her squirming and held in another gasp at the insinuation of his words. Had he been thinking of kissing her? Why would he ever consider kissing her, an old spinster? "Reverend Bedell—"

"Christine." At the sound of her name on his lips, she shivered as a strange warmth came over her. "Will you call me Guy when we're alone? After working together these past weeks, we don't have to be so formal anymore, do we?"

Her mother had never called her father anything other than Mr. Pendleton their entire marriage. "I don't know . . ."

"I'd like it." He brought his hand to her chin and tipped it up so she had no choice but to meet his gaze, which was such a warm blue that it evaporated any doubts like sunshine upon the dewdrops.

"Very well."

"Then say it." His eyes were focused on Christine's lips, and she had the distinct feeling he was indeed imagining kissing her. But why would he want to kiss her? He was surely jesting with her as he liked to do from time to time.

His thumb slid up from underneath her chin to along her jawline, then slowly down again to the tip of the chin. The touch was so gentle she shivered once more. She had the sudden urge to launch herself at him, to press against him and let him kiss her if he so wished.

But he couldn't possibly want to . . .

"Please, Christine," he whispered.

"Guy," she breathed shakily. "But you're a pastor and deserve my respect."

"I'm just an ordinary man, Christine." The way he said her name was like a caress. His face then dipped nearer so that he was only inches away. "An ordinary man who seems to have fallen prey to the charms of one very pretty woman."

Fallen prey? Pretty woman? She couldn't hold back a laugh. "Reverend—"

His brows came together in a scowl.

"I mean, Guy. I think you may be ill."

His scowl melted away into another beautiful smile. "I think you have a hard time accepting compliments."

He didn't realize how true his words were. Her father had specialized in doling out criticism and spite. And Mother had been too consumed with herself to think about what her daughter might need. It wasn't until Ridley had entered her life that she'd had a single positive word spoken to her.

"What will it take for you to believe me when I tell you I think you're amazing?"

He'd called her amazing before, and she hadn't been able to accept it then or now. "I'm just ordinary too," she said.

"Not to me." The sincerity in his simple statement made her breath catch. And when he bent just a little closer, she stopped breathing altogether. "I've never met a woman like you before."

She could only swallow. Hard. Surely this wasn't happening to her. Surely she'd fallen into a blissful daydream and would be woken up to the cold truth of her reality soon.

His nose touched hers, and the warmth of his breath brushed her lips. "Christine," he said, his voice filling her with longing, "may I kiss you?"

A warning sounded from the far corners of her mind and told her she ought to say no, that she should retreat while she still retained her dignity. But he stroked his thumb from her chin back to her jaw again, and the caress lit a flame inside her like the strike of a match to a wick soaked in oil.

She gave him her answer by moving into him and closing the distance between them. Although she'd never even embraced a man much less kissed one, she lifted herself to him and trusted he'd do the rest. She was rewarded by the sweet touch of his lips against hers. The sensation was soft and exquisite and brief. She found herself disappointed when he began to pull away.

"Guy," she whispered and pursued his lips with hers.

He stilled as if he hadn't expected her response. For an instant she regretted her boldness, wondered if she'd somehow broken a rule, and felt the heat of embarrassment creep into her cheeks.

"I'm sorry—" she mumbled, pulling away.

Before she could move more than a fraction, his hand slipped to the small of her back and his mouth returned to hers, cutting off her apology with another soft, feathery kiss. She didn't know why he was being so careful with her, kissing her as though she might break. So she cupped his cheeks with her hands and pressed her lips harder.

His hand against her back tensed and his fingers splayed, drawing her against his chest. He matched the pressure of her lips, tentatively at first. But when she melded against him, his kiss deepened and she could feel the power and strength of him. She relished it, craved it. And she didn't want it to end.

"Eh-hem." A forced cough came from the stairway.

Christine broke free at the same time that Guy jerked back. "Oh, dear!" she said before she could stop herself.

It was Ridley. Standing on the top step and staring at them. His hat was off, and he had a hand on his head as though he'd been in the process of smoothing down his hair when he spotted them kissing. He averted his eyes, but from the awkward way he held himself, Christine guessed he'd seen the most impassioned part of their kiss.

Mortified, she said, "I'm sorry, Ridley. This isn't what it seems—"

Guy's touch on her arm stopped her. "No, Christine. It's exactly what it seems, and I'm not embarrassed by it in the least."

The tension in her chest eased a little.

"I know we haven't known each other long," he continued, "but it's been long enough for me to realize that you're very special and that I enjoy being with you in a way I haven't experienced with anyone else."

How could that be true? Even if he'd enjoyed her company so far, surely he would eventually come to realize that she was no one special.

"I'm a man of forty years and have already lived a full life. I don't know how many days I have left on this earth. Therefore, I see no reason to wait to express how I feel, or to play the flirtatious games of the young, or to prolong getting to know each other in a lengthy courtship."

"If you'll allow me, and if Ridley approves"—Guy nodded at Ridley, and by doing so she saw that he understood how Ridley was much more to her than just a coachman—"I'd like to marry you."

Had she heard him correctly? "Marry me?" The words squeaked high and off-key.

He released a chuckle that rumbled with nervousness. "My proposal is rather sudden. But at my age, I know myself much better and have a great deal more wisdom now than I did when I was a young man. And I've become more proficient at judging the heart and character of others."

"You may be a good judge of character." She fumbled to slow

down the conversation. "But you can't possibly know the real me in so short a time." It had only been a month since the first Sunday she'd gathered enough courage to speak to him.

"I know you're the most incredible woman I've ever met." His expression was so sincere that for a moment she could almost believe him. "I admire so many things about you—your determination, unflinching spirit, practicality, humility, and so much more."

She gave a shaky laugh. "I'm not sure if you're describing the right person, Reverend."

"Not to mention . . ." His voice dropped an octave. "You're beautiful."

Heat flared in her cheeks. "Now I know you're telling tales."

"I'd like to spend the rest of my life proving to you that I mean every word." He held her gaze, and she saw something in his eyes that pricked her with fear. Was it love?

No one had loved her like this. Why would Guy be the first? Unless of course he didn't really know her as well as he thought he did. Once he was with her long enough, he'd grow tired of her and regret his decision.

Guy didn't say anything for a moment but watched her expectantly as if waiting for her answer to his proposal.

Panicking, she darted a glance at Ridley, hoping her friend would have some words of wisdom written in the lines of his face and radiating from his eyes. Instead he only shrugged his shoulders as if to say she needed to make up her own mind this time.

"Christine," Guy said quickly, perhaps sensing her fear, "I can see that I've put you on the spot today. And I'm sorry for that. It's just that at my age I have no need of conventionalities. However, you're still young and may wish to approach things more traditionally."

"It's not that. It's just that I'd already resigned myself to a life of singleness."

"As had I. After my wife died, I hadn't the desire to remarry. In fact, I resolved to have the mind-set of the Apostle Paul in missionary devotion to spreading the gospel. But from the moment I met you, I've thought of little else but you. Although I've tried to deny my growing attraction, I can't help but think that God has brought us together to serve Him in this ministry side by side. In His Providence, He saw that the two of us working together would have much more of an impact than we could ever have individually."

Guy's rationale made perfect sense, and everything within her was keen to believe him. Yet she couldn't ignore the whispers of doubt, the echoes in the corridors of her mind telling her she was worthless and unwanted and that his special attention was simply too good to be true.

Guy reached for her hand, his strong fingers enveloping hers. "Don't give me your answer today," he said. "Take some time to think about it. Please."

She nodded, knowing she could do nothing less. He deserved that much from her. Next to Ridley, Guy was the kindest man she'd ever met. Over the past month he'd become her friend, someone she could trust and talk with openly. And he was right that they did indeed share a passion for the poor, lost immigrants of the city. Working with him in developing the garment shop had brought her immense joy, and she didn't want that to come to an end.

"I'll think about everything you've said," she promised.

He squeezed her hand. "Thank you, Christine."

At the hope that flared in his eyes, she had to look away before he saw her guilt. If her own flesh-and-blood mother and father couldn't love her, Guy would realize soon enough that a husband wouldn't be able to either.

7

————◆————◆————

"I have something special for you all." Elise approached Marianne, who was sitting against the tenement building and reading a book she'd borrowed from a friend.

Sophie and her two young charges were playing with a marble Nicholas had discovered in the gutter. But at Elise's words, the three scampered toward her.

"What is it? What is it?" little Olivia asked, peering up at Elise with hungry eyes. Always hungry.

Nicholas toddled behind her, and Olivia reached for her brother's hand. Standing side by side with their straight brown hair and brown eyes the color of rye bread, no one could mistake the fact that the two were brother and sister.

"What do you have?" Olivia asked again while tugging at Elise's skirt.

"Be patient, my dears." She slid down the brick wall until she was sitting next to Marianne on the sidewalk that was littered with tattered papers, empty cans, broken boards, and other foul refuse.

The June heat and humidity had forced them out of the apartment for the afternoon. But even outside, the temperature was stifling. Elise wiped the perspiration from her brow, but it was only replaced by more. She prayed the weather would turn cooler by tomorrow or they would have to suffer through another unbearable workday as they had yesterday.

"Come closer," Elise instructed. She tucked her legs under her skirt and made room for them.

All around came the calls and laughter of play. Younger children were clustered on the sidewalk. Older girls were sitting on the sidewalks or tenement stairs, while a group of boys played baseball in the street. Parents and grandparents had brought chairs outside and occupied every spot of shade that could be found.

Sophie kneeled in front of Elise and then drew Nicholas and Olivia to her sides, putting an arm around each one. Sophie's butter-blond hair had pulled loose from her braids and was plastered to her flushed cheeks.

Elise dug in her pocket and pulled out a brown paper package. She unfolded the paper, and the ensuing gasps of the children were sweeter than the music of an entire orchestra. She didn't have to force a smile this time. She carefully unwrapped the wedge of cheese and let its aroma stir memories of the days when they'd had more than enough to fill their bellies.

She reached into her other pocket and retrieved the two hard rolls she'd also found. She'd gotten lucky today. Usually when she went scrounging for food on Sundays, the garbage canisters behind the grocers were already picked over. But today she'd discovered a barrel that hadn't been touched. Even if the cheese had been moldy when she'd first come upon it, she was able to scrape the mold away. She divided the cheese four ways, split the rolls in half, and passed out a piece to each of them.

"You have some too," Marianne said, breaking her piece of cheese in half.

Elise shook her head. "No. I'm not hungry." It was an outright lie because even as she spoke, her stomach rumbled.

"Are you sure?" Marianne said.

The others were devouring theirs in ravenous bites. Sophie, of course, had already broken off half of hers. She always claimed she was saving the portion for another time. But Elise knew she gave the saved portions to Olivia and Nicholas later, after their little bellies began to complain once more.

"I'm fine, Marianne." Elise looked away before Marianne could read the truth in her eyes. She watched the friendly face of Reinhold as he walked down the street with his purposeful stride. At the sight of her, he waved and veered toward her.

Reinhold's overlong, unkempt hair curled over his collar, and he'd hooked his suit coat over his shoulder with his thumb. His face was ruddy from his days spent in the hot sun. He was one of the few from their building who didn't sew. Instead he'd found work on a construction crew erecting new tenements. The pay was better, but the work was brutal. Reinhold came home every evening at dark utterly exhausted, usually sustaining one injury or another.

At nineteen he was the primary earner in his family, taking care not only of his mother and five siblings but also his mother's sister and her two children. While his mother and aunt were both seamstresses for Mr. Schmidt, working alongside Elise and Marianne, they couldn't bring in enough to support their families.

Reinhold wasn't overly tall, yet he was brawny and broad-shouldered. His strength and agility had earned him the job doing construction in the first place. Months of grueling work had honed his muscles and chiseled away the roundness that had once defined his face, leaving lean angular features instead. Gone was the boy. In his place was a man. A good and kind man.

He greeted Sophie and Marianne with his usual teasing while at the same time he picked up Olivia and Nicholas, one in each arm. He blew bubbles into both of their bellies and earned their delighted giggles. Over the tops of the children's heads, he caught Elise's gaze and grinned at her. When he returned the two infants to Sophie's waiting arms, he tickled Sophie and gained a laugh from her as well.

Elise relaxed against the warm brick wall and for just a moment pretended that all was well. With Reinhold there, it was an easy fantasy. He always made her feel safe. She supposed that was why they'd had a faithful friendship the past three years since her family had moved in with Uncle. She'd met Reinhold the first day here, and she'd found him to be a good listener. His steady, unwavering spirit had kept her from drowning in sorrows many times, especially in recent weeks.

He pulled a pouch from his pocket and gave each of the children a gumdrop. He had no money to spare for such an extravagance, not when his family counted on him. But he always found ways to make life more bearable, especially for the children.

"There now," he said, tousling Nicholas's hair. "Make it last."

Nicholas touched the piece of candy to his tongue carefully, his eyes wide with adoration for Reinhold.

"And I have one for the queen too." Reinhold's eyes sparkled as he held out a piece of candy to Elise.

She shook her head. "Save it for your siblings."

"Elise." He tone dropped in reprimand even as his smile widened. "Don't make me force this into your mouth like I did with the licorice last week."

The others watched her expectantly. They would enjoy seeing Reinhold follow through on his threat. It would make them laugh, just as it had the last time. With so little laughter in their lives, she decided to play along with Reinhold. Sure enough, as Reinhold wedged the gumdrop between her pursed lips, their sweet giggles filled the air around her.

Only after the fruity piece of candy was melting on her tongue did she glimpse a shadow in Reinhold's eyes, a shadow that expanded when he stared back at her once more above the heads of the others. The mirage of peace dissipated as wariness took its place.

After Marianne left to take the children to get a drink of water, Reinhold slid down next to her on the sidewalk. His shoulder brushed against hers, and she tried to take reassurance from the solidness of his presence. He was more than just a friend. He was like a brother.

"Tell me what's wrong," she said quietly, "and don't try to protect me."

He sighed and stared straight ahead. Now that the others were gone, the curtains were pulled back to reveal his true feelings—despair and frustration. "Your uncle has found another family to board with him."

The gumdrop turned sour as Elise's mind spun with the implications of Reinhold's revelation.

"I'd heard he was looking for someone else," Reinhold continued, "and this morning I learned that the family is moving in this week."

"How many?"

"Six."

"Uncle won't allow us to stay much longer," Elise said.

Reinhold nodded as though he'd already come to the same conclusion. "I want you to come live with us."

"We've been over this before, Reinhold. And we both know it won't work." When Reinhold had seen the bruises on her face after Uncle hit her a couple of weeks ago, he'd been angry enough to kill Uncle. But, as usual, Uncle was lying unconscious on the bed.

"I'll look for a bigger place that will fit all of us." The thread of desperation in Reinhold's voice told her how unlikely that was. She guessed that was what he'd been doing all morning on his day off—searching for an apartment.

"Even if you could find something," she said, "we wouldn't be able to afford it." She hadn't told Reinhold she'd already been trying to find another place to live. Uncle hadn't made mention of prostitution again. In fact, Elise wasn't sure if he even remembered his vile suggestion since he'd been so drunk. But ever since he'd mentioned it, fear had sprouted inside her and taken root. She didn't think she'd ever rest peacefully again until they were safely away from the man.

The sunshine beat down on her with unrelenting heat, making her feel suddenly faint. She'd promised her mother to protect and take care of everyone. And she'd vowed to herself that she would do whatever it took to give them all a better life, to get back to the way things used to be when Father was alive, before Count Eberhardt had destroyed their lives. But so far she'd failed to do anything to improve their situation. Now, with Reinhold's news, it appeared things would only get worse.

"I've been trying to think of a solution," Reinhold said, "and I could come up with only one idea."

"What?"

"Marry me."

A burst of laughter tumbled out of her. At the flash of hurt on Reinhold's face, she cut the laughter short. "You're serious?"

"Yes, why wouldn't I be?" he responded.

"Because that would be really awkward."

"It wouldn't have to be." His brows came together in a scowl. "I'd make a good husband, Elise."

Seeing he was, in fact, being serious, all the humor she'd found in his suggestion fell away. She studied his profile for a moment, the rippling muscles of his jaw, the maturity that had developed in his face in recent months. He'd been the man of his house for the past year, shouldering more responsibility than most other young men his age. Not only was he faithful and hardworking, but he was tender and kind. She'd seen the sweet way he treated his younger siblings, the same way he did Nicholas and Olivia and Sophie. He'd not only make a good husband, but he'd make a good father too.

But marry him? She couldn't imagine it.

"You'll make an excellent husband," she said cautiously. "But you're my brother and friend. It would seem strange—"

"You mean more to me than a sister." His voice cracked over his raw confession.

"Reinhold, please don't." She didn't want to hear that he had feelings for her. If he admitted he liked her beyond friendship, things would become uncomfortable between them, and she couldn't bear that.

"It doesn't matter how either of us feel," he said quickly, changing his tone back to the brotherly one she needed. "The fact is, if we get married, then my mother can't say no to you coming to live with us."

Mrs. Weiss wasn't unkind. She was just anxious. About everything. Having five more children move into their family's cramped apartment would give Reinhold's mother an attack of nerves. The attack might lead to her inability to work, which would only make the anxiety worse. It was a vicious cycle that Elise had witnessed Reinhold deal with on other occasions.

Elise didn't want to cause Mrs. Weiss undue stress and anxiety. All the more reason not to discuss marriage with Reinhold.

"If Uncle Hermann forces us to leave," she said, "I'll find someplace for us to live." She had no idea where. All she could do was pray for a miracle.

8

Christine circled the table, stopping to offer a word of encouragement to each woman. After almost a week, she could see improvement in their handiwork and she wanted to make sure she let them know.

Their steady chatter filled the upstairs workroom, which was a change after the first two days of tense silence. She prayed she'd finally convinced them that even though she was their supervisor, she had their best interests at heart.

Yes, she'd been strict. She'd made it clear from the first day that she wouldn't tolerate laziness or sloppiness. In fact, Guy had laid down several rules too. The first was that the women had to cease from prostituting themselves. The second was they must make a pledge of total abstinence. And the final rule, they must regularly attend worship services. Anyone who came to work intoxicated or who relapsed into former vices would be immediately discharged.

So far they'd only had to dismiss one woman. The rest had adhered to the rules with exemplary effort. They'd shown an eagerness to learn the honest trade that had even impressed the seamstress Mr. Devlin had sent over to supervise their training.

While Christine was pleased with their progress, she was surprised that her burden hadn't gone away. If anything, her heart was heavy with the need to do more. On the first Monday they'd opened the workshop, over forty women had lined up at the door. They were able to accept only twenty.

She hadn't wanted to complain to Guy about her discontent. She should be happy he agreed to have the shop at all. But she couldn't deny that something inside was still stirring her to do more. When she mentioned this to Ridley, he shook his head sadly and said she didn't have access to any more of her funds.

"Your stitches are very even, Mrs. Watson," Christine said to the tall woman who'd stood up that day at the chapel service and so passionately begged for employment.

The woman glanced away from her work for just an instant and smiled up at Christine. Her gaunt face was too thin and still streaked with grime and sweat. Though the windows were wide open, the room was wretchedly hot, and Mrs. Watson's listless hair clung to the perspiration on her neck. Even so, there was a gratefulness and relief in the woman's eyes that caught at Christine's heart.

At the familiar purposeful footsteps on the stairway, Christine's pulse charged forward and her hand flew to her cameo pin. Guy was finally returning. He'd been gone all morning to meetings. He'd been absent all day yesterday too. And she found that she'd missed him more than she cared to admit.

A tiny, secretive thrill wound through her every time she thought about his kisses and then his proposal of marriage. Half the time she told herself he'd only made the offer out of guilt for kissing her, that he hadn't really meant it. The other half she wondered if she'd dreamed the whole incident.

She didn't want to be thrilled for fear she'd indeed discover that his proposal wasn't genuine. But she couldn't help herself. She couldn't stop thinking about the way his lips had felt upon hers, and she was embarrassed to admit she longed for it to happen again.

As he climbed to the top step, she eagerly took in his broad, stocky build. His unruly hair was tamed momentarily by his hat. His face was clean-shaven and tanned in contrast to the white collar of his shirt. He scanned the room before his eyes landed on her. At the warmth in his expression, she could almost imagine that their relationship really could work, that she could say yes to his proposal. While he hadn't said anything more about it all week, Ridley assured her numerous times that Guy was only giving her time to think it over, that he didn't want to pressure her.

"Miss Pendleton," Guy said across the now-silent room, "may I have a word with you in private?"

The women looked first to him and then to her, and Christine ducked her head lest they see anything in her expression that could be deemed inappropriate. "Of course, Reverend Bedell. I shall be right down."

As Guy descended the stairs, she continued around the room with her inspection. She didn't want to appear overly enthusiastic to be with him, even though she was. When sufficient time had passed, she regulated her steps, slowly and evenly, until she was finally away from the women. Then she flew the rest of the way down.

She stopped abruptly at the sight of him on the front bench of the chapel, his elbows on his knees, his shoulders slumped, and his face in his hands. Her pulse skidded to a halt, her anticipation doused with dread.

Something was wrong.

She started hesitantly toward him. Had he changed his mind about marrying her? Was that it?

Stopping in front of him, she twirled the narrow gold bracelet that encircled her wrist. When he didn't acknowledge her presence, she twisted the bracelet faster. Her heart warned her to run before he could speak words that would hurt her. But she pressed her lips together, determined to stay and be brave. After all, this was why she'd resigned herself to spinsterhood so that she wouldn't get her hopes high only to have them come crashing back down.

He expelled a long sigh.

"I can see you have difficult news to share with me," she said, deciding that at the very least she could make this easier on him. After all, he hadn't really known her well enough when he proposed. "Whatever you want to say, I give you leave to speak your mind. I'd rather have the truth now than later."

He nodded but still didn't look at her. "I was praying things wouldn't come to this."

Her stomach began to tie itself into little knots. "I understand."

"I'd hoped they would listen to reason. But they are so stubborn."

"They?" What was he talking about?

He lifted his face from his hands to reveal a haggardness that hadn't been there before. "I met with the Ladies Home Missionary Society yesterday, along with their board of advisors. They're against our workshop."

She had to hold back a sigh of relief as the cause of his distress became clear. He wasn't withdrawing his proposal after all. "We knew the Society might oppose our plans. But after a week of watching the transformation in the women, how can we doubt God is behind the work?"

"Yes, I met with the board again this morning hoping to convince them of that."

Did she dare reach for his arm? She wanted to offer him a measure of comfort, to reassure him. But would he think her inappropriate if she touched him? "Perhaps we should invite them to come down and watch the women at work. Then they'll see for themselves—"

"They won't come. I begged them to visit, but they want nothing to do with the workshop. Until . . ."

Something in his tone put her on edge. "Until what?"

He reached for her hand and tugged her toward him, leaving her little choice but to sit down on the bench next to him. She overcame her shyness and placed her other hand on top of his. She had the sudden urge to lean into him further, comb his hair back, and kiss his cheek. Surely that would distract him from the seriousness of his thoughts. Surely it would help him remember that they were in this together, that he wasn't alone.

He abruptly shifted so he was looking at her, his face only inches away. His eyes were wide, revealing his frustration and fear. "Until they find a different donor."

A chill rippled up her back. "That makes no sense. I'm giving freely. Without any stipulations."

"I didn't want to mention the truth to you, Christine. But I've always been honest and I can do nothing less now." When he looked at her again, this time the pain in his eyes was undisguised. "I don't know anything about your father or his business practices, but apparently the chairman and several other board members don't want to be a part of a charity that involves working with you or your father's money."

She sat in stunned silence, unable to move. While it was true her father had made more enemies than friends during his life, she never expected anyone would oppose charitable efforts as a result of past grudges.

"I'll step down," she said.

"Even if you walk away, they won't take the money." Guy shook his head. "They've made up their minds to close the workshop for now, with the possibility of opening it again if they find a different donor. But who knows if or when they'll do that. After all, they're not convinced they need to shift the focus of this ministry."

And Guy wouldn't have been either if she hadn't pushed him with all her new ideas and convinced him that was what God wanted. Guy was humble and kind enough to listen to her. He'd granted her freedom to make the changes she thought were necessary. He'd trusted her wholeheartedly. And now she'd caused him problems.

"They'll allow you to stay on here at the chapel, won't they?"

"It doesn't matter now. I gave my notice—"

"No. You can't quit."

"It's more of a mutual parting of ways." He gave her a weak smile. "I don't agree with their decision, and I let them know it a little too adamantly."

Her mind spun trying to find a solution, anything. "I'll go and explain things to them and tell them it was all my fault. I'll tell them they need to keep you here. They can't let you go—"

"Christine." His voice cut through her panic. "I need to move on."

Maybe he'd thought he cared about her before. But now he would surely change his mind. He'd see her for the nuisance she really was. If he'd once thought of marrying her, he wouldn't have any desire to do so anymore—not after she'd ruined his job and ministry.

"I'm sorry, Guy," she managed through a tight throat, extricating her hand from his and standing.

He didn't try to stop her. Instead he buried his face in his hands again. When she walked away, he didn't call her back.

She'd hurt him. Why would he want her now?

A sob caught in her throat. She should have known a relationship with him was too good to be true. She shouldn't have allowed herself any hope. She should have kept the door locked on her spinsterhood and hidden her emotions out of reach where she would be safe.

"I'm sorry, Miss Pendleton," a stocky maid said as she approached her in the sitting room, "but the advisory board won't be able to meet with you after all."

Christine stood and smoothed a hand over her best black-silk bombazine. She'd been waiting for half an hour at least. She wanted to throttle the maid and force her to turn around and speak with the men again, who were holed up in the study. Instead she did what was socially expected of her. She inclined her head graciously.

Ridley met her at the door of the large brownstone home, and once it was closed behind her, she exhaled an exasperated breath. "That was a waste of time."

Ridley quirked a brow. "So they won't change their minds?"

"They wouldn't even meet with me." She tilted her hat to keep the hot sun off her face.

"I'm sorry, Christine." Ridley walked next to her down the brick path to the waiting carriage.

Her heart felt even heavier than it did when she'd left Guy at the chapel. All her dreams and plans had disappeared in one moment. Her hands and chest ached with an emptiness she'd never experienced before. Even though she'd grown up lonely and empty, this was different. She supposed she'd tasted of what a full and purposeful life could look like, and once having tasted it, how could she go back to the way things were?

She halted halfway down the path. The spacious lawn spread out before her, as did the many other large homes belonging to New York City's elite. "There has to be some way to access more of my fortune, Ridley," she said again.

Ridley strode two steps ahead of her before pausing and sighing. "We've already been over this, Christine. Your father tied double knots around your trust. I've already extracted as much as I can for now."

Her father had probably thought that, as a woman, she wouldn't be able to handle her own finances, likely considering her inept or frivolous or both. Even in death he continued to criticize her.

"I wish there was more we could do," Ridley said. "I'm afraid that legally we're at a loss."

Was her situation entirely hopeless, then? Was she doomed to a life of frivolity after all? How ironic that her father had wanted to prevent her from wasting her money on foolish things, yet his regulations were forcing her away from a truly worthy pursuit. Although she doubted he would have approved of her endeavor; he'd never had a charitable bone in his body.

The snort of her horses and the constant swishing sound of their tails reminded her that the team had been waiting in the sun for far too long. She may as well admit defeat and go home. But now that she'd witnessed what life was like for the thousands of people who resided only a few miles away, she could not sit idly by and pretend their plight didn't exist. And the thought of her big empty house waiting for her made her shiver in spite of the heat. She didn't know how she could bear returning to endless days of doing nothing meaningful in the mausoleum that bore all the glory of her father's wealth but none of his love.

Ridley was already at the team, feeding each of the horses an apple and murmuring endearments to them.

She didn't want to go home. Her pulse sped in resistance. Well, what if she decided not to return? No one was making her.

She started at the thought. Then she smiled. "Ridley, I think I may have a solution."

9

E lise jerked Sophie behind her, forcing her back under the kitchen table. "Don't you dare lay a hand on either of my sisters or you'll have to answer to me." Elise ground out the words through clenched teeth.

Friedric laughed into her face. His hands found her waist, and he yanked her against his body. "I don't mind having you instead," he whispered against her neck, even as his hands began to roam in places they shouldn't.

Elise brought her knee up swiftly and caught him between the legs. He yelped and fell backward, bumping into the kitchen table and causing a chair to topple over.

"Stop the noise!" Aunt Gertie called from the bedroom. "Some of us are trying to sleep."

The past week had been a nightmare living with the new boarders. Elise had hardly slept since the family had arrived. She'd been too busy keeping watch over her sisters, protecting them from the roving hands and eyes of Mr. Kaiser and his two oldest sons. Mr. Kaiser enjoyed frequenting the beer halls as much as Uncle and so he'd rarely been around. But she'd been dodging the two boys all week, and that was hard to do with their sleeping only feet away.

She'd moved her family under the kitchen table, thinking the chairs would provide a barrier. But they hadn't stopped Friedric from attempting to paw at Sophie.

Friedric groaned before straightening. She guessed that he was younger than her. But he was wiry and strong, and she was afraid that at some point he would overpower her.

In the darkness of the apartment she could see only the outline of his body. But when he lunged for her again, she sidestepped and he fell into the stove with a crash. His curses filled the air, and this time his own mother spoke up from her spot on the sofa.

"Stop pestering the girls, Friedric, and go to sleep."

"Shut up, Ma."

Behind her, Elise could feel Sophie curled up and trembling against her legs. Elise stuck her hand in her pocket and found the small sheathed knife that Reinhold had given her earlier in the week when she complained to him about the new boarders.

Friedric shuffled toward her. "If Sophie's too young," he said, "then you can be my girl, Elise. You're a looker."

"None of us are going to be your girl," she shot back.

He advanced closer. "Your uncle told us he's throwing you all out of here soon. But if you're my girl, I'll make sure you stay."

Elise was surprised Uncle Hermann hadn't forced them out yet. She'd known it was only a matter of time before he did. Since Reinhold had brought her the news of Uncle's plans, she'd been asking around the neighborhood for a new place to live. But whenever she found an available space, no one wanted so many young dependents, especially when over half weren't wage earners.

Friedric drew close enough that she caught the smell of beer on his breath. "You know you want me." He leaned in and attempted to kiss her.

She dodged him and at the same time thrust out the knife. When the sharp tip pricked him in the chest, he froze.

"Don't try to touch me or my sisters again." She attempted to keep her hand from trembling. "If you so much as breathe on us, I won't hesitate to cut you up."

He was silent for a moment as though trying to grasp the meaning of her words in his beer-fogged brain. Finally he stepped out of her reach and said, "You'll regret turning me down, princess," and his voice rumbled low with menace.

"Never."

"You just wait and see. I'll make sure that next time you're not here when I want one of your sisters."

Elise fought back panic and forced herself to remain calm. She drew in a steadying breath. "Okay, Friedric. You're right. You're my best option. I'll consider being your girl so long as you promise to get Uncle to let me and my sisters stay."

Her words must have taken Friedric by surprise because he was speechless for a minute before giving a triumphant laugh. "You have a deal. You'll have to get rid of the two snot-nosed babies. But I won't have any trouble convincing your uncle to let you and your sisters stay." He fumbled for her again.

She stopped him with her knife.

"You said you'd be my girl," he whined, backing away again.

"Only after I have proof that Uncle won't throw us out. If you touch me before that, I'll hack off your fingers."

He grumbled under his breath before finally muttering, "Fine."

Once Elise was lying down again under the table, she felt Marianne's shaking hand brush against hers. Elise raised a finger to Marianne's lips to silence her. They had to pretend for now that everything was all right and that they were going to sleep as usual.

But the truth was they had to leave as soon as possible. She didn't care where they went or how they would survive. All Elise knew was that they weren't safe here any longer.

Later, long after Uncle and Mr. Kaiser had returned and fallen asleep, Elise dared to whisper the escape plan first to Marianne and then to Sophie. She thanked God that it was summer and warm outside. Running away would be hard enough with such a large group of them, but at least they wouldn't have to battle the cold.

At the first light of dawn, they awoke as usual and did their toiletries and grooming behind the makeshift blanket they took turns holding up for one another. Elise made sure they ate every crumb of their sparse breakfast of bread and butter. As she and Marianne left for work, Elise prayed that Sophie would remember her instructions and be able to make her escape with the few coins Uncle hadn't yet spent on beer.

Elise could hardly focus on her needle and thread in the dim light of the morning. Now and then when she glanced at Marianne, she could see her sister's fingers were shaking and her tiny stitches were uneven as a result. Elise knew they couldn't wait too long. But she also needed to give Sophie enough time to get away.

Sophie had to leave first with Olivia and Nicholas. She had to be well on her way to the appointed meeting spot by the time Elise and Marianne slipped out of the garment shop under the guise of using the privy behind the tenement. Once both of them were absent for only a short while, Aunt Gertie would realize something was amiss and alert everyone. She couldn't chance Friedric finding out they'd left until they were well on their way. And if Uncle realized they were running away, he'd stop them from taking any money.

Marianne made the excuse to use the privy first. As the minutes dragged by, Elise hoped none of the other women could hear her heart thudding against her rib cage. When enough time had passed for Marianne to safely leave, she finally stood and said, "I'll go see what's wrong with Marianne. She was complaining of a stomachache earlier."

The rehearsed lie fell easily from her tongue. Every inch she moved through the apartment felt like a mile. Although she tried to remain nonchalant, her back felt like a target, and she waited for the first arrow of accusation to pierce it, for someone to call her a liar and force her to stay.

She didn't breathe until the apartment door closed behind her. In the dark, windowless hallway, she paused to draw in a sharp breath of the familiar scents of fried fish and sauerkraut. She debated crossing the hallway and making sure Sophie was gone. But to do so would risk discovery by Uncle.

Elise tiptoed so she wouldn't draw any undue attention. But as she descended, her footsteps on the squeaky wood floor threatened to alert others to her presence.

Finally reaching the bottom landing, she let out a sigh of relief. Yet before she could push the tenement door open, it was jerked wide by someone else.

It was Friedric.

"There's my girl," he said, breaking into a grin.

"Not yet." She decided her best course of action was to brush past him and pretend he didn't worry her. She made it out the door and was almost to the sidewalk when his fingers encircled her upper arm and forced her to a halt.

"Where do you think you're going?" he growled.

Did Friedric suspect she was running away? Her hand crept toward her pocket, and Reinhold's knife.

Friedric twisted her to face him. In the morning light she could see he'd taken the time to clean himself up. His dark hair was damp, the comb marks making trails through the thick waves. He smelled of soap and musk, and his jaw was shaven. She guessed he'd taken a trip to one of the public bathhouses, and she smoldered at the thought he could afford such a luxury when she could hardly keep her stomach from grumbling.

Where had he come up with the money anyway? Surely he must work somewhere. And if so, why wasn't he there now? Perhaps he was a member of one of the many gangs that roamed Kleindeutschland.

She yanked her arm to free herself. Nothing about Friedric Kaiser mattered. The sooner she could get away from him and never see him again, the better.

But his grip was unrelenting. "You can't go anywhere without me. Not if you're my girl."

"I'm going to the privy, Friedric," she said flatly, hoping he'd buy her act. "Give me some space, will you?"

All she could think about was getting away from the tenement before Aunt Gertie realized she and Marianne weren't coming back and that Sophie was gone too.

"Why aren't you using the back door?" Friedric asked.

"Mr. Glatz is still using it as his bed." She didn't know if the man was still there, but prayed he hadn't moved since before breakfast when she saw him blocking the doorway.

Friedric's grip loosened. "Fine."

She guessed he'd seen the old drunk there earlier as well. She pulled away from Friedric with a calmness that belied the frantic fluttering of her nerves. Proceeding down the steps, she veered toward the side of the tenement next to theirs, a route that would take her to the narrow alley behind the buildings that was crowded with privies and shacks made out of whatever solid material the homeless could piece together.

"I'll expect my repayment tonight," he shouted after her.

"You'll get it," she said without glancing back at him.

Once in the alley, she peeked over her shoulder to make sure he hadn't followed her. Then she disappeared into New York City's masses of depraved humanity.

10

Guy ran his fingers along the spines of his books. The flimsy shelf sagged under the weight of all the commentaries and classics. He needed to start packing them. He'd brought crates up from the cellar for that purpose. But he'd dawdled all morning, unable to find any motivation.

Tomorrow he'd preach his last sermon. He'd decided to deliver the news of the chapel and workshop's closing then. He and Christine had agreed they'd let the women complete this week without devastating them with the news that after only two weeks on the job, they would be losing their employment.

"God," he whispered into the stale air of his office at the back of the chapel, "I thought your hand was in this project. I thought this was what you wanted me to do. It all seemed so right. So clear . . ."

He lowered himself to his desk chair. He'd been praying all week that somehow God would intervene. He'd felt so strongly that if God was behind this newest venture, He'd provide for their needs. On this last day before their eviction, however, he could only conclude that maybe he'd been wrong. Maybe God hadn't wanted him to open the garment shop after all.

At a soft rap on the doorjamb, he glanced up to see Christine standing in the doorway. As usual the sight of her stirred him. Even if her expression had been somber this week, she was still as lovely and composed as always in her black gown and hat.

"Reverend Bedell," she said hesitantly, clasping her reticule in her gloved hands. She'd been in and out of the workshop quite often over the past several days, and although they'd talked together during the week, she'd been more reserved and formal with him.

Had he disappointed her? She'd badly wanted their effort to succeed. She had invested her time, energy, and capital into the project. She'd done her part. But he'd failed to maintain the connections they needed. If she'd been hesitant about accepting his proposal before, she certainly wouldn't agree anymore that God had brought them together to be partners, to work side by side in the ministry.

Maybe his proposal of marriage had been somewhat spontaneous, a reaction to the way her kisses had stirred him, but once it was offered he knew then he wanted to be with her. She hadn't just tolerated his kiss the way Bettina had always done, and she wasn't so delicate and breakable as he'd imagined. Rather she'd responded to him with true affection. He recalled how she had felt pressed against his chest, how she'd kissed him back with such passion. . . .

He didn't realize he'd been staring at her lips until she shifted. The clicking of her reticule clasping and unclasping filled the air. "Christine," he said, rising from his chair and trying to quell his longing before he scared her away.

Maybe his offer to marry her had taken them both by surprise, but now that he'd brought it up, he couldn't imagine his life without her. In fact, dread tightened his chest at the thought of what life would be like after tomorrow. If only he could find a way to be with her even though this project of theirs was coming to an end.

He'd considered his options. Perhaps he could assume a position with a new church. With his pastoral experience, surely he'd be given a larger congregation with a salary that would allow him to offer Christine a comfortable life. Or he could apply for a professorship at the seminary, which hopefully would be prestigious enough for a woman of Christine's social standing.

"Reverend," she began, "I know you've been praying for a miracle this week."

He nodded. He'd spent hours on his knees. Whenever he was in a crisis, prayer was his first and most important task.

"Rather than waiting for a miracle, I felt God prompting me to be one again." She glanced over her shoulder, and Guy had no doubt she was drawing strength from Ridley.

"I bought the old brewery on Seventh Street." She lifted her dainty chin as though daring him to defy her.

But he couldn't speak past his astonishment.

"I have workers coming here tonight to move the sewing supplies over to the new workspace."

He could only stare at her as a thousand thoughts rained through his mind in a torrential downpour, flooding him with doubt, amazement, excitement, fear, and wonder.

"Of course, the working conditions will be much less than ideal until I can have the place cleaned and renovated," she continued. "But I don't want the women to lose a day of work if at all possible. They're counting on the income. And Mr. Devlin has entrusted us with the work being done in a timely manner."

Guy grabbed the desk to hold himself up. How had she managed to obtain the old brewery? He knew she was wealthy. That much was obvious from the first day he met her. But apparently she had much more than he'd realized. And how was she able to wrest such a valuable piece of property away from the contractors who'd been vying for the dilapidated building in order to tear it down and build more tenements?

Currently the old brewery was one of the most dangerous sites in lower Manhattan, overrun by thugs and gangs. Even if Christine had indeed purchased the place, how would she be able to clean out all the vermin and vice there? And how would she make the changes necessary to have a workshop?

"The police went in yesterday and forced out all the trespassers," she said as if reading his concerns. "Officers are there again this morning to provide protection to the men I've hired to start the cleanup of the facility."

Guy sat back down in his chair before his legs gave way. He was being impolite to sit in a lady's presence, but he was too shocked to do anything else.

She moved away from the doorway and into his office. "Please say something." Her voice dropped to a distressed whisper.

Only then did he notice the vulnerability in her eyes. For as confident and determined as she appeared, underneath she was frightened and wanted his assurance.

She hadn't decided to shut him out of her life. At least not yet.

His relief at that realization gave him renewed strength. "Just when I'd believed our plans had come to naught, God has provided a way."

"These women finally have hope," she said, nodding. "Have you seen the change in their faces, the joy? The way they hold their heads a little bit higher? After giving them a chance to leave the chains of sin behind, how could I take away that hope? How could I throw them back into the life they loathed?"

"You couldn't" was his simple reply.

She visibly swallowed hard. "I had to do something, so I had Ridley research all the available buildings in the area. He discovered that the old brewery was owned by a businessman my father had once bailed out of debt."

"Just like Mr. Devlin?"

"Apparently my father liked having men in his pocket."

"And I take it Ridley isn't afraid to ask for a return favor."

She smiled then, and even though it was small, it was beautiful. "He's still a smart businessman himself, and I've learned a lot from him over the past month."

"Even so, I'm impressed that you were able to buy the brewery building when so many others were vying for it."

"I paid the right price is all."

In the process of saving the women, had Christine reduced her fortune to nothing? God forbid that she end up in their situation, forced into hard labor and needing the charity of others to survive.

As though seeing the worry on his face, her smile widened. "At the moment I'm currently homeless—"

"You sold your home?"

She nodded. But her smile remained.

"What will you do? How will you live?"

"I'll be just fine. I will always have a steady income from my trust. And Ridley assures me that if everything comes together as planned, our business will turn a profit and eventually I'll be able to expand. There's enough room for it."

"You'll have enough room for twice the workers."

"Maybe even triple. And the women have talked about needing safe, clean places to live. I hope to turn the third and fourth floors into a dormitory. I'll charge the workers a small fee to stay there and another small fee for a hot meal."

He was genuinely pleased at the way God had worked out the situation for her. "I'm happy for you, Christine. It looks like God has richly blessed your efforts."

A cloud seemed to pass in front of her eyes. She twisted her reticule and stared down the floor. As the silence stretched between them, he could sense she wanted to say something.

At last she cleared her throat. "I hope the Society's advisory board will reconsider allowing you to resume your work at the chapel now that I'm moving the workshop."

Guy leaned back in his chair, not caring that his large frame pressed the old wood to its breaking point. He folded his arms across his chest and tried to decide the best way to answer her.

"Since I'm to blame for all that's happened," she added, "I'll gladly do what I can to help you until you're reestablished here—"

"Christine," he said, interrupting her, "you're not at fault for anything that happened to me."

"I hold myself entirely responsible." Her voice was an anguished whisper, and when she looked at him, she revealed eyes that were equally tortured. "And now you're free to return to your ministry the way it was before I came along and ruined it."

He stood then, the sudden movement causing his chair to tip backward. It would have fallen to the floor, but in the narrow space it banged against the wall instead. "I am my own man." He rounded the desk. "And I make my own decisions before God. It's to Him and Him alone that I hold myself accountable."

Her eyes widened as he closed the distance between them. "But I coerced you—"

"Christine, you are a beautiful and charming woman. There's no doubt about that." He stopped in front of her, having to hold himself back from crushing her in his arms. "You move me like no other woman ever has, but I'm not so shallow or so weak as to blindly follow a pretty woman. I wouldn't have agreed to the plans if I hadn't felt God's approval of the endeavor."

"Really?" Her lashes fanned upward, revealing her lovely eyes.

"Really. I know it's time to move on. If God has closed the door of this building, who am I to stand against Him? Especially when He appears to have opened wider and better doors elsewhere?"

Confusion mingled with sadness in her expression. "Then what will you do?"

"I'm not sure." He glanced at his books, still needing to be packed. "I'm considering various options."

She nibbled her lip and then spoke in a rush. "Would you consider opening a chapel at the new building?"

As much as he wanted to be with her in this project, he wasn't wealthy. He was a working-class man and always had been. He didn't have a trust that would purchase food and pay his landlady for the room he rented. Of course, he didn't require much. The salary from the Ladies Home Missionary Society hadn't been large, yet it was enough to sustain him and cover his needs.

At his hesitancy, embarrassment flushed her cheeks and she started to step away. "I shouldn't have suggested it. I'm making a nuisance of myself again—"

He stopped her with a touch to her hand. He was being presumptuous again. But he had to make sure she understood, that in spite of everything that had happened, he didn't blame her in any way. He laced his fingers through hers and drew her back. He took courage when she didn't resist. With his other hand he tenderly lifted her chin to gaze into her eyes. "You have never, and could never, be a nuisance to me."

What had happened to her to make her think so little of herself? He caressed the smooth porcelain of her cheek. "Every second of every minute I've spent with you over the past weeks has brought me immense pleasure."

"I've brought you trouble."

He rubbed his thumb across the delicate arch of her cheekbone, relishing the silkiness of her skin. "God has used you to help me grow. And I thank Him for that. I wish we didn't have to part ways."

"Then will you think about opening a new chapel and helping me to run the workshop?"

He hesitated once more, which only caused her to break free and retreat to the door. "Wait, Christine. Could you give me a few days to pray about it?"

She halted.

"Perhaps I just need to have more faith that God will provide for my needs. After all, other missionaries have stepped out in faith, those with much less than me."

"I shall find a way to provide you a salary," she said, understanding lightening her features. "I'm willing to pay you myself—"

"I can't accept your charity."

She paused and considered his statement for a moment. She had to know she was already giving enough. Besides, he was a man of some pride.

"As I said, Ridley has assured me that eventually we may be able to earn a small profit from the workshop and dormitory," she said. "But even so, we shall seek sponsors for our endeavors. I have to believe there are good and kindhearted people who would like to help the poor but simply do not know how. We shall appeal to them."

He nodded. Perhaps it could be done. With the numerous accounts of murders, thefts, and other problems among the burgeoning immigrant communities, the wealthy of New York City were growing more alarmed about the need to stop the spread of crime and poverty. "I could arrange speaking engagements at churches around the city to draw awareness to your ministry."

"*Our* ministry."

He inhaled a deep breath, and a sweet sense of peace settled within him. "Yes, *our* ministry."

She smiled, and he whispered a prayer of thanksgiving. He couldn't hold back a grin any more than he could hold in the relief that God was allowing her to remain in his life—at least for a little while longer.

"Then shall we tell our dear workers to plan on attending chapel tomorrow morning at the new building?" she asked.

"I like that plan."

"It will still be quite a mess, however."

"I believe in you. You're such a capable and determined woman that you can make just about anything happen."

She nodded and started to turn away. Then she paused. "Guy?"

"Yes?"

"Thank you." Her absolute sincerity told him she'd been given few compliments in her life.

As the sound of Christine's footsteps faded with her retreat, he realized that next to the new ministry, the thing he wanted to do most in life was spend every day telling her how special and beautiful and precious she was.

Now if only he could convince her to let him do that.

11

Elise pressed her finger to her lips in warning to the others to stay silent as a gang of boys passed by their hiding spot. After almost a full week of living on the streets, her fingers were deplorably dirty, her nails cracked, and her clothes so filthy that she could hardly stand the stench of herself.

But she was too busy trying to keep her small family alive to worry about how clean they were. Their lack of cleanliness was the least of her concerns. The four pairs of frightened, hungry eyes staring at her told her that their problems were growing bigger every day, especially because she suspected that Friedric was searching for them.

No matter what abandoned doorway they slept in or what pile of garbage they buried themselves behind, eventually someone would spot them. And whenever that happened, they had to move on because they didn't know who to trust to keep their location a secret from Friedric.

"I'm hungry," Olivia said again. Sophie cupped her hand over the little girl's mouth. But the tears forming in the wide eyes taunted Elise. The hunger and discomfort of their situation wouldn't go away no matter how hard they wished it would.

She knew she should be glad that they'd all escaped from the tenement without any trouble. But part of her wondered if she'd done the right thing in leaving. Even with all the dangers of living with Friedric and Uncle, was it safer than living out here?

Once the rowdy group of boys turned the corner of the alley, Elise leaned back against the brick wall with a bone-weary sigh. The four pairs of eyes were still upon her. Waiting. They trusted her to come up with a solution to their problem. But she hadn't been able to do anything all week but attempt to keep them alive.

She had to do better. But what could she do? They'd spent all the money they'd taken from Uncle's purse and now they had nothing.

Nicholas was curled up on Sophie's lap, in her arms. He was growing more listless. Today he'd hardly moved, hadn't made a sound, not even a whimper of complaint.

"We need to take them to the Orphan Asylum, Sophie," Elise said. "That will be the best place for them until we find jobs and a place to live. Then we'll go back and get them."

Rather than protesting the idea, Sophie finally gave in and nodded this time. The tears that escaped down her cheeks rolled onto Nicholas's head. Elise guessed that Sophie had come to the same conclusion. That in order to save the infants' lives, they would have to give them up.

Marianne dug into her skirt pocket and fished out a handkerchief that was already brittle with use. She reached over to dab Sophie's cheeks. A wadded paper separated from the handkerchief and landed on Nicholas's head.

Marianne picked it up and lifted her arm to toss it onto the pile of rubbish that hid them, but then stopped. She smoothed out the wad with her cracked and dirty fingers. It was a gospel tract. She stared at it a moment and then looked up sharply. "Elise, this is it."

Elise wanted to cling to the knowledge that God was still with them. Mutti always had turned to God no matter how desperate their circumstances had grown. But Elise couldn't keep from wondering if God had abandoned them long before they'd set sail for America.

Marianne held out the rumpled pamphlet to Elise. "This is the answer we've been looking for." For the first time all week, Marianne managed a weak smile.

"We need food and shelter." Elise didn't move to take the paper. "Not a gospel lesson."

"No." Marianne rose to her knees. "The woman who gave this to us. Do you remember her?"

The visitors had come weeks ago, right after Mutti had died. Elise had been filled with too much anger and grief to pay them much attention.

"The woman said her mother had recently died too," Marianne continued. "She told us if we ever needed anything, we were to contact her." Marianne flipped the tract over. There on the back in neat print was a name. "Centre Street Chapel."

As Marianne's words began to penetrate the haze in her mind, Elise sat forward. Centre Street. It was several long blocks away. But perhaps under cover of darkness, they could make their way to the chapel. Then in the morning, they could locate the visitor.

"Her name was Miss Pendleton," Marianne said. "Remember she said that if we ever needed a friend, to come find her there at the chapel."

At the time, Elise had lumped the woman together with all the other wealthy people she'd ever known. But now she was too desperate and hungry to care about the disparity of their stations in life.

Many hours later, after the streetlights had been lit and the shadows of night provided a disguise, Elise led the others toward Centre Street. Every step was harrowing. The dangers lurking in the dark were every bit as deadly as hunger and thirst.

A sprinkling of rain had started and had cooled them from the summer heat. But soon the sprinkles had turned into a downpour, thoroughly soaking them. Elise couldn't breathe normally until they arrived at the brick building with a sign that read *Centre Street Chapel*, painted on a plank that hung above the door. She rattled the door only to discover it was locked.

"We'll have to find a place to hide until morning," she said to Marianne, who was holding a sleeping Nicholas. Elise's arms ached under the weight of carrying Olivia most of the distance. The little girl was now shaking from the cooler temperature.

"Maybe we can find a place in the alley behind the building," Marianne said wearily.

Loud, coarse laughter spilled out an open doorway across the street, along with a band of light that reflected on the puddles that had formed on the sidewalks. For so late an hour, the street was alive not only with drunks and roving gangs, but also with homeless children, some of them no older than Olivia.

"Elise, Marianne," came Sophie's voice near the front window of the chapel, "come look at this."

They both stepped closer. Sophie pointed to a paper wedged into the corner of the inside window. On it were words bold and big enough to see even in the dark. "'Chapel closed until further notice.'"

"No!" Marianne's cry rose too loudly. Elise clamped a hand over her sister's mouth to shush her, and Olivia wiggled down until she stood next to Sophie.

Though Marianne's pained declaration matched the silent cry inside Elise, she held it in and tried to make her mind work. But with the lack of sleep and food, her thinking had grown dull. She was afraid if she wasn't careful she'd make a mistake and they'd get caught by Friedric or even the police.

With a sigh she rested her head against the cool glass of the window.

"Since the building isn't in use, maybe we can find a way inside," Sophie whispered.

Trespassing was a crime, and if they were caught, they'd face jail. At least she and Marianne would. Sophie, Olivia, and Nicholas would probably be taken to the House of Refuge, a reformatory for children accused of crimes. Elise had heard it was a foul place, and she didn't want to risk her sweet children being forced into the same environment as hardened criminals.

Elise started to shake her head, but Sophie peered up at her with such a pleading expression that she knew her sister was thinking about being safe, dry, and warm, somewhere they could actually sleep without noise or filth or fear of attack.

"I'm sure the owners of the chapel won't mind," Sophie insisted. "Just for one night. Please?"

Elise couldn't resist Sophie's plea. They wouldn't be able to find a dry place tonight on the streets, not with the rain. Perhaps inside an abandoned building they could finally sleep for more than a few minutes at a time. Perhaps in the morning her mind would be sharp again and she would be able to think of a better plan to protect everyone.

They found a rear entry to the chapel, which was also locked. But

Elise managed to break a small window that appeared to have once been a closet or office. They lowered Olivia carefully through the window with instructions to find the back door and unlock it for them.

They soon found themselves inside the chapel. Except for the pulpit and rows of benches, the chapel was empty, which only made Elise's heart sink lower. Miss Pendleton, their one possible friend, was gone.

After locking the door behind them, Elise led them to a deserted room on the second floor that looked like it had been recently painted. There wasn't a single piece of furniture, but at least it was clean and dry. They huddled together on the hard floor. Elise covered Sophie, Olivia, and Nicholas with the one ragged blanket Sophie had managed to sneak out with the bag of their possessions. Even though the covering was slightly damp, it provided the young ones some warmth, and soon the soft rhythm of their breathing told Elise they were asleep. Even Marianne next to her had fallen into an exhausted slumber.

In spite of her resolve to stay awake for a while and make sure no one had spotted their entry into the building, Elise couldn't hold her eyes open any longer. She was so tired.

So tired of running. So tired of being hungry. So tired of living in fear. This wasn't the kind of life they were supposed to have. What had gone wrong?

Elise's mind began to shut down. Her last thought before falling asleep was that they would rise early and leave the building before anyone could discover them. They couldn't afford to get caught.

12

◆——•——◆

Christine glanced again at each of the faces in the tenement sweatshop and felt the sting of disappointment. She didn't know why she should feel it so keenly, except that she'd been hoping to see the two young women who'd lost their mother. In fact, she'd specifically asked Guy if they could visit that particular apartment because she wanted to see the girls again and offer them another word of encouragement.

Guy stood next to Mr. Schmidt, the shop's supervisor. The air in the room was thick with humidity, which magnified the scents of mildew, chamber pots, and unwashed bodies. Christine tried to breathe through her mouth so that she wouldn't gag and embarrass herself.

Guy raised a questioning eyebrow at her, and she shook her head. As she wound back to him, he pumped hands with Mr. Schmidt, said good-bye, and then ushered her into the hallway.

"The girls are gone?" he asked quietly after the door closed behind them.

"It's all right," she said. "I guess I didn't really expect to see them again."

"The community is so transient," Guy said. "People are constantly moving due to new jobs or illnesses, even death."

"Thank you for allowing me to check." She hadn't thought of the young grieving women since that first meeting, so the impulse to visit them again had been unplanned. And now appeared to be a waste of time.

They had more important things to do today, namely to spread the word that their new facility was ready for additional workers. After laboring around the clock all week, the workshop was ready for additional business. They would start hiring more seamstresses Monday morning at seven o'clock.

They didn't have the dormitory ready yet, but they were making progress at cleaning the place up. For now she was living with Ridley. Yet she hoped to eventually have a room of her own in the building so she could live on-site.

A door across the hallway opened, and a short man stumbled into view buttoning his trousers. At the sight of his bulbous nose, Christine recognized him as Mr. Jung, the uncle to the young women she'd come searching for.

"Mr. Jung," she said.

He glanced up at her with bloodshot eyes.

Christine tried not to notice how unkempt he was, his matted hair, tobacco-stained shirt, and the foulness of his breath. "I'm looking for your nieces."

He rubbed a hand across his eyes, clearly having just awoken. "That makes you and me both."

"Oh." Then that settled it, the girls were indeed gone. "So you have no idea where they might be?"

The man shook his head and grumbled something under his breath about their ungratefulness.

Guy handed Mr. Jung one of their tracts with the address of their new facility. "If you see them, would you give them this?"

Mr. Jung wiped the back of his hand across his overlarge nose. "If you see them, tell them they need to repay the money they stole from me."

As she descended the dark pit of the stairwell ahead of Guy, Christine closed the door on the possibility of seeing the girls. Although she'd felt the strange burden to reach out to them again, she would be busy helping so many others that she would soon forget she'd ever met them.

After another hour of visiting and spreading the word about the additional employment opportunities and new chapel location, the drizzle began to change into a steady rainfall. With her shoes already soaked and her gown damp, Christine didn't protest when Guy insisted it was time to go.

Instead of taking the carriage seat opposite her as he'd done earlier, Guy sat next to her. There was hardly enough room for them both, and his arm pressed against hers in a way that made her much too aware of his overpowering presence.

They'd been busy all week and had so much to talk about regarding their ministry plans that she hadn't given much thought to their relationship, other than that she was relieved he'd made the decision to continue working with her.

Now with him so close, she was conscious of the hardness of his muscles, his musky scent, and the rise and fall of his chest. She chided herself for thinking about him as anything more than a business partner. Maybe he hadn't rejected her for what had happened at Centre Street Chapel, but he certainly hadn't made any further indication that he cared for her. Not that she expected him to.

"I was thinking," he said after a moment, "what we thought was failure was really God moving us on to what He had planned all along."

"How so?" His hand rested on his knee, and she wished she was brave enough to lay hers upon it.

"We thought the closing of the Centre Street Chapel was a disaster to our carefully laid plans. But if God hadn't pushed us out, we wouldn't have embraced the larger vision He had in store for us—not only a bigger workshop but sleeping quarters as well."

She nodded. "And I think He's only begun to reveal all that is possible with that larger vision." They'd already talked about opening a Sunday school for children and offering classes in the evenings to the women who wanted to learn to read and write.

"Does this mean you're starting to believe in miracles?" he asked with a teasing note to his voice.

She smiled. "Maybe." She shifted slightly to look at his face. He'd also turned his head to smile at her. Suddenly she was aware their faces were mere inches apart.

"He did more than we ever asked for or dreamed about," Guy said softly.

She tried to concentrate on his words, but the only place she could focus was on his mouth. He had a charming smile. Her insides filled with warmth at the remembrance of the way his lips had moved against hers with both tenderness and barely restrained power. She couldn't deny she'd relived their kiss every day since it had happened and had dreamed about kissing him again.

She didn't realize she was staring or that he'd grown silent until his fingers slid to hers. She dropped her attention to his large hand.

"Christine," he started, "is it possible that God can do more yet between us?"

Was that a note of hope in his voice? Did he still care for her after all? She couldn't look into his eyes for fear of what she might see. Instead she focused on the way his hand wrapped so perfectly around hers.

"If you say no, that you don't want me, I promise I'll respect your answer—"

"I do want you," she said. The words came out before she could halt them, and she was mortified at her confession. She hurried to cover up her embarrassment. "It's just that I don't understand why anyone would be interested in me. I'm nothing—"

"You're everything to me. I love you, Christine. I think I've loved you from that first day you spoke to me."

He loved her? Her lashes flew up, and she met his earnest gaze, seeing nothing but honesty there. She started to shake her head, but he stopped her by dipping down and catching her mouth with his. The pressure was decisive yet tender.

She was surprised by the need that surged within her. She rose into the kiss. She could no more stop herself from opening her lips to him and deepening the kiss than she could prevent herself from pressing into him. Her hands moved to his face, then to his hair and the back of his neck. With each touch, his kiss grew stronger and more fervent until it was finally consuming her the way she'd dreamed about.

Finally he tore his mouth from hers with a groan. His sound of pleasure only stirred her so that she found his lips and kissed him again. And again. Until her lungs were seared and her lips bruised. Still she wanted more of him.

"Christine," he mumbled between their lips, "we must be married soon."

She couldn't find the words to answer him. She'd never imagined anyone would ever want to marry her. And now Guy had asked her not once, but twice. And he wanted it to be soon. Surely if anything were a miracle, this was it.

She smiled, and the movement caused him to pause and pull back a fraction so that their noses touched.

"What?" he asked breathlessly.

"You've finally made me a believer in miracles."

"I have?"

"It's a miracle that you want to marry me."

"I have witnessed miracles," he said, letting his fingers linger at the nape of her neck, driving her mad with his caress. "And my desire to marry you is the furthest thing from one. Any man would want you; I'm just glad God brought you to me first."

She leaned in, wanting once more to feel the warmth and closeness of his lips. But he pulled away, his brows creased. "Christine," he said, "you're a treasure worth more than anything I've ever had or could hope to have. And I want to spend the rest of my life showing you that."

His affirmation was difficult for her to understand. "Perhaps if you tell me often enough, I'll finally believe you," she whispered.

"Does this mean you'll agree to marry me?" His eyes overflowed with anticipation of her reply.

What reason did she possibly have to say no? Not when she loved him. Yes, she loved him. She raised her chin, hoping he'd claim another kiss. And when he did, she arched into him and met his passion with her own.

At the carriage door opening, Guy broke away from her. Neither of them had noticed the vehicle rolling to a stop or the handle rattling. With the rain pattering around him, Ridley stood hunched under an umbrella, his lips twitching against a smile. Once again he'd caught them in a passionate embrace.

Guy cleared his throat and shifted on the seat in an attempt to put space between them.

Christine slipped her hand over Guy's and then straightened her shoulders and faced Ridley. "I'm getting married to Reverend Bedell."

Ridley nodded. "Very soon I hope." The mirth in his tone sent a flush to Christine's cheeks.

"As soon as possible," Guy agreed eagerly, clamping his other hand over Christine's.

"My congratulations to you both," Ridley said.

Christine could only stare between the two of them. It was clear Ridley had anticipated this. He'd seen Guy's attraction to her all along, and she was relieved that he approved.

"Shall I go inside and retrieve the missing item, Reverend?" Ridley offered, nodding at the door of the narrow building.

Only then did Christine realize Ridley had driven them to the old chapel on Centre Street.

"I left my pulpit," Guy explained to her. "And I'd like to have it before the service tomorrow."

"I'd be happy to get it for you," Ridley said with a smile, "and allow you more time with Christine."

Guy grinned. "As much as I'd like to accept your offer, I do believe I'd better resist the temptation for the moment." Guy's large frame tipped the brougham as he descended. He made a dash for the front door.

Left with Ridley, Christine began to squirm. "I think I'll go in too, if you don't mind, Ridley," she said, feeling the need to hide her embarrassment. "I'll have a look around and make sure we didn't forget anything else."

He didn't respond except to hold the umbrella above her, though his widening grin was enough to bring another flush to her cheeks.

Once inside, she shook rain droplets from her skirt and then took stock of the room that had served as the chapel. In comparison to their new spacious building, she saw now that this place was tiny, only big enough to hold a few dozen people. And the workroom upstairs was equally small.

Gratefulness welled in her chest. Guy had been right. She'd thought their ministry had failed, yet God had only moved them on to bigger plans. If they'd given up or stayed here . . .

Guy stepped from his former office into view. "I think someone broke in," he said.

Christine glanced around but didn't notice anything amiss or damaged.

"The window's been broken," he continued. "And I heard some scuffling upstairs."

She started to speak, but when he put a finger to his lips, she stopped. He motioned toward the stairs. Somehow a knife had appeared in his hand, hidden by the bulk of his arm. While they tried to creep up the stairs without making a sound, several planks creaked. When Guy reached the top, he stopped abruptly, forcing her to halt behind him. His eyes widened. And then his shoulders relaxed.

"Miss Pendleton, if you don't believe in miracles yet, then you will now."

She hurried up the remaining steps past him. At the sight that met her, she stopped again with a gasp.

Cowering in a corner were a group of children and two women. One young woman had blond hair and the other brown. They were the very same women she'd been searching for only that morning in the tenements.

They stared at her with frightened faces that were smeared with the filth of the street. Their black mourning clothes were wrinkled and unkempt, their hair tangled, their cheeks too thin. The older sister had her arms around the others in a protective gesture that tore at Christine's heart.

Tears sprang to Christine's eyes as she reached for Guy's hand. "Yes, I most certainly believe in miracles."

The youngest of the children, a boy, gave a piteous wail that one of the girls quickly smothered with her hand.

Christine's heart wrenched again.

The brown-haired woman broke away from her sister and stared at Christine with recognition dawning in her eyes. "Miss Pendleton?"

"Yes," Christine answered, "I'm Miss Pendleton. And you're all safe now."

A sob escaped from the young woman's lips before she covered her mouth with her hands, leaving visible only her eyes that pooled with tears.

"I'll help you," Christine said. She knew she could do nothing less than continue to be the miracle people needed. But from now on she'd do so knowing that God was greater than any of her efforts and could work beyond all that she could ask or imagine.

Guy's fingers slipped through hers. Yes, God certainly worked in ways she couldn't imagine. Not only had He orchestrated the meeting with these girls, but He'd brought love into her life, a love she never thought she deserved.

She squeezed Guy's hand, and her heart swelled with gratefulness that she'd have a lifetime to love him in return.

⬥

Elise pressed her face against Marianne's and Sophie's heads and gulped back a cry of relief. She wouldn't weep. She had to stay strong. Even so, her heart wept silently, echoing her sisters.

Miss Pendleton crossed the bare room, her footsteps loud but reassuring. When she reached for Nicholas, Sophie relinquished the lethargic child with a sob. "Please help him." Her voice was desperate. "He's so hungry."

Miss Pendleton gathered the boy in her arms. He reached back for Sophie with only a whimper before falling silent and still against Miss Pendleton. "We need to go at once," she said to Reverend Bedell. Although she'd kept her tone calm, Elise caught the flash of anxiety in her eyes.

"Will he be all right, Miss Pendleton?" Sophie asked. She wiped the tears from her dirty cheeks but only smeared more grime on her once-creamy skin.

"We shall do our best to revive him," she said simply, her expression honest.

Sophie's lower lip trembled. Elise reached for her sister's hand and squeezed it.

"Let's be on our way." Miss Pendleton started moving toward the stairs. "We don't have room in the brougham for everyone, but we shall squeeze in as many as we can."

"I'll stay here," Reverend Bedell insisted. "Ridley can take you and the children over to the mission and then come back for me later."

Elise knew she ought to offer to stay behind, but she was too weak from hunger and too exhausted to consider her manners. Instead she reached for Olivia and hefted the girl onto her hip. As they headed downstairs with clattering footsteps, Elise felt light-headed. Was she dreaming? Was this really happening to her? To them? Would she wake up and find herself back in an alley in a deserted entryway?

It wasn't until she was sitting on one of the cushioned seats of the waiting carriage with Olivia on her lap and Marianne beside her that she allowed herself to hope. On the seat across from her, Miss Pendleton crooned over Nicholas. Sophie sat next to her holding the little boy's hand. As though sensing Elise's concern, Miss Pendleton glanced up and gave her a smile, a smile that said everything would be okay now.

"God placed you on my heart this morning, and I went to your tenement looking for you," Miss Pendleton said.

"You did?" Marianne asked through her sniffles.

Miss Pendleton nodded. "When I learned that you were gone, I didn't expect to see you ever again. But God apparently wanted to orchestrate the meeting in order to show me how good and powerful He truly is."

Good and powerful? Could Elise believe that? Tears flooded her eyes, and she had to blink them back rapidly. She turned to look out the carriage window, and as they lurched forward into the tide of traffic, Elise couldn't help but offer a prayer of thanksgiving.

She didn't know what would happen in the days to come. Where would they live? What work would they find? Even with Miss Pendleton's help, surely they would still face trials and hardships. After all, they couldn't depend upon this woman's kindness forever.

But for now, Elise expelled a long breath and settled back against the plush seat. If God had helped her this time, she prayed she would find the faith to trust Him with her future, whatever it held.

TOWARD
the SUNRISE

AN
UNTIL THE DAWN
NOVELLA

ELIZABETH
CAMDEN

1

*S*ometimes ten seconds is all it takes to change the course of a life.*
Julia Broeder had learned that lesson the hard way last week
when an impulsive decision triggered a string of events that now had
her waiting on this hard bench outside the conference room at the
Women's Medical College of Pennsylvania. Behind the closed con-
ference-room door sat the twelve people who were deciding her fate.
She would either be allowed to continue her education and graduate
in the spring as a fully licensed physician, or she would be expelled
and sent home in disgrace.

Dean Edith Kreutzer was a celebrated trailblazer in the crusade
to get women admitted to the medical profession, but this morning
she had looked as cold as an ice queen as she convened the college's
Board of Trustees to determine Julia's fate.

Julia curled her fingers around the rim of the hard bench, the
only furniture in the small foyer outside the conference room. Every
impulse urged her to stand and press her ear to the paneled door to
hear the board's discussion, but she forced herself to sit still. There
was nothing she could do to influence the board's decision.

It didn't matter how badly she wanted to become a doctor. Or that
she ranked at the top of her class in academics and was eager to go

out and be a physician in some of the poorest areas of the world. All that mattered was what she did last weekend.

It was Saturday morning when all the trouble began. Like all Saturdays, she was working at the college's pharmaceutical laboratory alongside six other ladies enrolled in medical school. As part of her coursework in pharmacology, she was making cinchonine pills by grinding the powder to the right consistency and pouring the medication into the tiny aluminum molds. At first she paid no attention to the intermittent bits of noise coming from outside the window, but finally a spray of pebbles hit the window glass and got her attention.

From the second-story window, she recognized the two young men standing in the slushy yard below. They worked for the Philadelphia Fire Department, and she knew them from Fairmount Park, where she and her classmates sometimes escaped to play tennis in balmy weather or go skating in the winter. Ross McKinney had a fine toboggan he often loaned her to go barreling down the slope when it snowed. The fireman and his friend seemed like decent young men, and she loved careening down the hillside on their toboggan.

She tugged up the window sash, chilly air flooding the room as she leaned outside. "If you hurl any more rocks at this window, I'll suspect you of being one of those tedious revolutionaries who rattle sabers and threaten to storm the ramparts."

Neither man laughed. One of them cradled a dog in his arms. Even from the second story, Julia could tell the dog was horribly mangled.

"I'll be right down," she said, slamming the window sash so hard the glass rattled.

The dog was a Boston terrier. One of her ears was partially torn off; her face was full of puncture wounds. Julia wanted to wince and look away, but doctors didn't have that luxury and neither did she.

"Have you got any drugs that might fix her up, Miss Broeder?" Ross asked.

It would take more than drugs to fix this dog. That ear was going to need to be anchored back on with a row of stitches, and even then she wasn't sure it could be saved. It was a Saturday, so the operating room at Olsen Hall should be available. The room was locked, but locked doors had never stopped Julia in the past. If one avenue was closed to her, she would go over, under, or around the obstacle until she reached her goal. In this case, it was by standing on the shoulders of one of the firemen to slip through the unlocked window of the operating room and then traveling through the darkened hallways to let the men, dog, and two of her classmates in through the front door of the building.

None of them had treated a dog before, but surely the principles of suturing a wound, cleaning to prevent infection, and stitching mangled flesh together were the same. Ross's friend had to dash off to his shift at the fire station, but Ross stayed and stroked the dog's flank, murmuring soothing words while Julia held a mask over the dog's snout, gently squeezing the rubber ball that fed a stream of anesthesia to the terrier.

Treating the dog's wounds took almost an hour, but she was satisfied with her work by the end. The dog would make a fine recovery.

After replacing the vials of anesthesia, antiseptic, and the suturing kit, she asked her classmates to sign her out of the pharmacy rotation for the day and accompanied Ross to the trolley stop, the slumbering dog heavy in her arms. The dog weighed at least twenty pounds, most of it pure muscle, but Julia refused to let Ross take it from her arms.

There was a bench at the trolley stop, but she was too nervous to sit. The clock on the bank tower across the street indicated she had nine minutes until the next trolley heading to the fire station would arrive. It was a good thing her classmates had not followed her to the trolley stop, for she was more likely to get the truth if Ross didn't have to own up to it in front of an audience.

"Where did you get this dog?" she asked. It hadn't escaped her notice that aside from the wounds she'd treated today, there were plenty of healed scars on the dog's chest, legs, and snout.

"He's my roommate's dog," Ross said. "You've never met Derrick. He works at the fire station, too."

"And does he fight this dog regularly?"

Ross's mouth tightened. "She's a good dog. Fighting is natural for her, and she doesn't usually get dinged up this bad."

Julia rocked the slumbering dog in her arms, cradling it almost like a baby. What did she know about Ross McKinney other than he was fun company at the park and that he was generous with his toboggan?

The odds were strong that if she released the animal back into his custody, this mangled, victimized dog would be forced into the fighting ring again. Ross's trolley wasn't due to arrive for another eight minutes, but the Red Line trolley had just rounded the bend on its electric rails and was heading straight toward them.

If she boarded the oncoming trolley, she could get the dog to safety. It had been a big risk to break into the clinic, but the deed was done, and it seemed atrocious to turn the dog back over to the brutes who had done this to her in the first place. Julia bit her lip, indecision giving her the start of a pounding headache.

The Red Line trolley would be here in ten seconds.

She had already done her duty by treating an injured animal. And Ross wasn't an altogether bad man. Clearly he cared for the dog or he wouldn't have looked so stricken when he flung those pebbles at her window.

Six seconds.

Ross must have noticed her watching the trolley's imminent arrival. "Here, I'll take her now if you want to head back to the college."

Three seconds, two seconds . . .

The trolley slowed, and the driver pulled a lever to open the doors. This was it.

She kept her eyes on the driver as she boarded the trolley.

"Hey!" Ross shouted. "That's my dog!"

The slumbering animal made it awkward to fumble for the lever controlling the door, but Julia managed to yank it shut before Ross could board.

"This dog has been badly mistreated," she said to the driver. "Please hurry. That man has no business owning a dog."

The driver hesitated only a split second before nodding in agreement and setting off down the street.

Dean Kreutzer discovered her transgression the following day when Ross and three friends from the fire station arrived at the college to ask for their dog back. They denied using the dog for fighting, but when Julia refused to turn over the injured animal, Ross threatened to get his friends from the police department involved.

Dean Kreutzer insisted Julia produce the dog. "You have already broken the rules by conducting an operation without supervision," the dean said tightly, going white around her lips. She ordered Julia from the office to go fetch the terrier.

Instead, Julia absconded with the dog to the train station, and an hour later she was heading toward the convent of the Sisters of Mercy outside of Philadelphia. The convent was located amid rolling hills and dairy farmland, a world away from the tough streets of Philadelphia. The dog rested on her lap the entire journey, staring transfixed at the countryside beyond the window. Had this dog ever seen countryside like this before? It might have been Julia's imagination, but it seemed the dog breathed easier as they moved deeper into the rural farmlands.

In any event, Julia left the dog at the convent, where the sisters agreed to care for it until they could place the dog in a decent home.

Upon returning to the college, Julia found two members of the Philadelphia Police Department waiting for her. When she refused to tell them or Dean Kreutzer what she'd done with the dog, a disciplinary hearing was ordered for the following Wednesday.

So now she sat on this hard wooden bench, awaiting her fate. She had been given an opportunity to address the board, but the charge was an ethical violation for the theft of a dog, and she couldn't deny that she was guilty as charged. Nor could she state with a clear conscience that she regretted her actions, which was what they needed to hear from her.

Julia had wanted to become a medical missionary ever since she was twelve years old and had pulled down a volume of *The Travels of Marco Polo*. Her world had changed forever. That creaky old leather volume, filled with hand-colored prints and maps of the Far East, sparked a spirit of adventure that lit her soul to this day. She dreamed of caravans traveling the Silk Road, of the austere beauty of the windswept Mongolian plains, of the perfumed gardens of Kublai Khan. She dreamed of someday seeing these lands with her own eyes, and why shouldn't she? She could combine her love of science with the craving for adventure by becoming a medical missionary.

Medical missionaries weren't charged with teaching the Bible or converting the natives. Julia would be useless in such a capacity, but by working in faraway places that had never seen a formally trained doctor, her life would be an example of Christian charity and selfless acts of service.

The unlatching of the door broke the silence of the room as Dean Kreutzer emerged. Julia stood, wondering if the others would follow, but the dean was alone, her steel-gray hair upswept into a stiff bouffant, her lips tight.

Dean Kreutzer closed the door. "Miss Broeder, it is the unanimous decision of the board that you lack the maturity and judgment to proceed with your education here. You are asked to leave the college immediately."

The blood drained from her face. The room tilted. Until this very second she hadn't truly believed they would expel her. How should a person react when every hope, ambition, and dream was crumbling into ash? For the first time in her life, Julia didn't know what to do or say. She stood rooted to the floor with her mouth hanging open, mute and helpless.

"The train to New York leaves at six o'clock tomorrow morning," Dean Kreutzer said. "I will make arrangements for you to be driven to the depot."

And with that Julia felt the door slamming on her entire world.

2

J ulia left the college the next morning with nothing but her two
battered old traveling satchels. After riding the train to New York
City, she took a steamship forty miles up the Hudson River to New
Holland, a village too tiny to be on most maps. She walked down the
rural lane toward Dierenpark, the historic estate where she'd been
born in the groundskeeper's cottage.

Tightly laced boots were never intended for walking long distances,
and her feet screamed for relief after trudging the two miles from town.
The traveling bags pulled on her arms, and she dreaded telling her
brother she'd been ousted from medical school only six months shy
of graduation. Emil was a good-natured fellow, but he had enough
responsibilities on his hands without the ignominious return of his
younger sister.

The November breeze was chilly, and her boots rubbed blisters onto
the sides of her toes, forcing her to walk gingerly. Why did women feel
compelled to buy such ridiculous footwear? She'd searched for practical shoes, but no shop in Philadelphia carried ladies' boots without
at least a two-inch heel, so now she limped home like a victim of a
Chinese foot-binding contraption.

She rounded the bend to Dierenpark, one of the grandest homes
in America. Rough-hewn granite pillars guarded the entrance of the
estate, but its gates were open, as was always the case at Dierenpark.

The mansion was still another half mile behind the gates, but the groundskeeper's cabin was only another hundred yards behind a stand of ancient hawthorn trees. Maintained by generations of Broeders, the cabin had a wide covered porch and a row of windows across the front. She mounted the steps, dropped the two bags with a thud, and knocked on the front door.

It felt odd to knock for permission to enter the home where she'd spent the first eighteen years of her life, but no one had expected Julia to ever live here again. After college she was supposed to become a doctor, venturing out into the world carrying medicine, hope, and a desire to do good things. She wasn't supposed to limp home with all her worldly possessions clutched in two sodden traveling bags and fall upon her brother's mercy.

The door jerked open, and Emil's broad frame filled the opening. "Julie!" he said with a wide grin. He tugged her into a rough hug, the air gusting from her lungs at the ungainly embrace. Sometimes men as big as Emil didn't know their strength. He brushed a swath of blond hair that fell into his eyes back from his forehead. "We didn't expect to see you so soon. Wait until you see the babies; they're as big as ham shanks."

She had to admit to being excited to see the twins again. They'd been born while she was home last summer, and they'd been so tiny they fit into the crook of her arm. She stepped inside the cabin, the familiar scent of apple cider and wood smoke in the air. The main room was spacious, with a wall of river rock framing a fireplace so big that when she was a child she could stand inside it without stooping over. Comfortable seating was scattered in clusters, and a battered old table doubled as a work surface and dining space. It was messier than she'd ever seen it, with baby nappies drying on haphazard laundry lines throughout the room.

Emil handed her a towel, and she swiped the damp from her hair and coat, but at the same time, she instinctively walked to the large crib to inspect her nephews. They had dark hair like their mother, but both had the round, innocent faces they'd inherited from Emil. One boy was sound asleep, but the other happily gnawed on a rag doll and gave her a drooly smile.

"Where is Claudia?" Julia asked.

"Oh, she's in bed. She hasn't been feeling so well."

Julia turned in concern. She had already completed her coursework in obstetrics, and four months after the birth, Claudia ought to be fully healed.

"What is the problem?" she asked.

"Morning sickness. I don't know why they call it morning sickness when she's got it all day long."

Julia's jaw dropped. "What do you mean, morning sickness? Is she with child again?"

"The doctor says she is two months along."

Julia sighed. It was none of her business how Emil and Claudia conducted their lives, but how on earth were they going to handle another newborn so soon after the twins? Had she been here, she might have recommended that Emil keep his hands to himself for a few more months. She would have thought Emil could have figured that out on his own, but he'd never been the brightest man in the valley.

"How long are you staying?" Emil asked, lifting a baby from the crib when the child started whimpering. "Things are pretty cramped ever since the twins came along. We still can't hang the laundry outside because of all the rain, but we can find someplace to stash you for a day or two."

She turned away, rubbing her thumb along the grainy surface of the fireplace rocks while she parsed her words. "I'm not sure. I am no longer enrolled at the college. One thing led to another, and well . . . I got expelled."

"Expelled?" Emil asked. "Is that a good thing? Like some kind of spelling contest?"

A lot of people in town laughed at her brother, who was as thick as a bowl of oatmeal about anything other than puttering about in the gardens. They'd both attended school in the village, but Emil dropped out after only a few years.

"No, it's not a particularly good thing. It means they don't want me back at college."

Emil looked confused. "Why wouldn't they want you back? You're the smartest girl in all of New York."

But also perhaps the most reckless. There was no point in trying to think of ways to soften the message. She told Emil everything, including how unlikely it was that any other medical school would accept her after she'd been expelled for moral turpitude.

Emil sat hunched over on a footstool, exchanging uncertain glances with Claudia, who had dragged herself from bed upon hearing Julia's arrival.

"So I've been expelled, and there is no going back," Julia explained to them as she nursed a cup of tea.

"What if you wrote a nice letter saying how sorry you were? Maybe then they'd take you back?" Emil suggested.

But she wasn't sorry. Even now, with time to reflect on her actions, she didn't regret taking that dog to safety in the countryside. If she told Dean Kreutzer where the dog had been taken, the dean would see it turned back over to Ross McKinney and his friends. "I think it's a little more complicated than that," she said to Emil.

"What about asking the Vandermarks for help?" Claudia asked. "My daddy says they have more power than the president of the United States. The president has to ask Congress for permission to get things done, but the Vandermarks just unleash their lawyers."

The Vandermarks had owned Dierenpark ever since two brothers sailed across the sea from Holland in 1635, staking a claim in the raw wilderness. It had been the Vandermark brothers who built this very cabin, and as their wealth expanded over the decades, they began building the grand mansion overlooking the Hudson River. Members of the Broeder family had been their groundskeepers since the early days, and the Vandermarks had always treated the Broeders well.

Not that Julia had ever actually met a Vandermark. The last Vandermark to live at Dierenpark had abandoned the mansion sixty years ago, after Karl Vandermark was found floating dead in the river. Three additional generations of Vandermarks had been born, and none of them ever came near Dierenpark, and Julia doubted they ever would.

But their lawyers came. An attorney for the family visited Dierenpark several times per year to inspect the estate, pay the taxes, and ensure the servants were performing their tasks. When Julia had been a child, that attorney was named Mr. Garfield, an elderly man with tremendous muttonchop whiskers who would pat Julia on the head and express amazement at how much she'd grown. He would pay the servants' salaries and always asked if they had need of anything, for the Vandermarks were generous people who would be sure to provide for their loyal servants.

But when she was fifteen, there was a change. Old Mr. Garfield retired, and the job was passed to a new attorney, a young man with light brown hair and eyes the color of the summer sky. Ashton Carlyle's elegantly chiseled face was handsome enough to make any young girl's heart flutter, but at twenty-three he was far too old and serious for someone like Julia. She was a country bumpkin and he was a Yale-trained attorney who seemed to find her interest in Marco Polo amusing. He lived only forty miles down the river in New York City, but they were from entirely different worlds. He was glamour and excitement and style. Even in the middle of nowhere, he seemed to carry an air of metropolitan sophistication with him. Was it his flawless attire? His neatly clipped hair? He always wore a silk vest, and the buttons on his clothing looked like real ivory. In the heat of high summer, when he shed his suit jacket, he still wore a starched collar with a vest and tie. For Julia, there was something appealing about a man who seemed so elegant in the middle of this abandoned, isolated estate.

It was Ashton Carlyle who had gotten Julia into college. The Broeder family had always been told that if they needed anything, they had only to ask the Vandermarks. Over the years, the Vandermarks helped with medical bills, repairs to the cabin, even funds for special occasions like holidays and weddings. But college? No one in her family had ever asked for such a substantial gift. And yet the Vandermarks were her only prayer of ever attending college, and when she'd turned eighteen, Julia had screwed up her courage to ask Mr. Carlyle if he could make it happen.

As was the custom, the lawyer was using the library to review the accounts and interview each of the servants to ensure all was running like clockwork. Mr. Carlyle was making notations in the estate's ledger when she knocked on the open door.

"May I speak with you?" she asked, hoping to keep the tremble from her voice.

Mr. Carlyle was the epitome of refined elegance as he pushed the ledger a few inches away and gestured for her to join him on the opposite side of the desk.

"Please," he said agreeably. "And what can I do for you, Miss Broeder?"

She was so nervous she couldn't tear her eyes away from his silk vest. The fabric was a pale blue, with an intricate pattern in deeper indigo. When she stared closely at the pattern, it appeared to be tiny figures of birds, each no larger than her thumbnail. Thousands of them embroidered into the silk. They reminded her of . . .

"Are those magpies?" she asked inanely, still staring at his vest.

He seemed startled at first, but the planes of his face softened in amusement. "Yes. The magpie is the Chinese symbol of joy."

That was where she'd seen the bird—in one of the books she feasted on while wallowing away the hours in the Vandermarks' library. The Vandermarks were great shipping magnates, and even in the eighteenth century they'd made tremendous inroads into China and the Far East. Their library was a reflection of their interests.

She jerked her gaze from his vest and looked him straight in the eyes. "I need money for college," she blurted out in a nervous rush. "I want to become a doctor."

He stared at her so oddly she felt like a butterfly pinned to a card. "Pardon me," he began delicately, "but it seems to me you are a female."

A snort of laughter escaped. "Honestly, Mr. Carlyle, you've known me for three years and are only figuring that out now?"

Humor lit his eyes, but he set down his pen and steepled his hands before his face. "Tell me why you wish to become a doctor."

She had a speech carefully prepared. It outlined the opportunities in modern medicine and her talents in math and science. It spoke of the nobility of the profession and her desire to do good things in the world. But in that stress-filled moment when she had the attention of the Vandermarks' attorney focused entirely on her, she couldn't remember a word of her prepared speech, and the truth tumbled out instead.

"I want to see the world," she said. "I want to live in the city and go to museums and soak up learning and knowledge and skills. I want to learn how to treat people and work wherever I'm needed, be it in the slums of Bombay or the steppes of Mongolia. I want to trace the routes of Marco Polo, climb the Himalayas, walk the Great Wall of China. I want to carry a medical bag at my side and feel needed wherever I go."

She ran out of breath. It was hard to keep looking at him, and her gaze strayed out the window. "And I don't want to live the rest of my life at this abandoned estate," she concluded, wondering if she had just spoiled her chance of going to college because she'd been too nervous to hold a proper speech in her head.

She need not have feared. Mr. Carlyle wrote her a check for her first semester's tuition and even offered to write her a letter of recommendation to attend the school. One week after she arrived at the Women's Medical College of Pennsylvania, a package from the Vandermarks came in the mail. With a letter of congratulations signed by the elderly Nickolaas Vandermark himself, the box contained a laboratory jacket, a set of blank notebooks, and a brand new copy of *Gray's Anatomy*. She was on her way.

Until that dog entered her world and an impulsive decision knocked her back to Dierenpark with no degree and no prospects.

"What about some other school?" Emil asked. "I'll bet any college would be glad to have you."

Not after being expelled from the world's most prestigious medical college for women. Besides, it was almost the Christmas holidays and she wouldn't be eligible to reenroll until January at the earliest.

"I was hoping I could live here until I figure out what to do," she said.

Emil and Claudia exchanged quick glances. "Well, we're not really set up for long-term guests," Claudia said.

Guests. If ever she needed reminding that she didn't belong in this house anymore, being labeled a *guest* did the trick.

"Maybe they can open up a room in the main house," Emil suggested. "I'll bet they've got at least a dozen empty bedrooms in that mansion."

There were twenty-five bedrooms in the mansion, and only a few were being used by the skeleton staff. It was pretty clear that Claudia didn't want her here, and the Vandermarks wouldn't care if she made use of a long-abandoned bedroom in the main house.

Julia sighed and nodded, and Emil jumped into action. "Let me help you carry your things," he said.

Dierenpark was one of the oldest and grandest estates in the entire country, but Julia knew it held a tragic and storied history. After Karl Vandermark was found dead in the river, a team of lawyers descended on the house and removed his fourteen-year-old son from the estate. That boy was now an old man, but Nickolaas Vandermark had never returned to Dierenpark. None of his children, grandchildren, or great-grandchildren had ever set foot on the estate, either.

Everything in the mansion was preserved precisely as it had been that terrible morning Nickolaas Vandermark fled the house. The Vandermark family clothing still hung in the wardrobes, a king's ransom in silver and china filled the cabinets, and even the papers in the desk drawers had been undisturbed. It was as if the mansion had been suspended in time.

It was so odd. The Vandermarks paid staggering property taxes to keep Dierenpark, plus the salaries of a small staff to maintain the estate, and yet none of them had set foot on the land in sixty years. Growing up, Julia had felt like she had the run of the mansion when she and her friend Sophie, the cook's daughter, explored the grand, stately rooms. Most of the furniture was covered in white sheets, and their footsteps echoed through the abandoned rooms, the portraits of Vandermark ancestors seeming to watch them from the walls. With their powdered wigs, military uniforms, and grim expressions, those Vandermarks always seemed a little scary.

As Julia walked down the path to the imposing granite mansion weathered by centuries of harsh New England winters, she was glad Sophie was still here to commiserate with her. Nobody knew of Julia's far-flung ambitions better than Sophie. As children, the two of them had prowled through the attics of the mansion, trying on old dresses from the eighteenth century and daydreaming about the grand balls that once would have been held at Dierenpark. They'd sprawled side-by-side on the floor of the library, gazing in wonder at the embossed leather books that towered to the ceiling.

Julia wished Sophie had been with her that day she'd run off with Ross McKinney's dog. Sophie would have had the entire Philadelphia Fire Department and Police Department in a puddle at her feet. That was simply the effect she had on men. With her blond hair, angelic beauty, and gentle demeanor, men simply adored Sophie. Sophie had a radiant kindness most people instinctively responded to.

Julia always felt she was pretty enough—she had a slim figure, chestnut hair, and fine brown eyes—but when she stood beside Sophie she felt like a rough hazelnut next to a luminescent pearl.

"There now," Sophie soothed as she drew Julia into the kitchen. "This won't seem so terrible after we have a nice cup of hot chocolate. Chocolate always makes everything better, don't you think?"

Sophie's mother had been the cook at Dierenpark until the older woman died of pneumonia not long before Julia left for medical school. With only a handful of staff maintaining Dierenpark, there wasn't need for a full-time cook anymore. Sophie lived in town with her father, but she came up to the mansion every day to prepare a few meals.

Julia accepted the cup of chocolate from Sophie, who joined her at the pitted kitchen worktable that had served centuries of cooks here at Dierenpark.

"Emil thinks the Vandermark attorneys might be able to help, but money isn't the issue," Julia said. "I was expelled for moral turpitude because they think I stole that dog."

Sophie winced. "Well, you did kind of steal her . . . not that I blame you! But you're right, money can't fix this."

"The Vandermarks have always been very good to me," Julia said. "Perhaps one of their lawyers would be willing to help me mount a legal challenge to get that decision overturned. I think it's my only hope."

Sophie fidgeted and sighed. "That's just it," she said gloomily. "I *don't* think the Vandermarks are all that decent. They didn't claw their way to the top of the world's shipping industry by being nice people."

It was true the Vandermarks had a ferocious reputation. Nickolaas Vandermark presented himself to the world as an elderly, dignified gentleman, but rumor had it he was as tough as Genghis Kahn in the world of business. And his grandson was even worse. The grandson was gradually assuming control over the Vandermark empire and lived somewhere in Europe. Julia was grateful she didn't need to deal directly with any of the Vandermarks, but they'd vowed to always provide for the Broeders, and for centuries they had been delivering on that promise.

And what she needed right now was a good attorney.

"Mr. Carlyle visits the estate each December," she said. "Maybe I should wait until his regular visit rather than barge in on him now. What do you think?"

"Don't wait," Sophie advised. "If the Vandermarks are paying your tuition, they need to know about your change of status immediately."

Money was going to be an issue. After the unexpected fees for traveling back from Philadelphia, Julia had burned through most of her funds, but what choice did she have? She felt like a supplicant going on bended knee to the Vandermark law offices in Manhattan, but if she ever wanted to become a doctor, she was going to have to appeal to Mr. Ashton Carlyle.

3

The law offices for Vandermark Shipping consumed the entire ninth floor of an office building on Broad Street. There was an elevator, but Julia preferred to walk up the stairs to burn off the nervous energy that had been accumulating while she'd been trapped on the streetcar ride here.

She'd never actually visited Mr. Carlyle at his Manhattan office, and she was stunned to learn that he was only one of twenty-five lawyers who worked for the Vandermarks.

"Is Mr. Carlyle expecting you?" the clerk at the front desk asked, peering over his spectacles with suspicion.

Dressed in a simple poplin frock with a square neckline and modest bustle, she felt a bit out of place in an office lined with mahogany walls, lit with green-shaded electric lamps, and smelling of old money. "No, but I hope he can make time to see me today." It hadn't even occurred to her that Mr. Carlyle might not be available, but a man of his responsibilities might be anywhere in the city today. Or the world, for that matter. The walls of the office were covered with maps showing all the great trading ports of the world: Rotterdam, Shanghai, Buenos Aires, Antwerp. It made her dizzy, this reminder of how big the world was. She drifted toward the map of the port of Shanghai, reaching out to touch the cold metal frame, her gaze traveling along the shorelines of the East China Sea, wondering if she would ever have the opportunity to see them in person. To listen to the cry of the kingfishers in the harbor. To feel the salty breeze on her face.

"Miss Broeder, what an unexpected surprise."

She jerked her fingers away from the map. Ashton Carlyle stood at the opening of a hallway leading to a suite of offices, looking as impeccable as always. His vest was made of shantung silk in the shade of carnation-red she always associated with the Chinese color of good luck. She gathered her breath and prayed for a bit of the good luck to rub off on her.

"May I say how dapper you look this afternoon?" she commented bravely. And indeed he did. His light brown hair was carefully groomed and in perfect keeping with his finely molded face. His trousers were pressed to a knife-edge seam and broke at precisely the correct spot over his fancy leather shoes. He must pay his tailor a fortune.

He dipped his head in acknowledgment. "Thank you. I am expecting a visitor shortly, but I have a few minutes if you would care to follow me to my office."

His office was as flawless as the man. There was no clutter in the room, but it was exquisitely decorated, with a wall of exotic maps, paintings of faraway places, and a large window overlooking Manhattan's skyline. He offered her a chair that was lined with tufted leather and deep-set squabs and faced his desk. She sat, clenching her beaded reticule in her fists.

"What can I do for you, Miss Broeder?" His voice was pleasant, but his face brimmed with curiosity. Always so correct, so proper.

"I need help. Money and a good attorney, for a start."

He coughed as he took a seat at his desk. He averted his gaze, adjusted his starched collar, then looked back at her again. "I'm sorry, could you repeat that, please?"

Heat suffused her body. This was awful—but had to be endured.

"I've been expelled from college. I'd like to mount an appeal, and I believe I need a good attorney to do so."

There was no change of expression on his face. It may as well have been carved from stone. "Explain yourself," he said quietly.

She owed him the truth and quickly told him about how the firemen expected her to patch up their dog so they could turn it around and fight it again. She admitted to taking the dog out of the city. She told him about the police becoming involved and her charge of moral turpitude.

"And what do you expect me to do about it?" Mr. Carlyle asked. The austerity in his tone was a surprise. He'd always been so pleasant and supportive in the past.

"Well, I know Mr. Vandermark has always taken a personal interest in my studies."

If anything, his face grew colder. But it was true! A semester did not pass without a large gift box directly from Nickolaas Vandermark himself. At first the old gentleman had sent supplies to further her education, but over the years the contents had grown more personal. Upon learning of her desire to work as a medical missionary in the Far East, Mr. Vandermark had sent more whimsical gifts: a bolt of batik silk, a set of calligraphy tools, even a case of Darjeeling tea from the wild mountains of west Bengal. She'd written him thank-you notes, always outlining her progress in school. Mr. Vandermark clearly read all of her letters and took care in the selection of these items to nurture and inspire her dreams.

"Do you know who Nickolaas Vandermark is?" Mr. Carlyle asked in a frosty voice.

"He is the man who has been paying my college tuition and supports my goal to become a doctor."

"Yes, he pays your bills," Mr. Carlyle said impatiently. "He is also among the most ruthless shipping tycoons of the nineteenth century. The 'kindly old gentleman' demeanor he wears like a snake skin is only an illusion, and he sheds it in the blink of an eye when angered. The man had a ten-year tiff with his only son over a violin. A stupid violin that neither one of them could even play. And yet that tiff lasted until the day his son died in a hotel fire. Even now, he is barely on speaking terms with his grandson, a man he raised from the cradle to be his heir. All of the Vandermarks are tough, driven men, and I can assure you they have no use for a woman who squanders the gift of a college education over a dog."

Julia had known she'd have to take a reprimand over the dog but still felt confident the Vandermarks would assist her in the end. She wasn't leaving without an agreement to get some help mounting an appeal.

"In ancient Japan, there is a practice called *seppuku*," she said. "It is used as a show of contrition in which a man slices his belly open to spill his guts on the floor. Would you like me to do that here, or shall I step outside to avoid the mess?"

His mouth tightened. "You may find this situation amusing, but I went out on a limb for you, Julia! Nickolaas Vandermark had never heard of a woman wanting to become a doctor, but I vouched for you. I assured him you were a good investment, that the future rested with people like you and not the hidebound rules of the past. He agreed to pay, and now you've gone and squandered it over a dog. *A dog!*"

She flinched at the contempt in his voice. She'd thought he was her friend. A strait-laced, starchy man who moved in entirely different circles than she, but still a friend. How quickly the tide could turn.

"Is there anyone else in this firm who would be willing to help me?"

He scowled, reaching into a desk drawer and withdrawing a slim book, thumping it down on his desk with more force than was warranted. After a moment of paging through the book, he closed it. "No, no one else can help. I am the lawyer charged with administering the business aspects of Dierenpark and all its employees. No other attorney in this office has time for such details. And quite frankly, I could not recommend they interfere. Getting you readmitted to school would be throwing good money after bad. You are on your own."

Julia grasped her reticule so hard the clasp dug into her palm. Her dreams were collapsing around her, but she kept her chin high. She stared at Mr. Carlyle even as he shifted in his seat and steamed, his face growing more flushed by the moment. She waited until he looked away first before she rose.

"Thank you for your time," she said quietly before leaving the office. She closed the door softly behind her.

Ashton listened to the whisper-soft rasp of Julia's skirt sweeping out of his office. The gentle *snick* as she closed the office door shamed him, but he couldn't afford to be soft about this. He'd risked a lot in persuading Nickolaas Vandermark to pay for her college. She had no idea how hard it had been or perhaps she wouldn't have been so careless. It was easy to be reckless with other people's money and professional reputation.

He could still remember the appalled look on Nickolaas Vandermark's elderly, narrow face when Ashton had first proposed sending Julia to college.

"I said to look after the financial and physical needs of the Broeder family," Nickolaas had said. "I didn't intend for that to mean funding a girl's jaunt around the world."

The Vandermarks were one of the wealthiest families in America and could afford whatever they wished, but asking for a college education for the daughter of the groundskeeper was an audacious request. Ashton had pushed for it until he'd earned the old man's reluctant consent.

And Julia had squandered it over a dog. Did the girl have no understanding of the gift she'd been given? Ashton hadn't had a benefactor to pick up his college tab. That burden fell entirely on his father—and his family endured years of struggle, heartache, and debt to get him through college.

Ashton would never forget the time he made an impromptu trip home in the middle of his third year at Yale, carrying two tickets to an afternoon baseball game. It was his father's birthday, and there was nothing the two of them enjoyed more than an afternoon watching the Brooklyn Dodgers at bat. Ashton had sensed money was tight at home, but he was working extra hours at the college library to afford the tickets and the train fare. As he vaulted up the steps to the brownstone townhouse where he'd been born and raised, he was stunned to see a *For Lease* sign hanging in the window.

He later learned his father mortgaged their home to pay his tuition at Yale. When the note was called in, his father had been unable to pay. He was evicted, moved to an eighth-story apartment, and was working two jobs in order to keep funneling money to Yale.

What did the intrepid Miss Julia Broeder know about that kind of sacrifice? Of the exhaustion that came from putting in a full day at an office and then manning a telegraph station at night? Or of seeing tears well in a father's eyes at the shame of being evicted from his home?

Ashton drew a calming breath. Debt and financial insecurity were a long way in his past, but the lessons he'd learned as a young man would be with him forever. Yes, he liked to dress well, but he had started living well only after he'd repaid his father every borrowed dime and safely banked a healthy reserve fund. Even today, he and his father shared a modest house to economize. Only a girl who never had to work for anything would be as reckless as Julia had been.

He clenched his fist and stared at the framed drawings on the wall opposite his desk. The pictures always soothed and inspired him. Most were of the various Vandermark properties he administered. The estate at Dierenpark, even though by far the oldest, was modest compared to the other investments. Ashton was responsible for administering a rubber plantation in Sumatra, a series of warehouses in the port of Rotterdam, and a castle in the Black Forest mountain range of Germany. He administered twelve Vandermark properties, and each of them was represented on the wall before him.

But one of the framed maps belonged to him alone: the map of Marco Polo's journey to the Far East and back. It was a humble map, taken from a book Ashton had read so many times as a boy that the binding broke and the pages tumbled free, but he saved the map. For years he kept it tucked into a drawer, where he occasionally unfolded it to relive those boyhood dreams. Only after he began earning a respectable salary did he pay to have it properly framed and displayed where he could see it daily.

It had been Julia's love of Marco Polo that had sparked the immediate sense of camaraderie when they'd first met all those years ago. She'd been only fifteen at the time but lively and curious and full of ambition. He had once shared her longing to see the world, but his fate had been settled long ago. He had responsibilities, and childhood dreams had been set aside when a golden opportunity at the Vandermark shipping empire became available.

Despite his prestigious job, he didn't want to spend the rest of his life being little more than a caretaker for the Vandermarks' far-flung properties. If he could execute the daring plan he'd been crafting for years, it would be the greatest triumph of his career. One only had to look outside his window to see the city bedecked with telephone wires, power generators, and the glowing electric lamps to see where the American economy was headed. They were no longer an agricultural nation, but an industrial one. And if his plan worked, it would give the Vanderemarks a hook into the burgeoning trade in electricity.

The clerk knocked on his door. "Mr. Stiles of the General Electric Company is here, sir."

Ashton drew a breath, pushing dreams of Marco Polo, incense-laden caravans, and an idealistic young medical student from his mind. This deal was three years in the making, and he could afford no distractions today.

He was relieved to see Mr. Stiles was alone. It was so much easier to deal with a fellow attorney without the engineers to complicate matters.

"Come in, Mr. Stiles," he said. "I hope we can sign those contracts today. It would serve both our corporations well if we could."

And he smiled when he saw the nod of approval from Mr. Stiles.

Julia sat on the pier at Dierenpark, the old wooden planking hard beneath her skirts. Before her, the Hudson River unfolded like a glistening ribbon, meandering northward through miles of verdant wilderness. The November morning was chilly despite the heavy blanket wrapped around her shoulders. She couldn't imagine how Sophie tolerated the frigid water as she waded into the river, casually plucking oysters from the reef near the pier and collecting them in a basket slung over her arm.

"I've never seen him so angry," Julia said, picking a sliver from the dry wooden planking that had turned gray with age. "I know he could help if he wanted, but he wouldn't even consider it. Shouldn't Mr. Vandermark be the one to make this decision, not his attorney?"

Sophie's face was closed as she leaned over to feel beneath the water, her hand emerging a moment later with another large oyster that landed in her basket with a clatter. "I don't think the Vandermarks even know we exist," Sophie said. "They live mostly in Europe and hardly ever come to the United States anymore."

Julia glanced upward, where Dierenpark perched at the top of the cliff above them, so picturesque it could have been placed there by a Renaissance artist. She'd never understood why the family held on to this estate when they clearly had no interest in it anymore. What must it be like to have so much money you could collect houses all over the world? Julia rarely wasted time being envious of people who had more than she; all she wanted was to be able to control her own future. She was willing to work hard for it. She *wanted* to work hard for it, for few great things in life were easily obtained. But the way Ashton Carlyle had dismissed her still smarted.

"All I've ever wanted was to figure out a way to escape this valley," she said, flinging the splinter of wood into the river. "I think I'll die if I have to stay in this nowhere village."

Sophie averted her gaze as she waded to the pier, setting the basket on the planking with a heavy sigh. Remorse immediately flooded through Julia.

"I'm sorry, Soph. I didn't mean it. Really."

"It's okay," Sophie whispered.

But it wasn't okay. All Sophie had ever wanted was to become a wife and a mother right here in this village, but last winter her fiancé had died only a month before the wedding. Sophie was now twenty-six and so heartsick over Albert's death she hid up here at Dierenpark, where she could be alone amid a universe of juniper trees and endless blue skies. Julia had often heard it said that despair of the soul was worse than pain in the body. She'd never believed it until she saw the way Sophie dimmed and withered in the year following her fiancé's death.

"Has there been no one since Albert?" Julia asked gently.

She immediately regretted the question. Sophie flinched and waded back toward the submerged reef, stooping over in search of more oysters, the slosh of water the only sound to fill the quiet morning.

"I still can't talk about it," Sophie finally said in a muffled voice, her eyes averted. "Not even with you. Most days I can pretend to be fine and go about cooking and tending the gardens, but everything is still hollow. And when I stop to think about Albert, the hollowness threatens to split wide open and sink me. So please . . . *please*, I still can't speak of it."

Julia had no experience with this kind of loss. She'd been too focused on her medical education to become sidetracked by a man, but she hated seeing Sophie so stricken with grief. If pretending to go about an ordinary life helped ease Sophie's pain, Julia would help.

She scooped up the basket of oysters and stood. "Come on. Let's go cook dinner, and you can show me how to make oyster chowder. I used to brag to my classmates about how you could make people weep over your cooking."

Sophie managed a bit of a smile, gentle gratitude softening her face. "Thank you," she mouthed and followed Julia up to the mansion.

Emil was waiting for them in the kitchen.

"Um, Julie? You know old Mr. Hofstad across the way from Dierenpark? The goat farmer?"

Of course she remembered Mr. Hofstad. Most of the Dutch settlers to the valley had been here for generations, but Mr. Hofstad had immigrated as a young man and never learned to speak English very well. His English might be poor, but he was a genius with goats, and they'd always gotten their milk and cheese from his farm.

"Well, he broke his arm last month, and his goats are getting ready to start kidding. He was wondering if I could help him out, but um . . . what with the twins and Claudia feeling so poorly . . ."

"I'd be happy to help!" Julia interrupted. She'd never helped a goat give birth before, but she was anxious to do something worthwhile while figuring out what to do with the rest of her life.

Because after today's meeting with Mr. Carlyle, it didn't look like she would be headed back to college any time soon.

✦

Julia stood in the middle of the goat pen, wondering what she'd gotten herself into. Mr. Hofstad had a lovely farm, surrounded by a white picket fence and plenty of pens, shelters, and barns. It looked picturesque from a distance, but now that she was inside the fence, it was a little more overwhelming than she'd anticipated.

The man had sixty female goats. Sixty goats! All of them pregnant, all of them due to give birth within the next two weeks.

Mr. Hofstad rambled in Dutch while he gestured to a pen. Two of the goats had already given birth, and the little baby kids looked so precious, standing on their wobbly legs and taking uncertain steps.

She waded into the larger pen. Goats were friendly and curious animals, and they immediately crowded around, completely encircling her within seconds. The bleating, the smell, the bumping of snouts against her . . . what had she gotten herself into?

Mr. Hofstad laughed. "They just say . . . hi!"

She nodded and said "hi" back to the goats. Claudia spoke a little Dutch and came over to translate. It took a while, but Sophie learned that the pens were divided into goats who were preparing to kid, which was most of them, and three smaller pens designated as kidding stalls, since goats preferred to be alone while giving birth. Julia needed to keep her eye on the goats to spot signs of labor and then guide the doe into one of the kidding stalls.

After the birthing, the mama and baby should be moved to one of the ten pens at the east side of the farm. The few billy goats were kept completely isolated. They were more aggressive and completely useless during birthing season. Mr. Hofstad would feed and water the billy goats but would be eternally grateful if Julia could tend his female goats until birthing season was over.

Well? What else was she going to do with her time and her talents? This was shaping up to be an adventure she would never forget.

4

Ashton's ears ached from the roar of shouts rising from the trading floor of the New York Stock Exchange. Watching from the gallery above, he had a bird's-eye view of the pandemonium below. Perhaps nowhere on earth did stately baroque splendor contrast so sharply with aggressive men who jockeyed, shouted, and wrestled for position around the trading columns. Overhead, a massive coffered ceiling featured leaded glass skylights of arabesque design, some of which were tilted for ventilation. An ornate bronze railing lined the gallery that encircled the top of the trading floor. Such grandeur, such commotion.

Ashton clung to the railing, leaning forward to track the movements of his agent on the floor below. Every twenty minutes, Grigsby came running to him with a fresh strip of tickertape. Ashton had to lie flat on the gallery floor and reach through the railing to grab the tickertape from below. His suit had been custom made in London, but Ashton didn't care. He paid one hundred dollars per annum for the privilege of this spot in the gallery, and he needed to see those tapes the moment they were released.

Shouts rose as another wave of orders were telegraphed in from Chicago, but Ashton didn't care about timber, beef, or corn prices. He'd come for one thing today, and that was to corner the market on the gutta-percha trade. Such a strange name for a commodity that was about to take the world by storm . . . only most people weren't even aware of its existence.

In the past decade, the economy of the United States had taken a steep turn from the world of agriculture into the dynamism of industry. The Vandermark fortune had been built on mighty ships carrying lumber, grain, fish, and fur all over the world, but that was not where the fortunes of the coming century would lay. Gutta-percha, the odd, milky liquid excreted by the rubber trees native to Malaya, was the perfect substance to catapult the Vandermarks into the twentieth century.

The Vandermarks already owned substantial gutta-percha plantations in Malaya, but they didn't own it all. After today, if Ashton played his cards right, they'd have a controlling interest in this little-used rubber.

A kind of rubber most people overlooked. A kind that was impractical for tires or raincoats or so many other uses. But gutta-percha was ideal for coating the wires of anything powered by electricity. Most of the electrical and telephone wires were currently protected by braided cotton cords that were subject to rotting, gnawing by insects, or even fire. Rubber made of gutta-percha latex was a perfect solution.

And if Ashton succeeded in pulling off this deal, soon every telephone, electric lamp, kitchen stove, and factory machine would be using wires coated with gutta-percha bought from Vandermark-owned properties.

He caught Grigsby's attention, and the man looked up at him with alarm in his eyes. From his trading column across the floor, Grigsby flashed the hand signals for the current price of gutta-percha commodities. The price was creeping higher. Ashton had been buying shares all morning. Traders were noticing the movement and joining in the stampede.

Ashton didn't care. It was still a gold mine.

"Buy!" Ashton shouted down. "Buy it all!"

Grigsby nodded and turned around to shout, gesture, and jostle for position in order to get the order placed.

❖

Was it possible to feel exhilarated and tired down to the marrow of his bones at the same time?

Ashton grinned as he waded through the crowds packed along Wall Street on his way back to the law offices. By the end of the trading day, the price of gutta-percha had tripled, but he still bought everything Grigsby could get his hands on. It was enough to ensure that the largest makers of electrical machinery would need to deal with the Vandermarks if they wanted the best and safest form of coating for their wires. It was a coup beyond anything he'd ever imagined when he'd first signed on to work for the Vandermarks.

This was the sort of deal he needed to specialize in if he was to get Nickolaas Vandermark's attention. Thank heavens for his interest in all things eastern, or perhaps he would never have known about the potential for the unusual type of rubber plant his predecessor had never capitalized on.

The scent of warm bread and spicy sausages filled the air as he passed a row of street vendors hawking their wares. He hadn't eaten since this morning. It was impossible to eat while trapped on the gallery of the trading exchange, but he dared not leave his post even for a minute. This had been the biggest triumph of his professional career, and it was worth a little hunger.

He passed the old German woman selling sausages from the back of a wagon and the fishmonger hawking baked eels and pickled whelks. He walked until he came to the Chinese woman turning out *jianbing,* an egg pancake filled with scallions, bean paste, and some kind of sweet-spicy sauce Ashton could never get enough of. He paid for the jianbing while his mouth watered and he felt dizzy from hunger.

"*Syeh-syeh,*" he said to the woman.

She smiled and corrected his pronunciation then replied in heavily accented English. "You are welcome."

He rolled the jianbing into a tube and took a hearty bite as he strolled back toward the Vandermark offices. This was what he loved about New York. He'd sacrificed his childhood dreams of seeing the moon rise over the Great Wall of China, but he had the thrill of riding the crest of the business world as it careened toward the twentieth century. And he could still indulge his love of Asian things at any street-corner vendor, at the art museums, and at the bookstores.

The jianbing restored his energy as he jogged up the stairs to the law offices. It was late, and some of the clerks and attorneys were already leaving, but Johnston was still at his post at the front desk.

"Mr. Vandermark is here to see you, sir. He is in the conference room."

Ashton smiled. Nickolaas Vandermark knew of his plan to capitalize on the gutta-percha market. Ashton never would have committed such a staggering sum without authorization. Nickolaas still had a sharp mind, but he was becoming less interested in commerce with each passing year. Most of the business administration was being turned over to his grandson Quentin, a grim, difficult man who rarely deigned to travel to the United States. Meanwhile, Nickolaas traveled the world and boasted of having personally set foot on each of the seven continents and all twelve Vandermark properties scattered from remote Malay plantations to a castle high in the Black Forest. Ashton hadn't realized Nickolaas had returned to the country or he would have asked the man if he'd like to watch some of the excitement from the stock exchange gallery.

He could hear the rumble of laughter coming from the conference room before he entered. This was it, then. The news of his triumph had already reached the offices. He swiped at the dirt clinging to the front of his suit from lying on the floor to reach down for the tickertapes. He couldn't get much off, but he straightened his cuffs and tie before entering.

"Here, here!" one of his colleagues shouted the moment Ashton passed through the doors.

A dozen attorneys were gathered at the table, and given the opened champagne bottles, it looked as if the celebration had already begun. Nickolaas Vandermark stood in the corner beneath a portrait of a seventeenth-century Vandermark general who had once led the Dutch in their failed attempt to keep New York out of British hands. The family resemblance between the grim, austere men was unmistakable. Nickolaas Vandermark was a tall man whose slender frame might be mistaken for gentility until one witnessed the pure steel in his eyes.

"Gutta-percha," one of the attorneys jested. "It sounds like a skin disease, but I understand General Electric and Bell Telephone are already clamoring for it."

The senior attorney for shipping contracts raised his glass. "I expect when we are all dead and buried, our children, grandchildren, and great-grandchildren will still be using wires coated with Vandermark gutta-percha. Congratulations, Mr. Carlyle."

Ashton smiled in acknowledgment. The financial security bought by this deal was priceless. Having been raised by a father who mortgaged his house and entire life's savings to get Ashton through law school, he didn't ever want to flirt with financial insolvency again.

A glass of champagne was pressed into his hand, but Ashton set it down, still looking at Nickolaas Vandermark, whose enigmatic expression was impossible to read. The old man watched the celebration from a distance, his sharp eyes scrutinizing the men in the room.

Ashton cleared his throat. "Thank you," he said. "We'll still need to finalize the contracts with a factory to produce the wire coatings, but we are now the only company that can guarantee an uninterrupted supply of gutta-percha in the United States."

Another round of applause and back clapping followed. At last, Nickolaas Vandermark pushed away from his spot in the corner and reached out to shake his hand. "Well done, Mr. Carlyle," he said simply. "It looks as though that suit has been through a stampede of buffalo—"

"A stampede of *bulls*!" another attorney jested.

"Indeed," Mr. Vandermark acknowledged with a tilt of his head. "Please send the cleaner's bill to me. It's the least I can do for such bravery in the face of corporate combat."

"Thank you, sir."

Those were likely to be the only words of praise he could expect from his employer, for the Vandermarks were famously stern and aggressive men of business. Their ships traveled in convoys complete with cannons and armed mercenaries to serve as protection as they sailed into the dangerous ports of the world. They leveraged their vast wealth to corner markets and intimidate competition. They had been this way ever since the seventeenth century.

Nickolaas glanced at Ashton's untouched glass of champagne. "I'd like a moment of privacy in your office, since it appears you have concluded your celebration."

That was abrupt. Mr. Vandermark's face was still expressionless and revealed nothing, but the signal was clear. He wanted everyone to move on. The good humor in the room evaporated as the other men set down their glasses and drifted away.

Ashton led Mr. Vandermark to his office. Perhaps the old man had reservations about praising such a junior attorney in public. Having just turned thirty, Ashton was considerably younger than most of the men here who had served the family for decades.

The moment the door to his office was closed, Nickolaas Vandermark's voice lashed out like a whip. "All well and good about the gutta-percha, but what's this I hear about your refusal to assist Julia Broeder back into college?"

Ashton blinked, stunned at the abrupt change of topic. "What?" He took a step back, bracing his hand against the surface of the desk while the older man paced like a caged lion in the confines of the office.

"My family has looked after the Broeders for centuries," he said in a voice simmering with heat. "I made it quite clear when you were assigned to manage the accounts at Dierenpark that you were to ensure that family had everything they needed."

Ashton felt poleaxed. He'd done everything for Julia! Wrote her tuition checks, provided money for books and supplies. He sent her regular packages filled with gifts and encouragement . . . all signed using Nickolaas Vandermark's signature stamp. What more could he possibly have done?

"I was informed Miss Broeder was expelled from college for legitimate reasons," he said stiffly. "Moral turpitude, to be precise."

"Well, I want her back in school," Nickolaas snapped. "If Miss Broeder wants a medical degree, you are to ensure she gets one."

"That may be difficult, sir. There are very few medical schools that accept women."

Nickolaas narrowed his eyes. "Allow me to be explicit. If the Women's Medical College of Pennsylvania refuses to reenroll Miss Broeder, I want you to persuade the Harvard Medical School to open their doors to females. Failing that, get Yale to do so. I don't care how you do it, but I want Miss Broeder reenrolled in a prestigious medical college with all haste. Have I made myself clear?"

"Yes, sir."

The door slammed behind Mr. Vandermark while Ashton's mind still reeled. He had no idea how this incident had come to Mr. Vandermark's attention, but it was well known the Vandermarks had people on the payroll to keep an eye on such things. In other words, they had spies. One of those spies must have passed this information on to Nickolaas, and it had set the old man off.

Ashton braced his palms against the surface of his desk, wishing he could stop the trembling in his hands. If he was fired by Nickolaas Vandermark, no other law firm in the city would hire him. He closed his eyes and scrambled to remember everything his predecessor had told him about dealing with Dierenpark and the Broeder family.

"Nickolaas Vandermark is outrageously superstitious," the former attorney had warned him. "He doesn't care about the other servants in the mansion, only the Broeders. It's strange, but I've never questioned the whims of millionaires. Give the Broeders whatever they want, but you will find them to be an easygoing lot. The Broeders are simple people who never ask for much."

Ashton sighed. There was nothing simple about Julia Broeder.

5

"You did fine, sweet pea," Julia murmured to the goat sprawled in the hay. The doe rested only a moment before turning to lick her newly delivered kid that already struggled to rise in the bed of sodden hay. It was just after midnight, and Julia leaned back on her haunches to watch the twin baby goats that had just been born.

She'd been here six days and had taken to sleeping in a cot set up in the corner of the barn. Goats could give birth at any time, and it was easiest for her to be close at hand. As soon as she recognized the signs of labor, Julia guided the doe into a kidding stall and made sure fresh hay was on the ground. Goats were legendary for their curiosity, and the goats in the pen behind the kidding stall tended to gather at the fence to watch.

What wonderful creatures these goats were! Aside from an occasional bleat and a smidge of hoof thrashing, goats were stoic as they gave birth, until the very end, when the doe's entire body seized up with tension. They seemed comforted by her presence, which was why Julia didn't mind hunkering down and chatting with them throughout the process. So far she had helped fifteen goats through their deliveries.

Twins were typical for goats, and as soon as Julia was sure both baby kids were doing well, she swept away the sodden hay and replaced it with fresh. Goats were finicky about cleanliness, and as much as she wanted to collapse into her cot in the corner of the barn, she cleaned the entire kidding stall before heading to a bucket of water to clean herself up before dimming the lantern and bedding down again.

She sat on the cot, groaning as she unlaced her shoes, but she froze at the telltale sounds coming from the kidding stall she had just cleaned.

Triplets? She had yet to see a goat deliver triplets, but it was possible. She scrambled to lace her shoes again then climbed back into the stall, swinging a leg over the top bar. After her first day on the job, she'd begged for some trousers from Mr. Hofstad, who presented her with a stack of clean pants and a belt. This work was simply too physical to be bothered with skirts, and she was becoming accustomed to the freedom of wearing trousers.

She knelt beside the goat, angling the lantern to get a better look at the doe's hindquarters. Sure enough, another glossy sac of fluid was nudging its way out of the birth canal.

"Well, look at you, triplets!" Julia smiled at the tiny snout that could be seen through the membrane. She shook off her exhaustion. No matter how tired she was, this goat had it worse. She stroked the doe's flank, staring at the miracle of birth happening before her eyes. There wasn't a lot to do at this point, just be on hand to sweep the baby kid away from the danger of the mother's thrashing hooves.

A gush of warm fluid spilled from the goat, and the kid slid out quickly. In short order, Julia cleared the membrane from the kid's snout, pleased to see how quickly this one sucked in a sloppy gulp of air. Moments later, it tried to stand. She watched, exhausted and entranced. That baby goat had a lot more energy than she had.

Julia glanced at the cluster of other goats watching from the neighboring pen. "I'll bet you are all praying you don't have to do this three times," she said as she began clearing out the soiled hay.

By the time she completed the chores, she was dragging from exhaustion. She plunged her hands into a bucket of cold water, scrubbed up, then flopped down on the cot and fell asleep with her shoes still laced up but a smile on her face.

———◈———

The bleating of goats awakened her.

Waking up was getting easier. Julia would never forget her first morning in the barn, when her muscles had been so stiff from squatting to deliver goats that she'd embarrassed herself when trying to rise from the cot. Her abused muscles refused to cooperate and she fell off the cot, smacked face first onto the barn floor, and sucked in a nose full of straw dust.

Now she rose from the cot with ease and settled into her routine. The first thing she did was go to the other barn and walk among the pens of pregnant goats, looking for signs of imminent labor. She spotted three that looked as if they'd probably deliver today, and by the time she got them moved into the kidding stalls, Sophie had arrived from the main house with breakfast, waving at Julia from across the pasture

"I've brought an omelet!" Sophie called out, holding the platter high. Julia left the barn and scampered across the field to the white picket fence.

"Bless you!" Julia said, nearly growing faint at the aroma of melted cheese and fresh herbs. Sophie propped her hip on the other side of the fence, passing her a bottle of milk and a basket of warm blueberry muffins as soon as the plate was scraped clean.

"Anything exciting?" Sophie asked.

"I had triplets last night. Rather, the sweet little Nubian goat with the floppy ears had triplets. I only helped."

But it had been exciting. Fulfilling. She had always assumed she was meant to be a doctor and treat people, but what about veterinary medicine? The livelihood of farmers like Mr. Hofstad was dependent upon the health of their animals, and there weren't many people who had formal training in veterinary medicine. Even treating that poor abused dog in Philadelphia had given her an unexpected surge of satisfaction.

She wanted to be a physician, not a veterinarian, but perhaps treating animals was the only option left. She was young and intelligent, and now that the blinding sense of panic she'd felt upon first being expelled had faded, she needed to consider her options. Perhaps God had played a role in what had happened, for how would Mr. Hofstad have managed without her? It was surely a blessing that she'd arrived home at Dierenpark when she did.

Sophie took back the empty bottle of milk and the basket. "Perhaps I can arrange to have some fresh clothes delivered," she suggested. "Do you have any I can take up to the house for a quick wash?"

"Is this your way of telling me I stink?"

Sophie's eyes sparkled. "It's my way of hoping I can provide you with some clean clothes soon. Very, *very* soon."

Julia rolled her eyes. "Sophie, even your insults are oddly sweet and kind." But she loped back to the barn and gathered up her mound of soiled clothes.

Sophie's beauty was as lovely and pristine as a summer's morning, but she winced and her eyes watered as Julia dumped the mound of dirty clothes into her outstretched arms.

"You are an angel of goodness and mercy," Julia said with a wink.

Sophie averted her nose from the noxious fabric. "I am Wellington at Waterloo," she gasped. "I am Washington crossing the Delaware. I can endure this until I get these clothes to the laundry, or die trying."

Julia watched Sophie retreat back through the gates to Dierenpark and disappear down the tree-shaded path. She wished Sophie would leave Dierenpark. Sophie was wasted here. The only thing Sophie truly wanted for her life was the chance to be a wife and a mother, and how was she going to meet anyone trapped in the lonely isolation of an abandoned mansion like Dierenpark?

The urgent bleating of a goat got her attention. There seemed to be some commotion in the back of the pen, and Julia ran back to the barn to wade into the midst of the forty-five female goats yet to give birth. Two does near the back were both antsy and beginning to cause trouble. They pawed the ground and bumped against the wall. These were the signs of labor, and their agitation was making the other goats nervous.

It took some doing to lead them out of the pen without the others wanting to follow. There were only three kidding stalls, meaning she was going to have to double them up. Goats preferred to be alone while birthing, but it wasn't a requirement.

The goat in the single pen was getting close. The doe had flopped onto the straw and bleated in distress. Julia rushed to her side, mounding some fresh hay up around the doe's hindquarters.

"Hello, Miss Broeder," a voice said from the far end of the barn. The voice was smooth, cultured, and familiar.

She whirled around, stunned at the sight of Ashton Carlyle in a goat barn. But there he was, framed in the open doorway, wearing a starched collar, shoes polished to a glossy shine, and a canary-yellow vest so fine its satin gleamed in the dimness of the barn.

She stood and rested her forearms along the top bar of the pen. "Did you get lost? Dierenpark is across the lane."

The corners of his mouth lifted an infinitesimal degree, but it could in no way be classified as a smile. His nose wrinkled as he scanned the dim interior of the barn. "The only business I have at Dierenpark relates to you, and I was informed I could find you here. If you could wrap up what you are doing, we can meet in the library at Dierenpark to discuss the issue."

She didn't take her eyes off him as she hunkered down to continue stroking the goat, who bleated piteously. Feeling down toward the doe's pin bones beneath her tail, Julia knew it would probably be only a few more minutes before this doe delivered.

"I'm afraid I'm rather busy," she said, trying to keep the amusement from leaking into her voice. "Why don't you tell me what's on your mind?"

He seemed annoyed by her refusal to leave the barn and follow him to the baronial splendor of the mansion. Nevertheless, he took a few steps farther into the barn so he could stand beside the kidding stall.

"It occurs to me I may have been hasty in my reluctance to intercede on your behalf with the dean of the college. This is a busy time on my calendar, but if you can be ready to leave on the eight o'clock train tomorrow morning, I will accompany you to Philadelphia in order to launch an appeal of your expulsion."

She sucked in a quick breath and stood. "You'd do that for me?"

"Yes. However, the smell in this barn is stupefying, so I'd prefer to discuss the details at the mansion."

She drew a few feet closer so that she faced him across the bars of the pen. "Thank you! I don't know what to say . . . except that this might be the nicest thing anyone has ever offered to do for me."

If anything, her words seemed to annoy him more. The corners of his mouth turned down, and he looked impatient. The handkerchief he used to cover his nose was embroidered with his initials.

"Please be prepared to leave Dierenpark by seven o'clock tomorrow morning if we are to catch the train by eight."

The goat behind her started thrashing. She turned and sank to her knees beside it. "Oh . . . well, I'm afraid I won't be ready to leave for a while. These goats really need me."

He seemed flabbergasted. "Do you mean to tell me you are passing up the shot at a college education over some goats? Last week it was a dog, now it is a goat. I can only hope Dierenpark doesn't suffer an influx of turtles or migratory rodents that might spark another round of sudden altruism on your part."

She kept rubbing the goat's flanks, grinning up at him. She was beginning to suspect there might be a wonderful sense of humor beneath all those fancy New York clothes. "What's the hurry? I probably won't get readmitted until next semester anyway."

The goat's bleats became more urgent, more insistent, like the warning blasts from a fire engine barreling down the street. The goat flexed her hindquarters and held up her tail. The glossy rim of the amniotic sac appeared at the birth canal. This goat was about to deliver.

She glanced up at Mr. Carlyle. "Do you want to see a goat give birth? It's about to happen."

The attorney drew his handkerchief higher. "Thank you, but no."

A goat in the neighboring pen started bellyaching. The way she whined and nudged her snout against the fence was a sure sign of growing discomfort. It was beginning to cause a problem, because the doe sharing the pen was getting agitated, pacing and banging against the fencing. That goat was likely to cause harm to the other doe if Julia couldn't get them pacified.

"Would you please go pet that goat?" she asked Mr. Carlyle. "She is kidding for the first time and is nervous."

Mr. Carlyle still clasped his handkerchief over his nose, but his eyes grew round. "And you think petting will help?"

"Oh yes. Goats are social creatures, and petting will calm her until I can get there. Would you be an angel?" She smiled up at him.

All trace of kindness and compassion evaporated from Mr. Carlyle's face, but he folded his handkerchief, stepped to the second pen, and cautiously touched the goat's head with his fingertips. The goat responded, butting her head against his palm, licking him, sniffing.

The air practically turned blue from the salty words of Dierenpark's famously proper attorney.

"She just wants to get to know you." Julia laughed, her attention split between the baby kid about to make its first appearance in the world and the sight of Ashton Carlyle trying to touch a goat with as little contact as possible.

The baby's snout appeared, distracting Julia as she leaned over to guide the new goat into the world. She used a towel to clear the mucus from the kid's nose.

"Look, it's a boy," she said. "What a little sweetheart he is with all those dark patches."

The doe turned her head to lick the newborn kid clean, but when the newborn should be responding to his mother, he remained motionless. Julia used the towel to pry his mouth open, scooping more mucus out, but still no sign of life.

Okay, be calm. Although it was hard while this baby goat lay unmoving in the straw. She knew from the farmer's instructions that if a newborn kid didn't breathe on its own, she should rub it hard.

"Come on," she urged, using the towel to briskly rub the sodden newborn's ribs and belly. "Come on, breathe!" she ordered.

Still nothing. She sensed Ashton moving closer to the pen, leaning over to watch, but she didn't need any distractions right now. In the past week, she had delivered almost twenty baby goats, and every one of them had lived. This was the first one that didn't know how to breathe.

It was perfectly formed. It was a beautiful little billy goat with a creamy white coat and patches of dark brown. Four tiny hooves, a cute little tail. She was going to make this goat breathe through sheer force of will.

She reached beneath the kid so she could massage both sides of his ribs at once. He didn't weigh much, and she lifted him entirely off the straw to rub hard.

"Come on, baby, take a breath." This was awful, just awful. It didn't seem fair for this little goat to die before it even drew its first breath.

The single bleat took her by surprise, and she froze. Then another squeak.

Her gaze flew to Ashton, who leaned over the fence with a rapt expression on his face. He met her eyes.

"I think he's alive," he whispered.

"I think so, too," she whispered back, afraid to move. This might be the most amazing moment of her life.

The smile he sent her over the rim of the fence was dazzling. He must have been hit with the same rush of exhilaration that swamped her. Inanely, she noticed how fine and white his teeth looked in the dimness of the barn.

The bleating continued, and she gently lowered the goat to the barn floor, moving aside so the mother could continue licking and prodding her baby. Even now, the kid was struggling to get his hooves beneath him, rolling and experimenting with his weight. It didn't work. He collapsed into the hay with a mournful squeak, provoking a spurt of laughter from both her and Ashton.

She sat back on her haunches and smiled with the sheer joy of being alive.

<hr />

It was surely the most amazing thing he had ever witnessed. As the only child of parents who had also been only children, Ashton had no siblings, cousins, uncles, or aunts, so he had never been around newborn babies. His mother's bad lungs meant they had never had a pet or come within an acre of a barnyard.

So he had never seen anything being born or watched a living creature experience the first few moments of life. He'd held his breath while Julia worked over the newborn goat, her expression fierce as she struggled to make that goat breathe. And it did!

Her determination came as no surprise to him. For years he had been reading the thank-you letters she penned to Nickolaas Vandermark, spilling her heart out as she recounted the wonders of anatomy and physiology classes, of visiting the museums and libraries, of her dreams to trek into the Far East as a missionary. A tiny piece of Ashton had fallen in love with the bright, ambitious girl who wrote those letters. Not that he had any real aspirations for her. He loved her the same way he loved reading about Marco Polo. The way he loved a Brahms symphony. With admiration, with awe, with the desperate need to know what was going to happen next.

He always sent back polite letters of acknowledgment, using Nickolaas Vandermark's autograph stamp, as was the custom for the office correspondence he handled. Mr. Vandermark had no interest in the academic progress of Miss Broeder. He'd never asked to see any of her letters or inquired about her grades. It wasn't until the royal scolding the other day that he'd learned there was something odd about the Vandermarks' need to keep the Broeders placated.

All Ashton knew was that he needed to get Julia readmitted to college, or he was probably going to lose his job. And the glory of completing the gutta-percha contracts would be passed to some other attorney who would reap the rewards of what Ashton had sown.

He watched Julia as she raked the soiled hay into the corner and replaced it with fresh.

"Well, this was a bit more of an adventure than I bargained for when I set out from the city this morning," he said, possibly the understatement of the year. "Now that it is behind us, when can we leave for Philadelphia? The sooner an appeal is mounted, the quicker we can get you back in school."

Julia didn't look at him as she cleaned her hands in a bucket of water. She seemed to take extraordinary care as she lathered a nail brush and scrubbed beneath and atop her nails, around the cuticles.

"I don't want to go to Philadelphia," she finally said as she swished the brush in a bucket of water then rinsed her hands.

His smile remained tightly in place. "I must not have heard you correctly. Would you repeat that, please?"

She fiddled with a towel. "I'm thinking of veterinary medicine. These last few days have been very fulfilling, and I've never given much thought to treating animals before."

Ashton had difficulty seeing through the haze of red, but he kept it out of his voice. The first technique in the art of negotiation was to never let the opponent know how badly you needed something. His father had retired from his job as an accountant three years ago due to the lucrative income Ashton was earning. He wasn't going to let the whims of Julia Broeder endanger his career or his family's financial security.

"It seems to me that medicine is not only more profitable but far more valuable to human happiness," he said with admirable ease. "Allow me to help you reenroll in medical school. We can have you back in college by next week if we both play our cards right."

She smiled and shook her head. "All of these goats will be delivering in the coming week," she said, waving her arm at the herd. "I've already committed myself to the job."

"Can't someone else do it? What about your brother?"

She wrinkled her nose. "Emil has never been too good with anything that requires a lot of thinking."

"Then let me hire someone from the city. I can have someone here by tomorrow."

It was maddening the way she blithely walked to the far end of the barn, cranking the rusty old arm of a water pump to fill a bucket. "I'd rather do it myself. I promised the farmer, and it's kind of fun, you know?"

He clenched his fists. This girl seemed to enjoy things that were *kind of fun*, like mingling with firemen she didn't know very well and squandering a college education to play milkmaid out in a barn.

He mustn't get angry. He needed to figure out the source of her reluctance, find a solution for it, and then get her on that train to Philadelphia. It was impossible to know what Nickolaas Vandermark's reaction would be if Ashton failed to get Julia back into medical school, but he didn't intend to find out.

"Miss Broeder," he began in his calmest voice, "you have three years of exceptional grades. When you visited my office last week, you indicated that your actions in Philadelphia were impulsive. I cannot believe you will derail your entire career over that decision. Tell me why you are reluctant to return to Philadelphia, and I will find a solution for it."

Whatever she needed, he would get it for her. Help delivering the goats, a recommendation from their congressman, a petition signed by every Vandermark in the nation. Whatever she needed . . .

She stood, indecision on her face. She was filthy, her hair spilling out of a sloppy braid, and yet she was oddly attractive to him. This was a girl who literally rolled up her sleeves to tackle whatever job was placed before her, and there was something terribly appealing about that sort of fearlessness.

"I want to deliver these goats," she said simply. "I gave Mr. Hofstad my word, and I am needed here for at least another week. I won't be able to sleep if I walk out on that commitment."

The bleating of a goat caught her attention. "Oh, twins!" she said as she climbed back over the pen to hunch down beside the goat that had just delivered the struggling billy goat minutes ago. Ashton clenched his teeth as he prepared to wait out the delivery of another animal, but things were about to get worse. The goat he had been petting earlier had also flopped to the ground and was kicking.

Julia noticed, and within a moment she had climbed over to the neighboring pen. "This doe has never delivered before, and it is going to be difficult for her. Could you please tend the goat I just left? It will be an easy birth since she just delivered, but she needs help. Please!"

He steeled himself. Hadn't he just silently vowed he would get whatever she needed? Julia was completely overwhelmed by a herd of goats at the moment and would be useless if he dragged her away from them while her heart was here in this barn. If he was going to persuade her to go to Philadelphia, he needed to meet her halfway.

He swung a leg over the fence as he'd seen her do, pausing at the sight of the ground. It was damp with mud and some other liquid he feared to name. His shoes, made of imported Italian leather and polished to a high shine, cost more than most people earned in a month. He tentatively set a foot down, wincing as he put his weight on it and felt it slide in the muck. Trying to ignore the squishing noise his shoes made as he crossed the pen, he stood over the struggling doe, ignorant of what to do next.

"Just have a towel on hand and be prepared to catch the kid as he drops out," Julia called out helpfully.

He grabbed for a towel, clinging to it like a lifeline. He'd rather not get a close-up view of the goat's exposed hindquarters, but her tail was raised and it was hard to look anywhere else. He should have taken off his coat. He was hot and this was going to be messy, but it was too late now. This was moving a lot faster than the last time.

He squatted down just in time to catch the warm newborn goat as it slipped from the birth canal into his hands. Ashton was too overcome to speak, couldn't even draw a breath. The newborn was slippery and struggling. Wriggling, bleating, glistening . . . and amazingly alive as it twisted in his hands.

"I did it!" he shouted, scrambling to wipe the mucus from the goat's already bleating mouth. "I did it!"

"Indeed you did!" came a shout of approval from the neighboring stall.

He set the newborn in the straw and scooted back as the doe licked her newest baby. He didn't know what to do with his slimy hands, but he held them aloft while he gazed at the new life he'd just delivered. Over the years in his role as an attorney, he had negotiated gifts for restless Tamil natives on their Sri Lankan tea plantations, risked rat bites and drowning to inspect the ports used by Vandermark ships, worked through the night, and lain flat on his belly in the gallery of the New York Stock Exchange. Today he had delivered a goat, and somehow it had been the most gratifying of all.

6

Ashton had vowed he would do whatever it took to get Julia to Philadelphia and back into college, and apparently that meant he was going to help her deliver dozens of baby goats. It was going to be a grubby, uncomfortable week, but if he wanted to keep his job with the Vandermarks, he must meet Julia halfway in order to earn her cooperation.

After delivering his first goat, Ashton shucked his coat and vest, unhooked his watch and chain, rolled up his sleeves, and set to work. There was nothing to be done about his shoes. They were a casualty of the war to get Julia Broeder back into college, but at least these goats would learn to appreciate a man with style as he moved around the barn.

He returned to Dierenpark only long enough to make arrangements for telegrams to be sent to his Manhattan office and to his father. His clerk knew where all the property files were located and could turn them over to a fellow attorney for administration while he was gone. It would cause some grumbling among his colleagues, but everyone was aware of Nickolaas Vandermark's eccentricities and demands.

One of those demands was a baffling sense of urgency to keep the Broeder family happy. Had a member of the Broeder family been kind to the old man when he'd lived at Dierenpark as a child? Or when a fourteen-year-old Nickolaas found his father dead in the river? It was hard to imagine what kind of trauma such an incident would have caused, but it was bad enough that Nickolaas Vandermark never returned to Dierenpark. Combine that traumatic experience with the mixed blessing of inheriting extreme wealth, and it was bound to cause some eccentricities. In any event, it meant that Ashton's job was to remain at the goat barn until Julia's mission was completed, and then get her back into medical school.

Over the next few days, Julia handled most of the birthing work, while Ashton carried water, cleared out soiled hay, and laid down fresh. He brought grain to feed the goats and shoveled dung. About once an hour, he waded into the large pen of pregnant goats, scanning for the signs of impending labor. At first they all looked alike to him, but Julia taught him to recognize a Nubian from an Alpine from a Toggenburg goat. It didn't take long to notice their personalities and quirks, as well.

And they were *smart*. One doe always seemed particularly curious, sticking close to him as he made his hourly inspection of the goats. She was a pure white Alpine goat with large eyes and alert ears that wiggled and rotated at every sound. It wasn't until he left the pen on his third visit that he noticed the Alpine carefully unlatching the gate exactly as he had done. The rascal had been spying on him! The gate was hanging open, and a dozen goats casually wandered into the pasture. It took half an hour to get them rounded back up and latched inside, but within minutes, the white Alpine was unlatching the gate again.

When he confessed what happened to Julia, she moved the Alpine to a different pen with a more complicated latch. "Mr. Hofstad warned me about that," she said. "Try not to let the goats watch you do anything you don't want them to emulate. They'll learn how to operate that water pump if they can get to it."

"I ought to teach them how to make me breakfast," Ashton grumbled, but he was secretly impressed with how these curious, gentle goats were starting to grow on him. He was sacrificing a week of his life for these goats, and he might as well learn to enjoy their company.

Mr. Hofstad came by a few times to check on their progress and bring them fresh clothing. The old farmer made sure they had plenty to eat and kept their lanterns topped off with kerosene, but for the most part, Ashton and Julia were on their own for the kidding.

The work was dirty, demanding, and never-ending, but he couldn't recall a time in his life when he'd had such fun. Goats had no respect for working hours and were happy to go into labor at any time during the day or night. Julia had been sleeping on a cot in the kidding barn, but Ashton stayed with the majority of the goats in the pole barn. Twice he'd been roused in the middle of the night when a goat needed transfer into the kidding barn.

He estimated they were delivering between ten and twenty baby goats per day. As busy as it was, there were still long stretches when there was nothing to do. He and Julia sat on the floor of the kidding barn, leaning against the wall and talking about everything from Julia's ambitions to see Mongolia to his love of baseball.

"It is the perfect spectator sport," he told her. "My father and I would find a spot in the bleachers, and the games are so long and boring we had time to talk about everything under the sun. And then would come the moment when the bases are loaded, a good batter steps to the plate, and that amazing, unmistakable sound when the crack of a bat echoes over the stadium. The whole world explodes in a roar, and we'd stand and scream until our throats were raw while the men rounded the bases. Then we'd take our seats again, and Dad and I would go back to the conversation where we left off."

"What about your mother? Did she ever go?" Julia asked.

He sighed. His mother's health had always been tricky. Sometimes she had to spend weeks in bed. Perhaps that was one of the reasons he'd always been so close to his father. "She was never well enough to leave the house that long," Ashton said, but he was careful not to paint his family in a negative light, for he couldn't imagine two better, more loving, more generous parents. "My mother couldn't go with us to the games, but she always wanted a blow-by-blow account when we returned. I think my father enjoyed that part almost as much as the games."

He picked up a piece of straw, shredding it while reaching back toward the golden memories that would always be a touchstone for him. They'd had a good life. Not perfect. They'd had more than their fair share of medical bills and illness, but it never dampened the sheer joy of a loving family. "She died when I was fifteen. After that, it was just Dad and me, but we still go to the park whenever the Dodgers are playing at home."

They still lived together, too. After Ashton earned enough money to get their house back from the bank, he climbed up to the shabby eighth-story apartment where his father had lived after losing the house. Ashton laid the title of their old Brooklyn townhouse on the table, alongside their rent payment book for the apartment.

"You can burn the rent stubs if you want," he said quietly. "We don't need them anymore."

His father had no idea how diligently Ashton had been saving to get their house back. When he picked up the house title and realized what he held in his hand, his father's eyes pooled with tears. His Adam's apple bobbed, and he swallowed several times before speaking. "Okay, son," he said quietly. "Thank you."

There was no need for thanks. His father was the great, generous foundation of his world. They would not have lost their house in the first place if his father hadn't mortgaged it to pay Ashton's college tuition. They never spoke of it again, but they both moved back into the modest townhouse where they'd been so happy. They still went to baseball games together. They went to church on Sunday, and afterwards to Chinatown to feast on gingered duck and fried dumplings. No man had a better father.

When he first went to college, Ashton dreamed of joining the foreign service to see the world. To be able to walk the Silk Road, to sail the seas of the Orient, to be an envoy to the ancient monasteries in Lhasa.

Those romantic boyhood dreams came to an end when he realized there were more important things than walking the Silk Road. There was the love between a father and a son. There was the obligation to repay a debt, to build a foundation of financial security and ensure they need never fear for next month's rent. There was the satisfaction that came from a job well done.

It had been a good choice, one he never regretted. And if he sometimes felt a twinge of envy when he read Julia's letters from college?

It was a minor thing. He looked forward to her letters that babbled of her soaring Oriental dreams and always wished her well.

Strange, but the only thing he and Julia never spoke about during their endless tasks of caring for the goats was her return to college. Each time he tried to broach the subject she diverted his attention to a kid who needed help learning to nurse, or a water trough that needed refilling, or countless other things. He finally gave up, figuring Julia would be ready to return to Philadelphia as soon as the last goat was safely delivered.

At least they were never hungry. In addition to the meals provided by Mr. Hofstad, once a day Sophie van Riijn came from Dierenpark with a huge basket of food. How could he have been visiting Dierenpark for years and never noticed this stunning woman before? The first time Sophie arrived, standing on the other side of the white picket fence with her basket, he had to blink his eyes to be sure he wasn't imagining the angelic vision that had just arrived on the farm.

"That's Sophie," Julia said as she set down a bucket. "You might want to close your mouth to be sure you don't attract flies."

"But who *is* she?" Ashton asked.

"Her mother used to be the cook at Dierenpark. Sophie isn't on the payroll, so that's why you've never met her before. Anyway, she likes it up here and can't stay away. Actually, I think she is hiding up here. She's still mourning her fiancé, so you might want to wait a half hour before you attempt to snatch her away like Paris absconding with Helen of Troy."

He'd have to be deaf not to hear the jealousy in Julia's tone. Which was ridiculous. Sophie was lovely, but that sort of willowy beauty had never appealed to him. Strangely, he'd go for the girl with straw in her hair and daring enough to deliver goats while still smiling.

❈

At first Julia didn't believe Ashton would actually stay for the duration of the birthing season, but he settled in without complaint and worked from dawn until dusk. Plenty of times he worked in the middle of the night when a doe went into labor.

When he knelt beside her by the warm glow of the lantern, his sleeves turned back to reveal strong wrists and capable hands, she thought he might be the most attractive man she'd ever seen. Wasn't that odd? She had never taken much notice of him when he was the prim attorney sitting across the desk at Dierenpark, but ever since he'd rolled up his sleeves and got elbow deep in goat birthing, she found him impossible to ignore.

They got along brilliantly together, laughing during the chores and chatting amiably during times of rest. And she loved looking at him. With his starched collar gone and shirt unbuttoned to reveal the strong column of his neck, he looked relaxed and happy. He was smart and fun and supportive.

The only dark cloud on the horizon was when he nagged her about getting back into college. It was annoying, and she wished he would stop. Didn't they have enough to contend with without worrying about Philadelphia?

Besides, the topic worried her. She hadn't exactly told Ashton everything about her expulsion. She'd pretty effectively burned her bridges on the way out the door when she gave vent to her temper before the Board of Trustees. The prospect of showing up on bended knee, appealing for their mercy . . .

It was too much. There was no way she could reenroll before January anyway, and she didn't want to talk about it right now.

But Ashton did. The issue came to a head one afternoon while he was helping her repair a wooden feed trough that tipped over when one of its legs rotted through. Neither one of them knew what they were doing, but Julia figured they had everything they needed in Mr. Hofstad's rusted old toolbox, and how hard could it be? She found a block of clean wood that could be cut to size, and Ashton sawed it to the appropriate dimension. They flipped the trough over to remove the rotted wood.

"This is a bit like surgery," Julia said as she pried out the old nails to remove the rotted piece of wood. She gave a crisp nod when she saw how perfectly the new leg fit in place. Maybe she didn't need to go back to medical school, after all. She didn't *need* to be a doctor in order to find satisfaction in life. She could work with animals. Or maybe become a nurse.

"Have you thought about how to approach Dean Kreutzer at the school?" Ashton asked as he pounded a nail in place. "You know her best, and any insight you can give me will help prepare our case."

"It's very impressive the way you wield that hammer," she replied. "I'd suspect you've done this before, were it not for that canary-yellow vest you wore the other day. No man who feels comfortable wearing that shade of yellow ought to be familiar with the wielding of farm implements."

"The dean?" he pressed. "What were her precise objections to the incident with the dog?"

"I'm thinking maybe Nickolaas Vandermark won't mind if I don't return to medical school."

"Don't talk like that." Ashton had stopped nailing, sitting back on his haunches to look her directly in the eyes. "He wants you back in college, and I intend to make that happen even if I have to pound on the door of every medical college on the eastern seaboard."

"I think Mr. Vandermark wants me to be happy and doesn't care if I become a doctor or not."

"You really don't know Nickolaas Vandermark," he said in a warning tone.

"I know that he is a decent, caring man. Almost every month that I've been in school he's sent me packages and little gifts. And I know he reads the letters I send because one semester when I mentioned we were about to start studying dentistry, he sent a leather-bound case of dentistry tools. When I mentioned that I grew up reading the tales of Marco Polo and hoped to someday see Mongolia, he sent me a watercolor of the palace at Xanadu. It was charming—and proves that he isn't as heartless as you think."

"I sent the gifts."

He spoke so quietly she wasn't certain she'd heard him correctly, but the odd way he looked at her confirmed it. She stilled, trying to absorb this new information as Ashton looked at her through cautious blue eyes. He looked part defensive, part vulnerable, and suddenly everything made sense. His knowledge of China and Tibet. His passion for Asian food. Even his vests that were usually embroidered with Chinese symbols.

244

"Why would you do such a thing?" she finally asked.

"Because I admired you," he said simply. His face flushed and he turned away, grabbing the hammer and pounding another nail into the leg of the overturned trough.

She blinked in confusion. "But you never said anything. All those years when you'd visit Dierenpark, you never breathed a word."

He didn't look at her as he put the tools back in the box. "It is common for Mr. Vandermark to send gifts and holiday remembrances to his business associates and the charities he supports. I usually handled such transactions, and of course he approved of sending you something now and again. But when I read the thank-you letters you sent, I wanted to do more. I still used the rubber autograph stamp because it would seem strange if you knew most of them came from me. But you shared my love of the Far East, and I wanted to send you something nice."

"I never knew . . ." Her heart squeezed. No one had ever looked after her or cared about her well-being like that, and it made her want to weep. He'd been doing these kind, thoughtful things for the past three years and never once asked for a thank-you. Part of her wanted to rush into his arms and plaster kisses all over his face, but she stayed rooted to the spot, overwhelmed by the surge of emotions welling inside.

Now that Ashton had started talking, it was as if the floodgates had opened. "My mother was always sick when I was growing up, and it terrified me," he said. "She and my father were my whole world. She had seizures, and when she suffered fits, it was horrible. I wanted to help, but my father always sent me to another room. There was nothing I could do for her, and I think it bothered them for me to witness her seizures."

He turned to look at her. "When I went to my room, I found comfort opening the pages into the world of Marco Polo. There I found no terminally ill mothers. No father struggling to hold back tears as he watched his wife slip away year by year. I found adventure and discovery. I found ancient monasteries and the perfumed courts of Kublai Khan and mountain peaks so high they seemed to pierce the heavens."

The wistfulness faded from his face as he turned to look at her. "My mother died when I was fifteen, and my dad still mourns her. I am all he has left, and I can't leave him, not after everything we've been through together. I'll never sail to China or anywhere else in Asia . . . but when I first read your letters, I caught a glimpse of those long-ago memories that once sustained me. Julia, I want you to live your dreams. I want you to sail the seas of the Orient and drink yak milk and listen to the sounds of the bamboo flute as you drift to sleep at night. I will do anything to see that you get there."

Her heart thudded faster as he spoke, all of her childhood dreams stirring and reawakening. It was almost as if she could feel the cool winds of the high Eurasian steppes on her face. She'd never met anyone else who understood these dreams, but Ashton knew. He understood.

It was going to hurt when this week was over. He would have been a good friend. A good partner. A part of her sensed that he could be much more than that, but she couldn't let herself toy with those dangerous emotions. Women who chose the life of a medical missionary rarely had husbands. When she'd accepted a commission to work abroad, she knew it meant she probably would be a spinster for the rest of her life.

She had never questioned that decision, but looking at Ashton, so handsome and earnest as he sat across from her on the floor of a goat barn, made her long for more. She longed for *him*.

"Did you know that female physicians who become missionaries are almost always spinsters?"

The question seemed to take him aback, but he recovered quickly. "It had never occurred to me."

"I think it strange . . . no, I think it *unfair*, that we are expected to tromp off into the world without knowing what we are passing up."

He quirked a brow. "What about that fireman in Philadelphia? You seemed quite friendly with him."

There was the faintest trace of jealously beneath his words, and it flattered her. "Ross McKinney had a fine toboggan I wanted, but nothing else."

She wanted Ashton Carlyle. His integrity, his intelligence. His willingness to roll up his sleeves and face the challenges of the day with humor and a sense of adventure. She leaned forward, tilting her face close to his, and was thrilled at the flare of attraction in his eyes.

"You know I can't leave New York," he said. "No matter where your adventures take you, I will remain in the city with my father."

"I know," she whispered. One of the things she now adored about Ashton was his big-hearted, affectionate relationship with his father. Ashton was a man of honor, one who could be trusted to care for his family. It made him even more attractive to her.

She leaned in to kiss him; he met her halfway. They grabbed each other so hard she almost fell off the stool, but he held her tight and kissed her until they were both breathless.

"This is probably a bad idea," Ashton whispered against her lips, but he was smiling as he said it.

"It's a wonderful idea. Kiss me again."

He did, but it didn't last long. The incessant bleating of a Toggenburg goat reminded them they still had two dozen goats to safely deliver. But as they tended to the arrival of six newborn kids that day, they laughed and kissed as though the rest of the world had stopped existing outside the safety of this idyllic goat farm in the middle of rural New York.

7

The moon was high and the night so chilly she could see her breath in the air, but Julia did not want to go to bed. There were a million stars overhead, and sometimes she simply liked to gaze up at them. She sat on the bench a few yards from the barn, where she would be close enough to hear a goat in distress but far enough to enjoy the blessedly sweet air. From here she could see Ashton moving inside the barn, dimly lit by the single kerosene lantern that gave the barn a warm glow and seemed to soothe the goats. It was cool enough that he wore his yellow vest and suit jacket, refilling all the water troughs in his Italian leather shoes. She really ought to go help, but she was so tired, and quite frankly . . . she liked looking at him. How many men could negotiate international contracts one day then deliver a baby goat the next?

He had been a good sport about things. After agreeing to help her with the kidding, he never once complained and they made a good team, but they were nearing the end of the grand adventure. Only seven more goats were still to deliver, and after that she would have to figure out what she intended to do with the rest of her life.

A thud came from the barn as Ashton replaced the water bucket by the pump then headed her way. All she could see was his silhouette as he crossed the yard. Crickets chirped in the distance, and it felt like the most natural thing in the world as he joined her on the bench. He followed her gaze upward.

"Sometimes it is hard to imagine those are the same stars and moon people look at from China," he said in a wistful voice.

Who would have guessed that Dierenpark's spick-and-span attorney would have this deeply buried streak of a romantic adventurer inside?

"Someday I'll get there," she said. "I don't know how, but I know I'm not destined to spend the rest of my life here."

He sighed and leaned forward, bracing his forearms on his knees. "Then what are you destined for, if not to get back into medical school?"

"Not that again." There weren't many things that frightened her, but the prospect of traveling to Philadelphia with a fine attorney at her side and still failing to be readmitted to college had been keeping her awake at night. If she failed, she didn't want an audience when it happened.

"I'm just not sure I'm meant to go back to medical school," she hedged.

"What's holding you back?" Ashton prodded. "And don't say it is because you are thinking of veterinary school. No missionaries are sent overseas to treat animals. If you want to be a medical missionary, you need to become a physician."

She fidgeted on the bench. "I haven't exactly told you everything about what happened at my expulsion hearing," she admitted.

Ashton stiffened. "Let's hear it," he said grimly. When she hesitated, he dropped some of the scary tone and spoke softly. "You've got the benefit of attorney-client privilege. I promise not to tell a soul, but I really do need to know everything."

Sitting on the goat farm's only bench, she told Ashton what she had said that terrible day. She had been invited into the conference room to make a brief statement and answer questions posed to her by the members of the Board of Trustees. She did her best to explain her actions, but Dean Kreutzer had been entirely unsympathetic, her face grim as she reprimanded Julia for operating on a living creature without supervision, compounded by the theft of the dog. Julia knew it had been wrong to break in to the operating room, but she had done the right thing in getting that dog out of the city. She called the dean a heartless and cruel woman who didn't deserve the title of "doctor" if she would knowingly consent to placing a living, breathing animal back in the hands of Ross McKinney and his dog-fighting friends.

Dean Kreutzer, a woman who had done so much to open the medical profession to women, had turned white when Julia insulted her. The college's entire board had been at that meeting, and Julia was stunned that every one of them supported the dean. How could men and women devoted to medicine be so heartless?

She stood at the end of the conference table and held up her pinky finger. "I've got more courage in this little finger than the lot of you put together," she had said.

Ashton's eyes widened, but he didn't condemn her, just waited in silence for her to finish the story.

"Things didn't go so well after that," she admitted. "They asked me to leave the room while they made a decision, and I did. It only took them five minutes to decide I wasn't a suitable candidate for their school."

She was embarrassed and ashamed. Not for saving the dog, but Dean Kreutzer hadn't deserved the childish temper tantrum Julia had unloaded on her. It had been a frightening and stressful situation, but doctors needed to learn to master their emotions, and Julia had not done so.

"After thinking about it, I really don't want to go back and face them," she said.

Ashton's laugh was mildly amused. "I imagine not."

She brightened. "You understand, then?"

"I understand, but you still need to do it. If you were childish and undisciplined, you need to go back and own up to it. That's more a sign of maturity than hiding on a goat farm."

Her gaze strayed back to the barn, where the muffled sounds of goats moving about mingled with crickets and the occasional bleat of a baby kid. It was safe here, and she'd relished every moment of this past week with Ashton. It had been a haven from the stress and disappointment of Philadelphia.

In her heart she knew Ashton was right, but for now she wanted to carve each moment of these last days on her soul, for she knew this week would forever linger in her memory as one of perfect, idyllic happiness.

⌒◆⌒

All the goats had been delivered. In the past two weeks, Julia had helped deliver over a hundred newborns and had only lost three kids that never started breathing. Her work here was probably done, but she and Ashton walked the grounds with Mr. Hofstad to be sure.

The old goat farmer still wore his arm in a sling but seemed quite pleased with the burgeoning herd. She wasn't sure what he babbled in Dutch, but Julia figured it must be good given the warm approval in his tone.

Claudia's morning sickness was no longer quite as bad, so she walked the farm with them, one of her baby sons draped over her shoulder. She did her best to provide translation.

"Mr. Hofstad says you have done a fine job," Claudia told them. "He offers you each the pick of the litter if you'd like to keep a goat."

Ashton spewed a mouthful of the cider he'd been sipping from a flask. He coughed, but Julia sensed he was covering a laugh as he swiped his mouth with the back of his hand.

"There is a very clever Alpine," he said. "My father could probably use her to chart baseball statistics."

Claudia provided the translation, and Mr. Hofstad took a few steps toward the pens of Alpines before Ashton interrupted and tried to communicate he was only joking.

Julia prodded him. "Go on. You know you'll miss her once you are back in the city."

"I'll miss you, and I'll miss Sophie's cooking, but I'll be glad to see the last of a goat who unties my shoelaces, noses into my pockets, and has learned to unlatch every gate on this property. As of today, she is officially Mr. Hofstad's problem again."

But he was smiling as he said it. She wanted to keep listening to him talk. Even when he was annoyed, Ashton couldn't hide the streak of humor that lurked just beneath the surface. It was fascinating and attractive and annoying. She wished she could stop her thoughts from running along these lines.

But most of all she hoped Mr. Hofstad would find something else that needed doing at the farm. She didn't want her work here to end. It would mean facing Philadelphia and Dean Kreutzer. It would mean confronting the possibility that her medical career really was over.

And it would mean losing Ashton Carlyle forever. He would go back to his office in Manhattan and forget his week on a goat farm with the country girl who could never fit into his world even if she wanted to. If she became a medical missionary, she would ultimately board a ship and sail toward the sunrise until she reached Asia. And Ashton would remain in the city, working in a skyscraper, living in his comfortable townhouse, and going to baseball games with his father. She would never see him again.

Even thinking about it was painful. She pushed the thoughts from her mind and looked to the old goat farmer.

"Are you sure I can't help with weaning the kids?" she asked Mr. Hofstad. Surely that would require a lot of work, and she wouldn't mind lingering in the village a few more weeks. Claudia translated, but the old farmer shook his head, letting out a stream of reassuring words.

Ashton peered at her through knowing eyes. "Perhaps you'd like to offer to paint his barn? Build a new pen? Help with the spring planting? If you play your cards right, you might even still be here for the birthing next November."

"I'm just trying to be helpful," she defended.

His eyes softened. "And you are helpful. You give everything your best, even if it means working on a goat farm when you ought to be finishing up medical school. You are driven and daring. If someone tells you no, you will always prove them wrong. You are sometimes tough, sometimes terrified . . . but I have faith in you, Julia. You are not destined to spend the rest of your life on a goat farm."

He was right, but the thought of returning to Philadelphia still intimidated her, for the one thing she had never learned how to do was fail, and her odds of failing her appeal were high.

She didn't know what she would do with the rest of her life if this door was finally slammed in her face.

❖

Ashton headed to the mansion, the wind causing the too-big clothes he'd borrowed from the farmer to flap in the November breeze. Yesterday, Sophie had offered to try to wash the worst of the goat filth from his tailor-made suit, which was now surely ruined, but it was the only thing he had to wear back on the train to the city.

Besides, he suspected that by now he would have had a response to the telegram he sent two days ago, and he wanted to read it without Julia hovering over him. Julia's brother couldn't read, which was the only reason Ashton had felt so comfortable sending Emil to town with his hastily drafted message. He needed answers, and he wouldn't be able to find them here at Dierenpark.

He continued walking down the path toward the mansion, its rough-hewn granite blocks coming into view around the bend of twisted old juniper trees. Each time he came here, he always pondered the same question: Why did the Vandermarks hold on to this grand old estate if they never intended to return to it? Dierenpark cost a fortune in annual property taxes. They paid a staff to ensure the contents of the house were not plundered, for it was well known that in their haste to leave Dierenpark all those decades ago, a treasure trove of artwork, silver, and jewelry had been left inside. All of it untouched, as though frozen in time.

He mounted the worn stone steps leading to the covered portico and knocked on the ornate wooden door inlaid with bronze castings. It wouldn't surprise him if there was a castle somewhere in Europe missing its front door.

Sophie answered his knock, looking as pretty as the morning sun with her blond hair worn in a casual braid over her shoulder and humor in her eyes.

"You look like a dirt farmer," she said with a glance at his homespun dungarees held up by a pair of suspenders.

"You look like the woman who is going to answer all my prayers by having a freshly cleaned and pressed suit for me."

She laughed, and even her laughter had a musical cadence that sounded pure and lovely. "Follow me. Florence worked miracles with the suit, but I'm afraid there wasn't much we could do about that silk vest. Oh, and a telegram arrived for you this morning."

It was on the mahogany table in the front hall. Ashton slipped it into his pocket, reluctant to read it before Julia's best friend. "Thank you," he said. "My suit?"

He followed Sophie to the back of the mansion, passing beneath gothic arches and wood-paneled walls until he reached the oldest part of the house, a charming room reflecting its seventeenth-century Dutch origins with a low-beamed ceiling and a few chairs and tables in quaint groupings. A row of diamond-paned windows overlooked the river, but all Ashton could think of was the mouth-watering aroma drifting from the nearby kitchen.

"What am I smelling?" he asked. "And please tell me you've made plenty to share or I may grow faint from hunger."

"It's Dutch *gevulde koeken*. Almond cookies, in English."

"They smell like food of the heavens."

She laughed again. "They are food of fresh butter, sugar, ground almonds, a little vanilla, and I like to add a dollop of homemade raspberry jam. Would you like one?"

"Sophie, I don't know if you noticed, but I am about to pass out from craving one of those cookies."

He followed her to the kitchen and was stunned to see the work table hidden beneath several feet of cookies. Florence Hengeveld, the housekeeper at Dierenpark since before Ashton had been born, was putting the cookies in little brown sacks.

"Are you feeding an army?" he asked. There must be hundreds of little bags of cookies.

"We sometimes provide food for travelers who sail up the river on the steamships," Sophie said casually. It was an odd comment, but he didn't have time to process it after he took his first bite of *gevulde koeken* and nearly fainted at the explosion of warm, buttery flavor.

He knew after a week of eating from the baskets Sophie delivered to the goat farm that she was a good cook, but these cookies defied description. He might never be the same man again.

254

But he hadn't come here to sample Sophie's baking. He just needed his suit so he could leave on tomorrow's train. The housekeeper brought him his freshly laundered clothes, and as Sophie had predicted, his silk vest was a rumpled, ruined mess, but his suit looked clean and, more importantly, it no longer stank like a goat barn.

With the clean clothes slung over his arm, he wandered toward the library, dragging the telegram out and flicking it open with impatient fingers. He drifted to a window, tilting the telegram into the light to read.

One of his former classmates from Yale was chief counsel for a hospital in Philadelphia and was familiar with the Women's Medical College. His friend confirmed that Dean Kreutzer was a decent woman, but one with a strict moral code. She could be reasoned with, but ethical standards were paramount.

It confirmed what he suspected. This was a winnable battle, and a rush of satisfaction filled him. It was true that he'd only come here on Nickolaas Vandermark's orders, but as time passed, it had become vitally important to make sure Julia did not derail her dreams. This telegram contained all the insight he needed to get Julia back into college.

A tiny piece of him—the small, selfish part—wanted to keep her in New York. If he got her back into college, she would eventually board a ship and sail to the other side of the world. He would never see her again, and that would be . . .

Well, it didn't really bear thinking of. He hoped she would continue writing him letters. He would never see the great sights of Asia, but Julia would, and if he could catch a glimpse of the faraway, wide, wondrous world through her eyes, it would be enough.

He set the telegram on the desk and changed out of the farmer's clothes. It was time to return to his world. The trousers fit him perfectly, lined with satin, the buttonholes smoothly finished. The freshly starched shirt still carried a trace of the clean smell of soap. He began to feel like himself once again. He clipped on his onyx cufflinks, straightened his collar, and rubbed his freshly shaven jaw to be sure he hadn't missed a spot. He smelled of new linen and men's cologne.

This brief, magical interlude at Dierenpark was coming to an end.

❖

Sophie insisted on hosting a grand feast to celebrate the end of the birthing season. It would be held on Dierenpark's magnificent terrace overlooking the river, and Sophie promised to make goat cheese tarts, along with clam chowder, lobster cakes, and apple pie.

As the sun began to set, Julia helped Sophie carry trays loaded with food down to the slate terrace overlooking the river. Candles were lit, Emil dragged out their father's old guitar, and the air was heady with laughter and celebration. Mr. Hofstad and his wife came, as did Ashton and the handful of servants who kept Dierenpark operating. Long after the food was consumed, they stayed to talk and laugh as the moon rose high and Emil fooled with the guitar.

Julia drifted to the far side of the terrace, leaning over the balustrade to watch the moonlight glisten on the river. She had been brave enough to set out for college in a new and strange city. While in Philadelphia, she'd landed her first paid job at a pharmacy, completed three years of demanding medical courses, and rescued a dog from angry firefighters. She had even performed three complete autopsies, yet nothing intimidated her as much as going back to face Dean Kreutzer and the possibility of complete failure.

There was a rasp of fabric and Ashton joined her at the balustrade. He smelled of pine soap and looked clipped and groomed, every inch the Manhattan attorney once again.

"You look very fine," she said, trying to inject a hint of light into her voice. "That little white Alpine goat won't even recognize you anymore."

One side of his mouth lifted in a faint smile, but it vanished quickly. "I plan on leaving for the train station at seven o'clock tomorrow morning. I trust you will be ready."

She turned away. She didn't want him to see the cowardice on her face. "I don't know . . ." Her voice trailed off, for she had no good explanation to give him other than that she was tired. And afraid.

"Don't back down on me now," he said, his face somber.

She sighed. "I still don't know if this is the right path for me, after all. If you saw the way Dean Kreutzer looked at me . . ."

His hand covered hers, warm and firm in the chilly night. "This is your first test," he said with quiet conviction. "Given the path you have chosen, there are going to be more, and it's going to be hard. There are going to be times when you will feel worn out, ground down, and you may begin to doubt yourself, but I have never seen someone run toward a dream with as much passion as you. Don't give up now, Julia. You've chosen a steep and daring path, and no matter how hard, how grueling, how intimidating . . . you are going to change the world wherever you go. You will leave a path behind you of people who have been healed and inspired because you came into their lives. Don't give up now."

No one had ever believed in her this much, and it was humbling. The lump in her throat made it impossible to speak. She turned her palm up to clasp his hand, and he squeezed it in return.

"Are you going to be at the train station tomorrow morning?"

She took a deep, fortifying breath. "I'll be there."

8

The conference room at the Women's Medical College of Pennsylvania was exactly as Julia remembered. Wood-paneled walls, the windows flanked by heavy maroon draperies, and a long table stretching down the length of the room. Julia and Ashton sat at one end of the table, Dean Kreutzer on the other. The dean wore her steel-gray hair in a bun, and her high lace collar made her look imperious, stiff, and sour, which was an accurate summation of Dean Kreutzer's personality. Along both sides of the table sat the men and women who made up the college's Board of Trustees. Rich philanthropists, renowned physicians, church leaders, and college professors. Not an ounce of humor on any of their faces.

Ashton had warned her to keep quiet and let him do most of the talking. "Miss Broeder's academic record speaks for itself," he said. "She has the academic abilities to soar through this program with distinction, but more importantly, she has the heart and stamina to work in the challenging field of medicine. Your college has a distinguished tradition of sending medical missionaries into the world, and Miss Broeder is eager to join their ranks. Such a calling will require a person of extraordinary passion and courage, and I believe Miss Broeder has demonstrated those qualities."

"It will also require wisdom and self-restraint," Dean Kreutzer said through stiff lips. "This is where Miss Broeder has been judged lacking."

Julia swallowed hard and gripped the seat of her chair. Although what the dean said was true, it was hard to sit mute while people discussed her fate, but she followed Ashton's lead and remained silent.

"Self-restraint is something that comes with age and maturity," Ashton countered. "Miss Broeder demonstrated a lack of both during the incident in question, and she is prepared to acknowledge such."

Dean Kreutzer pierced her with a stare. "Well, Miss Broeder? Do you regret your actions?"

She glanced at Ashton, who gave her a tiny nod to speak. Her knees were weak as she stood, and she braced her hands on the table to keep them from trembling. None of the members of the board had a glimmer of sympathy on their faces. These were the people before whom she'd arrogantly held up her pinky finger and declared she had more courage in that single digit than the lot of them combined, so she hadn't expected much sympathy.

"I regret insulting the courage of the members of the board," she began. "I don't personally know any of you and had no right to cast aspersions on your character. But I cannot make a liar of myself and say I regret saving the dog." She looked Dean Kreutzer in the eye. "I wish I could have found a way that complies with both the laws of man and the dictates of my conscience, but the situation was—"

Ashton grabbed her hand and tugged her back into her seat. This wasn't good. She'd probably just blown her chances by mouthing off again.

"As I'm sure we all agree," Ashton began, the embodiment of diplomacy, "Miss Broeder has an admirable desire to combat suffering, be it in a dog or in a human being. I would ask the board to consider the qualities of intelligence, compassion, and adaptability necessary for a medical missionary to succeed. However unconventional, Miss Broeder's actions in regards to the dog displayed quick thinking and ultimately rescued the dog in the face of firm opposition. Such qualities will serve a missionary well."

"And what has Miss Broeder learned from her experience earlier this month?" the dean asked, directing the question at Julia. She would have to answer for herself. She couldn't hide behind Ashton's eloquence.

"It taught me the advantages of a good attorney."

Laughter rumbled from a few board members, but it was quickly stifled when Dean Kreutzer shot them a warning glare.

"And if you do not have a good attorney whilst dealing with the sultan of Oman? Or the tribal leader of a Bengali village? As a missionary, you will encounter people of different backgrounds and perspectives, some of which you may find repugnant, and yet these are the people you shall serve. How shall you comport yourself in such trying circumstances?"

Flippant answers weren't what the dean needed to hear. Nor would hot-headed tirades work any better. The dean made an excellent point about the need for cool-headed tact when she ventured into a world that would surely have different norms and customs.

Over the past week, Ashton had left his cosseted life in the city to work alongside her in a goat barn. He didn't like it, but he handled the situation with patience and humor. He learned and adapted, and ultimately he accomplished his goal.

"I am learning patience," she began. "There is a Chinese proverb that says the best fighters are never angry. I will learn to manage my impulses and my temper. I cannot say I regret saving the dog, but I wish I had handled my anger better so as not to have offended the people who were most likely to be my staunchest allies."

She risked looking into the faces of the individual board members around the table. All of them were forward-thinking people who believed in education for women, who dedicated their lives to the care of the sick and the poor. They didn't deserve the broad brush she'd painted them with merely because they hadn't fallen in line behind an impetuous girl with more bravado than wisdom.

"I know I have much to learn from every person in this room." She looked directly at Dean Kreutzer, a woman who had been at the forefront of the battle to clear the way for women in medicine. "And I truly hope I have the opportunity to return to school so that I may do so."

It felt very different this time when Julia was asked to step outside to await the board's decision. For one thing, she had Ashton sitting on the hard bench beside her. The hallway was cramped and uncomfortable, with a bench designed more for beauty than for comfort. Whoever thought carved mahogany scrollwork on the back of a bench was a good idea? All it did was dig into her spinal column and make these few minutes even more exquisitely awful.

She glanced over at Ashton, who looked as uncomfortable as she felt. The waiting was torture, and she needed something to unwind the tension that ratcheted higher.

"Did you ever get a good scolding when you were a boy?" she asked. "Come on, let's hear it. I'll bet you were reckless and disorderly at least once in your life."

"I was the perfect child."

She snickered. "And what would your father say about that?"

"He would agree." He tossed the comment off blandly, but a hint of a smile threatened to ruin the straight line of his mouth.

She rolled her eyes. Someone like Ashton Carlyle probably wore a suit and tie even as a toddler, while she was making mud pies with Emil.

The door to the conference room opened, and the dean herself came out of the room, her manner still stiff and commanding. Julia stood, her mouth suddenly dry and her heart threatening to leap from her chest.

"The board has voted," Dean Kreutzer said. "We have concluded that there are times when the laws of man are in conflict with basic human decency and compassion. We believe you are now more sensitive to this issue and have the makings of a fine medical missionary. Welcome back to college."

Julia shrieked and leapt into the air. Her feet didn't even touch the ground because Ashton snatched her in mid-jump, shouting for joy and whirling her in circles.

<hr />

It was time to say good-bye to Ashton. The dean wanted her back in class tomorrow morning, so there was no opportunity to return to Dierenpark. Ashton offered to walk her to a nearby apothecary shop where they would send a telegram home, asking Emil to forward her belongings to the college.

The scent of menthol and tobacco surrounded them as they stepped inside the shop. While Ashton dictated the note to the telegraph operator, Julia gazed at a display of elegant soaps on the glass countertop. Most were in paper boxes or tins featuring sumptuous illustrations of the soap's fragrance, such as jasmine or roses. Other pictures depicted the soap's main ingredient: beeswax, rose oil, or cream. One of the larger tins had a bucolic scene painted on the lid, an Alpine goat standing in a green field with a pristine blue sky overhead. She opened the tin lid and ran her finger along the milky smooth cake of soap inside. She paid for the tin and joined Ashton outside.

"The trolley stop is at the corner of the street," he said, and they walked with impossibly slow, measured steps toward the corner. They both knew this was where they would say their final good-byes. She would stay in Philadelphia, while Ashton would take the trolley to the train station and then return to New York City this afternoon. They would have only a few more moments together before they both returned to their normal lives.

The street corner was crowded, with a vendor selling pretzels and a boy hawking newspapers. A passel of school children had just been released for the day, and they scampered down the street in a flurry of boisterous voices.

She reached inside her pocket for the tin of soap. After all the unique and wonderful gifts he'd given her over the years, a bar of soap seemed terribly humble, but she couldn't bear the thought of Ashton disappearing into the vast city and forgetting their magical week together. In a goat barn, of all places.

"Here," she said, pressing the tin into his hands. "A bar of goat-milk soap to remember our time together."

His eyes softened. "I won't need any help remembering, but thank you," he said, his voice rough with tenderness. He tucked the tin inside his suit pocket then clasped both of her hands. "I hope you will continue to write. I can't tell you how much your letters have always meant to me."

"I'll write." The trolley was already making its way down the street toward them.

Ashton turned to face her, longing carved onto every line of his handsome face. "This is it, then."

"I know. I won't ever forget you."

He pulled her into his arms and kissed her. Some of the schoolchildren hooted, but she didn't care. This was probably the last time she would share a kiss with a man in her life, and she wanted to savor every second of it. She clung to him, trying to memorize the moment. She was going to have to live on this kiss for the rest of her life.

The trolley stopped, and she heard the door open. Ashton looked down at her, love and wistfulness gleaming in his eyes. "I wish things had been different," he said.

She shook her head. "I don't. Everything about these days together was perfect. Simply perfect."

He nodded. Then he boarded the trolley and headed out of her life forever.

9

MAY 1898

Ashton surveyed the array of goods mounded on the kitchen table, wondering how he was going to get them all inside the modest packing box.

"What's this?" his father asked, picking up a brown bottle and holding it to the window in a vain attempt to see inside.

"It's a blend of lemon and eucalyptus oil," Ashton replied. "When dabbed on the wrists, it is supposed to act as an insect repellent."

"Clever." His father replaced the bottle alongside the broad-brimmed hat and rain gear. Compared to the whimsical gifts Ashton had given Julia over the years, this final box was sadly pedestrian, filled with practical items a woman should have as she ventured out into a mountainside jungle. Julia's last letter had said she'd accepted a position in Malaya, a British colony in the South China Sea. An Anglican mission group was establishing a number of medical clinics throughout the Malayan islands, and they were eager for Julia to join them. She would leave the week following graduation.

She had invited him to her graduation, of course. She and her twenty-three classmates would accept their medical degrees in two weeks. Ashton would send a gift but could not bring himself to attend the ceremony.

A clean break was best. He would probably dream and wonder

264

about the adventures of Dr. Julia Broeder for the rest of his life, but it would be from a distance.

"Use the mosquito netting to protect the eucalyptus oil," his father suggested. "If this bottle breaks, she'll have a stinky mess on her hands."

Ashton smiled as he folded the mosquito netting into thirds then rolled up the bottle of oil. His father could have no idea what *stinky* meant until he'd lived in a goat barn for a week. He used another swath of mosquito netting to line the bottom of the box and then began laying in the compass, the Bible written in three languages, and the broad-brimmed hat that could be folded and rolled for easy transport. His father helped assemble the box, but Ashton turned away to prepare the one deeply personal item he didn't want his father to see.

It was his map of the travels of Marco Polo, taken down from his office wall just this morning. For years it had hung alongside pictures of Vandermark properties all over the world. On a wall of expensive etchings commissioned by a millionaire, Ashton's one piece of art was this humble map taken from a book he'd loved as a boy.

Julia shared his love of Marco Polo, and he didn't really need this map anymore. It was already engraved on his soul for all time, and he liked the idea of Julia having it with her as she ventured forth into the world.

He slid the map into a wooden tube, the quiet rasp barely audible over the normal city noises drifting in from the open kitchen window. Some girls played hopscotch in the alley, a vendor hawked German sausages, and the steady clomping of horse hooves and carriage wheels never seemed to stop. The mountains of Malaya seemed like another world. He tucked the tube deep into the box where his father would not see.

"Why are you giving her your Marco Polo map?" his father asked quietly.

Ashton's shoulders sagged. He didn't like hiding things from his father, but this was too painful to discuss. "It's nothing, Dad. Just something I want her to have."

His father took the tube from the box, wiggling the map out and unrolling it. The edges were worn with age, its faded lines as familiar as his own face.

"I remember when you used to disappear into your room with that book about Marco Polo," his father said. "I felt bad that you were an only child and had to find escape in books rather than having a brother or sister to play with. Especially after your mama got so sick, I wished you'd had someone—"

"Dad, I was fine."

His father's eyes lightened with a spark of humor. "It was probably a blessing to have only one child. It spared me the sin of having a favorite," he said with a wink. "Are you going to deliver the box in person? I'm sure Miss Julia would welcome your company should you attend her graduation."

"No, my life is here now." Ashton rolled up the map again and placed the tube in the box.

"Ash . . . I know what that map means to you," his father said, his voice serious again. "It is your every boyhood hope and dream. And if you are giving it to a girl, that means she is someone very important to you. You would not give this map away lightly."

He couldn't deny it. Not that he intended to do anything about it. Julia was free of encumbrances and could do with her life as she wished. He had obligations. "I don't think Julia will spend the rest of her life overseas." The words spilled out before he could stop them. "She may come back in ten or twenty years, and then perhaps we can have some sort of life together. This isn't the right time for me to go hopping off to Malaya."

His father drifted to the open kitchen window to stare outside. "I may not have been the world's best accountant or the perfect husband, but I am confident I did a good job raising my son. Above all, I wanted to make sure you had a strong foundation of faith and intelligence, but I also hoped you'd be able to chase those high-flying dreams of yours. I hoped you'd someday become a good husband and father. I wanted you to grow straight and tall and strong enough to withstand the storms that inevitably come into any man's life." He turned to face Ashton, a wistful smile on his face. "After everything we have been through together, it would be a shame if all I raised was a nursemaid for my old age."

Ashton rocked back on his heels. "I don't think of you like that—"

"Ash, the years go by quickly. I don't think you fully understand that yet. Don't wait ten or twenty years for this girl to come home. Trust me, I will be fine. I'm fifty-eight years old and have more friends than most men my age. The barbershop quartet meets three times a week. I play gin rummy twice a week—"

"You've only got one son."

"Yes, and I raised him to go after what he wants in life." Tears pooled in his father's eyes, but he was smiling. "Go find that girl while you are both still young. You'll never regret it."

Ashton turned away and braced himself with the back of a kitchen chair. He hadn't expected this, and it hit him hard. He squeezed his eyes shut. If ever he doubted he had been raised by a brilliant, kind, and generous man, those doubts were now blasted to pieces. A bittersweet pain bloomed in his chest. This might be the happiest, saddest moment of his life. He didn't know what was going to happen, but Ashton had his father's blessing to follow his heart.

⸻ ❖ ⸻

In response to Ashton's urgent message, Nickolaas Vandermark breezed into his office the following afternoon, a small boy at his side.

"Good morning, Mr. Carlyle!" Nickolaas Vandermark boomed, a surprising amount of energy in the elderly man's voice. Ever since Ashton's triumph with the gutta-percha contracts last autumn, Ashton's star had been rising high in the corporation. His success in getting Julia back into college had solidified his position. It didn't mean the Vandermark patriarch was going to agree to his audacious request, but at least he was in a decent negotiating position.

"Have you met my great-grandson, Pieter?" Mr. Vandermark asked. The boy was probably eight or nine years old and seemed oddly pale, sickly, and sullen. "Stand up straight and greet Mr. Carlyle," the elder Vandermark instructed.

The boy complied with barely concealed anxiety and then Nickolaas barreled ahead. "Pieter and I are headed to England to see Stonehenge. Won't that be fun, lad?" He gave the boy's shoulder a bit of a shake.

The boy mumbled something too quiet to hear and seemed to shrink even more. Ashton supposed there were problems and responsibilities being born into a family of such wealth, but Pieter seemed abnormally timid. It was hard to envision such a shy lad growing up to assume command of this mighty shipping empire. Perhaps that was why old Mr. Vandermark seemed to be taking him under his wing on his world travels.

"We may be gone for several months," Nickolaas continued. "While I am gone, all business is to be funneled through my grandson. You have his address and telegraph codes in Germany."

Ashton tried not to grimace. Quentin Vandermark had an even worse reputation than Nickolaas for grouchiness. "Very good, sir."

"Now, what's this I hear about a new proposal?" Nickolaas asked.

Ashton rounded the desk to stand before the bank of engravings of Vandermark properties. They ranged from Ceylon in India, Cape Town in Africa, and scattered islands throughout the Malayan kingdom.

"The gutta-percha deal I orchestrated last fall happened only because I've always had a curiosity about life in the Far East. I knew the rubber plantations were beginning to struggle around the world, but I believed the Vandermark plantations would profit by shifting our operations toward gutta-percha. It worked."

A spark of curiosity gleamed in the old man's eyes. "And . . . ?"

"And I'd like to take a more active part in your overseas operations. There is only so much I can deduce from an office in Manhattan. I'd like to become an overseas agent for the Vandermark investments in Asia and Africa, with a base in Kuala Lumpur in Malaya."

He seemed to have caught Nickolaas Vandermark by surprise. "Have you ever *been* to Malaya?" the man asked. "It is hot, putrid, and the white man's grave. I've never been able to pay someone enough to be willing to do it."

Ashton's heartbeat kicked up tempo. "I'd do it," he said, and for once in his life, he and Nickolaas Vandermark came to a quick and speedy agreement.

Julia scanned the crowd assembled in the college auditorium but couldn't find Emil or Claudia among the guests. Emil had warned her they might not be able to attend her graduation. Claudia was large with child, and with the twins not even a year old, it was asking a lot for them to travel to Philadelphia. She hadn't really expected them to come, but it would have been nice to have someone here for her. Everyone else seemed to have parents, siblings, or friends to watch them cross the stage to accept their diploma from Dean Kreutzer.

It didn't matter. She straightened her shoulders and adjusted the position of the square mortarboard on her head, its silky tassel swinging alongside her cheek. This was *really* happening. The groundskeeper's daughter from a rural village too small to be on most maps was about to be formally declared a physician within the space of a few seconds.

Her graduation robes swished as she crossed the stage. She smiled like a maniac, still having trouble believing this day had finally come. Even Dean Kreutzer's famously austere face brightened a bit as she shook Julia's right hand and pressed the diploma into her left.

"Bon voyage," Dean Kreutzer said with a tip of her head.

"Thank you, ma'am." A smattering of applause followed as she crossed to the far end of the stage and descended the three steps. She stood alongside the other recent graduates as the remaining women accepted their diplomas.

What a long journey they had been through together. Within the next few weeks, most of them would be boarding ships or heading out west to begin their new lives. It was doubtful she would ever see any of them again.

From here on out, her life was likely to be filled with good-byes. The thought hurt, but this was the path she had chosen for herself. Without warning, the memory of Ashton's voice popped into her mind. "You've chosen a steep and daring path," he had said. "No matter how hard, how grueling, how intimidating . . . you are going to change the world wherever you go. Don't give up now."

The memory of his words warmed her. As soon as the ceremony concluded, she took off the mortarboard and headed outdoors, where sunlight flooded the courtyard garden. Most of the new graduates stood alongside parents or other family members, some of them lining up for the photographer who was taking portraits at the far end of the garden. These things were always so awkward, but she wanted the chance to say good-bye to everyone.

"Congratulations, Dr. Broeder."

She whirled around. "Ashton! You came!"

"Of course I came. A week of hard labor in a goat barn ought to at least earn me a spot at your graduation."

He looked crisp and dapper in the sunshine, his tie artfully arranged and tucked into a lapis-blue satin vest. She was *not* going to get emotional about this, despite the sudden lump in her throat. He was here merely as a courtesy, as Mr. Vandermark's representative.

She cleared her throat. "Thank you for the graduation present. It was very thoughtful. I hadn't even thought of mosquito netting, but it will be very useful, I am sure."

Why was he looking at her so strangely? Everyone else in the garden was laughing and embracing, but Ashton gazed at her cautiously, as though he feared she were about to burst into flame.

"I brought another gift," he said hesitantly.

"You did?" His graduation gift had been overflowing with highly practical goods: yards of mosquito netting, good rubber boots, insect repellant. It was thoughtful but impersonal and, she had to admit, a little disappointing.

"Yes, I have another gift," he said. "The problem is that it is something that should belong only to my wife—"

She couldn't hear anything else he said. The world tilted and swayed. "You have a *wife*?" she shrieked.

She planted both hands on his chest and gave a little shove, pushing him off the sidewalk and into the patch of crocuses. "You have a wife and didn't tell me? You let me go all that time in the goat barn . . ."

She was shouting now, and everyone in the garden swiveled to stare at them, but she didn't care. He deserved the public embarrassment for misleading her so. His face flushed crimson, and he tugged at his collar.

"I *hope* someday to have a wife," he clarified hurriedly. "Why must you always be so literal?"

She was dizzy with relief and thankful to see he was already starting to laugh at her outburst. "You nearly scared a year off my life."

270

Ashton stepped back onto the path, kicking some mulch from the soles of his fancy shoes. She felt a little bad about the shoes; Ashton did put a lot of stock in nice shoes.

"Come here," he said quietly, tugging her into a warm embrace. "Your face is still white, and I think we both need this."

She hugged him back. Groups of spectators were still looking at them curiously, but let them look. Ashton cared enough to come to her graduation and he didn't have a wife, so suddenly everything seemed a little brighter in her world.

He kissed her cheek and whispered in her ear. "In my left pocket I have my mother's engagement ring. My father asked me to give it to the woman I intend to marry. So I've come to Philadelphia, hoping I can convince you to try it on."

She couldn't quite believe her ears. This wasn't good. The prospect of marrying Ashton Carlyle was beyond her wildest dreams, but he had made it plain that his future lay in New York.

She pulled back and looked up into his face, wincing at the anticipation she saw. "I've already accepted a position in Malaya," she began.

"So have I."

It seemed impossible, but as they stood in the garden, he outlined his new position for the Vandermark shipping empire. "I will be traveling a lot but will be based in Kuala Lumpur," he said. "We'll be able to live in the same place, except for when I make trips to the other properties."

"I don't understand . . ."

"I love you," he said hoarsely. "I've loved you ever since you were eighteen years old and started sending me letters about the joy of pulmonary functions and ice skating in the park and why Chinese spices have never been properly used in American cuisine. You are the woman I want to marry." He swallowed nervously. "And I really hope you'll be willing to try on my mother's ring."

Her heart swelled and threatened to burst. She loved him too, for their week in the goat barn had been the most joyous week of her life.

"I don't need to try it on to know that it fits," she said. Somehow, since the moment Ashton had showed up in the goat barn, she'd known they would fit together beautifully.

They were married the following week in New York City, with his father standing as best man.

It had been the most hectic week of Ashton's life. Between planning a hasty wedding, closing up his office, and packing to travel to the other side of the world, Ashton's life was already more adventurous for having married Julia.

His final responsibility before heading overseas was training a new attorney to handle the affairs at Dierenpark. He drove with Mr. Grady up to the estate to tour the old mansion and the historic pier where the Vandermark shipping empire had been launched almost three centuries ago. When he showed Mr. Grady to the groundskeeper's cottage, he took extra care to explain the importance of tending to the needs of the Broeders.

"I was warned about how superstitious and eccentric Nickolaas Vandermark can be, especially where the Broeder family is concerned. I didn't realize how imperative this was until I ran afoul of one of the Broeders." He smiled secretly. The Broeder he'd run afoul of was now his wife. Julia was still in the city, packing their final trunks before they both set sail tomorrow. "Emil Broeder isn't the brightest man you will ever meet, but he's harmless and shouldn't cause any trouble."

Ashton hoped to sample a bit of Sophie's baking before heading back to the train station, for Sophie was to baking what Michelangelo was to the Sistine Chapel, but he was destined for disappointment.

"Sophie isn't here," the housekeeper said when they entered the kitchen. "She's up on the roof."

When he asked what she meant, the housekeeper assured him that the widow's walk made the roof perfectly safe and that ever since her fiancé had died Sophie had been spending an inordinate amount of time up on the roof.

Ashton hesitated. He didn't want to intrude on her privacy, but he worried about Sophie. She was probably the kindest, gentlest person he'd ever met, but she seemed too fragile to survive in the world. And he didn't like the thought of her alone on that roof. He'd probably read too many gloomy Russian novels, but grieving women and rooftops did not seem like a healthy combination. He glanced at Mr. Grady.

"Give me just a moment," he said. "I need to say good-bye to Sophie."

Stepping out onto the roof of Dierenpark was a breathtaking experience. From here he could see miles up the river, to endless forests blanketing the hillsides in a thousand shades of green. He scanned the roof until he spotted Sophie.

What in the world? She sprang to her feet, a guilty flush on her face. The notebook she'd been writing in flopped to the ground, its pages fluttering in the breeze. He looked at the contraptions on the table beside her—thermometers, weird brass dials, and equipment he couldn't begin to name.

"What's going on up here?"

"It's n-nothing," she stammered.

"Funny, it looks like a scientific laboratory to me. What have you been doing up here?"

This might explain Sophie's near-constant presence at Dierenpark. Julia had assumed it was because Sophie was mourning her lost fiancé, but it appeared there was something else drawing the lovely Miss van Riijn to Dierenpark.

He listened to Sophie explain herself and agreed that her activities up here were probably of little consequence, but he still felt obligated to report them. The Vandermarks were notoriously private people, and they had a right to know of all happenings at Dierenpark.

He told Julia about his odd encounter with Sophie the next morning as they stood in line to board the steamer that would take them on the long journey, first to India and then on to Malaya. Julia told him he was being paranoid.

"Sophie is completely harmless," she assured him. "She's been operating that weather station for nine years, and no one has ever complained."

"That's because we didn't know about it." The Vandermarks would know about it soon. Immediately upon returning to the city, he'd made arrangements to notify Quentin Vandermark via telegram about Sophie's activities. Quentin's reputation for ferocity was even worse than his grandfather's, but rumor had it that Quentin was living in some remote hideaway tucked deep into the forests of Austria, so with luck, Sophie would never have to deal with him.

They walked up the steep planking to board the steamer, getting higher with each step. As they climbed, he felt his worries and concerns about Dierenpark fade and dissolve as he looked toward the future. From the deck of the ship, they had an excellent view of the Manhattan skyline, which was growing taller every year. He pulled Julia against his front, his arms around her waist so they could both take a parting view of New York. It was an amazing city: bold, brawling, alive, and vibrant. It was commerce and innovation, a marvelous city where on any block dozens of languages could be heard haggling, planning, arguing, and celebrating. It had been an extraordinary place to come of age, but it was in his past now. His future lay in the Far East.

He and Julia stayed at the railing as the ship left the harbor. Fading into the distance he could see the awe-inspiring Brooklyn Bridge. No matter how far or wide he traveled, he doubted he would ever see another bridge so magnificent. He hugged Julia close as the ship passed the Statue of Liberty, Fort Hamilton, and Gravesend Bay. In a few minutes, the crowded, joyous, wonderful city would be only a speck on the horizon. A piece of his soul would always love New York, but for now he and Julia were going to chase their dreams. He had a woman whose far-flung ambitions matched his, and together they would head toward the sunrise as it rose over a distant shore.

ABOUT
THE AUTHORS

Christy Award finalist and winner of the ACFW Carol Award, HOLT Medallion, National Reader's Choice Award, and Inspirational Reader's Choice Award, bestselling author **Karen Witemeyer** writes historical romances because she believes the world needs more happily-ever-afters. She is an avid cross-stitcher and shower singer, and she bakes a mean apple cobbler. Karen makes her home in Abilene, Texas, with her husband and three children. To learn more about Karen and her books and to sign up for her free newsletter featuring special giveaways and behind-the-scenes information, please visit www.karenwitemeyer.com.

Jody Hedlund is the Carol Award-winning, bestselling author of multiple novels, including the ORPHAN TRAIN and BEACONS OF HOPE series as well as *Captured by Love*, *Rebellious Heart*, and *A Noble Groom*. She holds a bachelor's degree from Taylor University and a master's degree from the University of Wisconsin, both in social work. Jody lives in Michigan with her husband and five children. She loves hearing from readers on Facebook and on her blog at www.jodyhedlund.com.

Elizabeth Camden is the author of nine historical novels and two historical novellas and has won both the RITA Award and the Christy

Award. With a master's in history and a master's in library science, she is a research librarian by day and scribbles away on her next novel by night. She lives with her husband in Florida. Learn more at www.elizabethcamden.com.

Books by Karen Witemeyer

A Tailor-Made Bride
Head in the Clouds
To Win Her Heart
Short-Straw Bride
Stealing the Preacher
Full Steam Ahead
A Worthy Pursuit

The Ladies of Harper's Station

No Other Will Do
Worth the Wait: A Ladies of Harper's Station Novella
Heart on the Line

A Cowboy Unmatched from A Match Made in Texas: A Novella Collection
The Husband Maneuver from With This Ring: A Novella Collection
Love on the Mend from With All My Heart Romance Collection

Books by Jody Hedlund

The Preacher's Bride
The Doctor's Lady
Unending Devotion
A Noble Groom
Rebellious Heart
Captured by Love

BEACONS OF HOPE

Out of the Storm: A BEACONS OF HOPE *Novella*
Love Unexpected
Hearts Made Whole
Undaunted Hope

ORPHAN TRAIN

An Awakened Heart: An ORPHAN TRAIN *Novella*
With You Always

Books by Elizabeth Camden

The Lady of Bolton Hill
The Rose of Winslow Street
Against the Tide
Into the Whirlwind
With Every Breath
Beyond All Dreams

Toward the Sunrise: An Until the Dawn Novella

Until the Dawn

Summer of Dreams: A From This Moment Novella

From This Moment
To the Farthest Shores
A Dangerous Legacy

Sign Up for Your Favorite Author's Newsletter!

Keep up to date with their book releases
and in the loop about upcoming events.

Sign up for Karen's email list at
karenwitemeyer.com.

Sign up for Jody's email list at
jodyhedlund.com.

Sign up for Elizabeth's email list at
elizabethcamden.com.

More from the Authors of
All My Tomorrows

When the man who killed her father closes in, telegraph operator Grace Mallory tries to flee—again. But she is waylaid by Amos Bledsoe, who hopes to continue their courtship. With Grace's life on the line, can he become the hero she requires?

Heart on the Line by Karen Witemeyer
karenwitemeyer.com

When a financial crisis leaves orphan Elise Neumann and her sisters destitute, Elise seeks work out west through the Children's Aid Society. On the rails, she meets Thornton Quincy, who suddenly must work for his inheritance. From different worlds, can they help each other find their way?

With You Always by Jody Hedlund
Orphan Train #1
jodyhedlund.com

Naval officer Ryan Gallagher broke nurse Jenny Bennett's heart six years ago when he abruptly disappeared. Now he's returned. However, with lives still at risk, he can't tell Jenny the truth about his overseas mission—but he can't bear to lose her again either.

To the Farthest Shores by Elizabeth Camden
elizabethcamden.com

BETHANYHOUSE

You May Also Like . . .

When unfortunate circumstances leave Rosalyn penniless in 1880s London, she takes a job backstage at a theater and dreams of a career in the spotlight. Injured soldier Nate Moran is also working behind the scenes, but he can't wait to return to his regiment—until he meets Rosalyn.

The Captain's Daughter by Jennifer Delamere
London Beginnings #1
jenniferdelamere.com

Growing up on the streets of London, Rosemary and her friends have had to steal to survive. But as a rule, they only take from the wealthy, so they've all learned how to blend into high society for jobs. When, on the eve of WWI, a client contracts Rosemary to determine whether a friend of the king is loyal to Britain or Germany, she's in for the challenge of a lifetime.

A Name Unknown by Roseanna M. White
Shadows Over England #1
roseannawhite.com

In 1917, British nurse and war widow Evelyn Marche is trapped in German-occupied Brussels. She works at the hospital by day and is a spy for the resistance by night. When a British plane crashes in the park, Evelyn must act quickly to protect the injured soldier, who has top-secret orders and a target on his back.

High as the Heavens by Kate Breslin
katebreslin.com

◆BETHANYHOUSE